CW00402429

Traitors to the damned

A.R. Stirn

Thank you God, for giving me a love of books. They granted me an escape when life got too hard.

This book is for anyone who is trying to escape from a world that is just too painful to be part of sometimes. I hope you are able to find peace, and adventure within these pages. I hope that I can grant you an escape from life, even if its only for a short while.

Chapter 1

This kingdom has the potential to be beautiful. I think at one time it was. Before hatred and violence flooded its streets. Before that cruel bitch of a woman became queen and made those like her practically royalty. Whereas those of us without magic in our veins became scum. We became unworthy, being used only to do the work sorcerers like her are too good for, or kept in pleasure houses or worked as slaves. Very few of us humans have been able to find freedom and control in our lives, even if it's not as much as we used to have. We lived once in harmony, as equals. Witches, warlocks, humans, elves; we coexisted for centuries. But queen Mortala turned this peaceful kingdom into a pit of hell that only the magical and strongest survived.

In the heart of Willowmore, children of magic chased one another through the crowded streets as their parents strolled in and out of shops, their laughter and joy filling the air. Some carried new dresses or hats, while others held fresh pastries and cakes made special for the festival tomorrow. I studied them as I wove in and out of the crowds. They were all so different but you can feel the same magic humming through their blood. Some of them were taller than any human, towering over all as they walked, while others barely came up to my knees. Some had beautiful wings that flowed and sparkled behind them, others had skin tinted with such vibrant colors it almost hurt to look.

My hands were stuffed casually into the pockets of my pants, they hung from my thin frame but they did well to hide my figure. I did my best to walk calmly, appearing unbothered by the scratchy, tight fabric binding my breasts flat and the large collared shirt and waist coat. I tipped my head low, the large brim of my hat casting my face in shadow. The worn, brown fabric hung perfectly to cover my face. Even without looking at me, you could feel my blood was different. Was wrong. Some didn't bother to acknowledge me as I passed, while others hissed or spat at my feet. Being human made me hated by all. Being a messenger for the kingdom of Willowmore had its perks though, I was able to come and go through the kingdom and it's streets as I pleased whereas most humans could not. I worked with the gutter of this kingdom, not only delivering messages but exchanging drugs and contraband forbidden even to the magical. I may loath those I work with, but they are the reason I have enough coin to have a roof over my head and a full stomach every night.

Dealing with the corrupt and evil of this land, has not only thrown violence into my life but also power. I knew everyone who dealt or bought drugs, I knew who was in debt to who, my knowledge of this city could burn it to the ground. But that also made me an even bigger target. I had been jumped and attacked more times than I could count. Learning to fight had to be gained at a young age by anyone who wanted to survive in this world. The scars covering my body prove that I have and will survive this retched city and its people. Even in the nicer parts of the kingdom, buildings were dull, withered and dusty. Around every corner there seemed to be misery.

I stalked through the city, doing my best to keep my head down as I made my way through the crowded streets until I reached the outer gates of the city. Humans never came to this part of the kingdom unless it was against their will. The narrow roads were lined with brothels. Enslaved humans and witches alike trapped within their walls. Drug dens, gambling houses and musty bars were filled with drunken wizards, each one worse than the last. A warlock stumbled past me and snarled a string of curses in my direction. I bared my teeth and gripped the dagger at my hip tightly in warning. He turned to follow me, his nasty words slurred and horrid. My anger boiled within me as I waited to see what he would do. Either he got smart and walked away, or I would get to have some fun.

I smiled wickedly as his hand clamped down on my shoulder. I whirled, spinning to face him. I grabbed the collar of his wrinkled shirt and pulled him into the alley. His eyes were a bright purple, magic hummed dully through his body. He tripped over his feet, stumbling deeper into the filthy, narrow strip. I slammed his body to the ground, my mind and body slowly being taken over by the rush and madness a fight always brought me. His purple eyes widened as I pressed the blade of my dagger to his throat. I smiled viciously, enjoying the fear I could see in his eyes. It would be so easy to kill him. So easy to cut open his throat and watch him bleed out. But I decided to give him the choice to live.

"Now is your chance to apologize." I snarled. His body went still under me for a minute but then a cocky smirk spread across his drunken face.

"And what's a fragile girl like you gunna do if I don't?" My smile grew as I stared at the cruel warlock. I said nothing as I slid the blade across the soft skin, tearing through the artery. Releasing a river of magic tainted blood. His eyes went wide, terror flowing through his body as his life slowly began slipping away. I stood as he began writhing on the ground, trying to stop the bleeding. I didn't bother wiping the blood from my hands, instead I tipped my hat and turned down the alley. He was dead before I had reached the street.

I finally reached *The Flower Bed*. The most popular whore house in the kingdom. I grimaced as I stepped through the front doors, the blood on my hands smearing onto the door handle. Sickly sweet perfume filled the air almost like it had replaced the oxygen itself. Clouds of smoke from pipes swirled in thick clouds creating a permanent fog. The entrance hall was overflowing with lovers entangled on couches, benches, against walls and even on the marble floor itself. The rattling of bed posts and loud moans of pleasure bounced off the walls and echoed through the ceiling from the bedrooms above. Silks in every color hung from the high ceiling and walls, wrapping the room in an orgy of color.

I glared at those around me and made my way into a small office to my left and shut the doors quickly behind me. The same silks covered the walls and a large desk sat at the opposite end with an enormous witch sitting behind it. She was the size of two human men. Her skin was the color of green moss and as leathery as my boots. Madame Scala, the owner of *The Flower Bed*. She counted a large stack of coins and ushered me forward without glancing up from her business. I didn't speak as I dropped a small letter onto her desk, blood soaking the corner. I plopped into an arm chair and draped my legs over the side. I pulled a handkerchief from my pocket and began wiping my hands clean while I waited. She broke her gaze from her income and inspected the envelope addressed to one of her girls.

"That little witch must be magic in bed to have a royal guard fall for her." She threw the unopened letter into a drawer and shut it with a chuckle. "Especially since she's fucked half the kingdom." I remained silent, my patience beginning to wear thin. She plucked a gold coin from her pile and twirled it between her fingers. Scala was one of the greediest creatures I had ever had the displeasure of meeting, and that was saying something in this kingdom. "I still don't understand why you hide such a figure under those dreadful male clothes and suits." She was one of the few who knew I was actually a female.

I gave her a shrug. "Its forbidden for females to carry weapons." My hand dropped the the hilt at my waist. "Magic or no magic." She nodded. Despite her hatred for my kind, she understood the dangers of being a female no matter what runs through your veins. She stared fondly at the gold coin flitting through her fingers. "Have you reconsidered my offer?" She smiled wildly, her yellow teeth were chipped and cracked. I remained silent and raised a single eyebrow in annoyance.

"You could make good money here. I remember what you looked like before you started disguising yourself." Her eyes traced my body. "You have a lovely figure, too thin in some places but I bet that can be fixed with regular meals." I gritted my teeth. "You would of course have to grow out your hair, nobody wants a woman with a shaved head." My blood began to boil.

"Anything else you want to change about me?" I growled. She eyed me again, ignoring my obviously growing temper.

"We would have to get rid of those things on your hands as well but that shouldn't be too difficult." My hand curled tightly around the hilt of my dagger, the metal tips of my fingers clinking against the hard metal. She could try to remove them, but I had spent my entire life trying to get rid of the damned metal encasing my fingertips. Unfortunately for me, there was no separating them from my skin. They were fused together. I glared at her, rage building within me.

"There is no *we* Scala. I'm no whore." I traced the side of the hilt, the smooth handle bringing me comfort. "Now, where is my payment? The usual fee to keep me from running back to that guard and telling him you're stealing his love letters, and add ten percent for running your mouth." I snapped. She shrugged her large shoulders and chuckled harshly. She flicked the gold coin through the air and I caught it easily.

"Keep the change. Consider it a preview of what you will have when you accept my offer." Her mouth twisted into a sickening smirk, showcasing her yellow teeth. I tucked the coin into my pocket and left the room. My rage simmered as the noises of the whore house surrounded me. The moon shown brightly as I stepped back into the streets. They were mostly empty, now only occupied by the drunk, high or desperate. Loud laughter from bars filled the air as I walked. I passed alleyways dodging drug dealers, fights and those offering themselves out for the right price.

I kept to the shadows and pulled my hat close to my face. The warm summer air kissed my face gently. I avoided the living and sneered at those who came close enough to see me. Most of Willowmore residents had returned home for the evening, preparing for dinner and excited about tomorrow's festivities. Prospers Day. The day celebrating queen Mortalas reign. The queen grew up the daughter of a duke. She married the king, king Dolant, he wasn't a warlock but from an ancient magic bloodline of powerful creatures. Their marriage was agreed upon, hoping it would help with peace throughout the kingdom. It worked for awhile. Until the queen learned of her husbands infidelity. Even though they had been married for political reasons and not for love, she became enraged. She killed the king and his human mistress and damned his entire bloodline, destroying all of them and took control of the kingdom. Her hatred for all creatures unlike her began and spread through the kingdom like a virus.

Peace no longer existed here. Violence against humans is condoned, celebrated even. Mortala stripped away our rights and gave us the worst living conditions and jobs and tomorrow is the day that we "celebrate" it. I haven't been to the festival since I was a child. Even through young eyes I hated it. So I stay in. I never venture out onto the streets on Prospers Day. Even a days worth of work isn't enough to get me out of my home. It's not worth the violence and ridicule we humans have to face.

I finally made it to the other side of the city to the *Pennly Inn*. I had found this place the day I escaped that dreadful orphanage I started my life in. I was bruised and starving when I demanded the owner, Mrs. Pennly, hire me. She had laughed but employed me in exchange for a room and meals. Now that I was a messenger and made my own money, she charged me a monthly rate for my room.

The warm glow of the fire and cheerful conversation greeted me as I opened the inn doors. Humans drank, ate and laughed together as I entered the dining halls welcoming atmosphere. The delicious smell of tonights dinner wafted from the busy kitchen and rose around me, causing my stomach to howl. I searched through the cheerful crowd for Mrs. Pennly, but she wasn't present in the sea of people. I made my way through the tables, nodding at familiar faces until I reached the bar at the back of the room. Mrs. Pennly sat in front of a stack of papers, making notes and filling in numbers as I approached. Her wrinkled face was drawn in concentration, her grey hair pulled onto the top of her head into a bun. A gold locket hung from her neck that contained a picture of her late husband. He died a few years after they married so I never had the pleasure of meeting him, but based on how fondly she talks of him, I know I would have liked him. She was a small, plump woman but had a soul that lived fiercely. I took the seat next too her and ordered a whiskey while I waited fo her to finish. Without looking up from her papers, she addressed me.

"Good evening Lorn. I was beginning to worry about you." I checked the watch in the pocket of my waist coat. I had arrived back later than usual. "I was begging to think I would find you bleeding in a alley again." The amount of times she had found me that exact way over the years was almost comical. I chuckled and took a drink of whiskey, the amber liquid burned its way down my throat and filled me with warmth. With a heavy sigh, she pushed away the papers and took the glass from my hand before draining it. I smiled softly and signaled to the bar keep for another.

"Rough day?" I asked. Her shoulders jumped in a shrug.

"Not as bad as yours I bet." Penn knew the illegal dealings I was involved in, though she never asked for details. She always told me the less she knew, the better. Her pale blue eyes scanned me for any injuries or blood. Some flecks stained my clothes, but she obviously figured it wasn't mine because of her lack of concern. It was a rare occasion that I went a day without either my own or someone else's blood on my hands. I pulled the gold coin from my pocket and placed it on the counter in front of her.

"My rent for the month. I'll take the evening meal every night as well." I took a drink from my new glass as she pocketed the coin. Her shoulders were tense, they had been since I sat down. I could tell there was something she was wanting to say but was too afraid to say it. "Out with it Penn." I hated when people refused to speak about what was on their minds. It was always so bothersome to pull information from others and the inn keeper knew how much it annoyed me. With another heavy breath she turned to me.

"I have a job offer for you." I remained silent, waiting for her to continue. "I need you to take a payment to Geran tomorrow." I took another drink.

"No."

"Ill give you a month rent free and include the evening meal." When I didnt say anything she continued. "I need that payment taken tomorrow or I wont get new comforters by winter." Geran was the son of a shepherd.

Penn had been paying for their services since I was a child.

"You know I don't work on Prospers Day."

"Yes I know but I haven't been able to get the money together until today and he needs the payment by tomorrow." Loud voices erupted from a table behind us. I turned to see where it came from. Three men sat at a table in the middle of the room. One of them obviously had his fill of drink tonight, his words were slurred and loud, disrupting the others in the room. "Please don't be angry with me, I wouldn't ask if I didn't need it done right away." Penn continued.

"Then find another to take it." I replied dryly without taking my eyes off the drunken man.

"You're the only one I trust to deliver that much money." One of the waitresses walked past the three men, and the one drunkenly smacked her backside roughly before laughing loudly. Rage sparked to life within me. Penn didn't say anything as I grabbed my glass and began making my way through the tables. The room fell silent as the other diners watched my silent approach. Most of those here were regulars and knew what was about to happen. I stopped at the edge of the table and waited for the three men to look at me.

They were dirty and sunburnt, probably farmers on the outskirts of the city. I recognized the two sober ones, their presence for dinner was frequent. They both knew me too, and their gazes immediately turned to their friend, their eyes filled with fear. I focused my gaze on him as well.

"Evening gentlemen." I said calmly. The two regulars nodded and the other eyed me through a drunken haze. "I think it's time to call it a night, don't you?" The room remained silent as all eyes were trained on me. I pointed my question at the drunken man. One of his friends spoke, but I didn't break my gaze.

"I agree. Its time to go John." So the drunks name is John. Now I had a name to the face, and he is no longer welcome back. John glared at his friend before turning back to me. Fury raged within me as he turned back to his mug of beer, dismissing me without saying a word.

"Did I just see you touch one of the waitresses without her permission?" His only reply was a disgusting smirk. I chuckled, excited to release the anger within me. His friends tensed, knowing what was about to come. I downed the last of my whiskey and took a deep breath, waiting for his eyes to find me once more. When they finally did, I smashed the thick glass on the side of his head. Broken glass pierced and sliced through his skin. I felt a sting in my palm knowing I had cut my own hand, but I wasn't done yet. John began to yell but I gripped his hair roughly and brought his face onto the wooden table in front of him hard, not once, but twice. The bone under his left eye cracked and the skin sagged, his nose lay twisted at an odd angle as his body slumped to the floor. The room remained silent as I stared at the unconscious man at me feet. I pulled a handkerchief from my hand

and wrapped it around the cut before turning to the other two who averted their gazes.

"Out." I ordered. The two scrambled from their chairs and hauled their friend through the door, throwing fearful glances back at me. I walked back to the bar, where Penn sat with a blank expression on her face. The bar keep had another glass of whiskey ready for me. I palmed it and turned to her. Penn had taken me in as a child and practically raised me. But our relationship had always been about business. What I can offer her, and what she can offer me in return. She knew I couldn't pass up a months rent, no matter how much money I was making these days. I took a deep drink of the bitter liquid.

"You really need to learn to control your temper." Penn said quietly. I ignored her.

"Leave the payment for Geran at the front desk." I turned my back and made my way to the staircase in the back of the room, my residual anger fizzling out. I took the steps two at a time and made my way to the end of the hall to my room.

The pale blue walls made the worn floors seem much older than they were. Books lay in piles around the walls and atop the dresser and small bedside table. Penn had taught me how to read and write when I first started working for her so I could take reservations and meal orders. My downtime was usually spent reading, my only escape from this shit life.

I had pushed my small bed into the corner of the room in order to have more room for my vast book collection. I made my way to the washing tub in the other corner and began stripping off my clothes, eager to bathe and wash the grime from the day off my skin. I hung my hat on a hook by the door. I pulled the small watch from my pocket and set it on the table and peeled off my boots and pants and shrugged my waistcoat off and to the floor. The small badge pinned to my chest clanked to the floor at my feet with my shirt. The gold messenger emblem of a dove holding a scroll stared back at me. It teased me. Mocked me for working for the very people that hated my kind. Mocked me for working for the evil of the world.

I grimaced and scrubbed myself clean quickly in the cold water of the wash tub, the cut in my hand staining with the movement and soap. I pulled on a clean shirt and pants as I shivered. Penn arrived shortly after I dressed and dropped of a steamy bowl of stew and thanked me before she left me for the night. I scarfed down the bowl quickly, my tongue and throat burning as I swallowed, too hungry to wait for it to cool down. I set the empty bowl outside my door and crawled into bed, the mattress old and lumpy beneath me.

I attempted to read from a book of poems but I found myself too distracted by tomorrow's events to concentrate. Annoyed, I tossed the book aside and extinguished the oil lamps lighting my small room. Dreading the idea of going out tomorrow, I tossed and turned restlessly late into the night. The muffled laughter and conversation from downstairs finally lulled me to sleep.

Chapter 2

I was in the dining hall the next morning drinking a cup of coffee when Penn found me. She gave me a thick envelope, about the same size as my palm and told me Geran would be in the city square. Geran and his parents live on the outskirts of the northern part of the territory. He comes to the city on days like today where he can sell to large crowds within the kingdom's walls.

He and his father have always been very kind to Penn and I, but I can only stand being around them for a short period of time. They lived easy lives compared to most of us. Their high-quality goods and charming looks have earned them as much respect as a human can get in this kingdom. Granted it isn't a lot but it's more than the rest of us.

Penn gave my shoulder a light squeeze and left me to drink the last of my coffee. I drained the rest of my cup, the metal on my fingers clanked against the glass as the bitter liquid heated my bones. I strolled into the streets and was greeted by the feeling of magic. The streets were packed with smiling and laughing faces heading to the square, where the official beginning of the festival will take place. Multi colored flags hung from lampposts and in between buildings. Lanterns burning with colorful fires floated magically above the crowded streets cascading those below in a shower of color. Music played softly in the distance. If it was any other day, in any other kingdom I would've joined in with the excited faces around me. But I will not be celebrating today.

I shoved my way into the ocean of people making their way north. The deeper into the city I walked, the angrier I became. I could sense the magic around me, feel it flowing through the veins of those I passed. Witches in lavish dresses spent their coins on the various different vendors lining the streets. Booths displayed goods from all over the kingdom aching to be bought. Wizard children begged their parents for trinkets and treats, and they obliged. I only saw a small handful of humans, all begging for coin on the side of the streets. The dirty, poor humans would be ignored today or fall victim to cruel taunts or violence. Today was a day for celebrating the discarding and degradation of humans, not for being generous or charitable.

It seemed to take a lifetime to enter the square, the sun had moved high over head and the excitement had grown. The queen would be arriving soon, so I needed to hurry and get out before she did. I shoved my way through eager warlocks and witches, snarling at them when they made a comment in my direction. Only a few dared to curse or challenge me. My reputation for fighting back and usually winning proceeded me even today.

I scanned the crowd three times before I finally spotted Geran. He was leaning against his small booth displaying his wool, fabrics, and clothing for purchase. His blonde curly hair shined like gold in the sunlight. He was tall and slender but muscles corded his arms, visible even from under his green shirt. He grinned at me as I approached.

"Lorn! I thought you didn't venture out on Prospers day." He teased. I stopped in front of him, ignoring the scoffing of several sorcerers. His blue eyes twinkled as he awaited my response.

"I don't." I held out the small envelope addressed to his father. He didn't drop his gaze from mine as he took the payment from me.

"But you made an exception for me? I'm flattered." His flirtatious eyes scanned my face, landing on my lips. His boldness irritated me.

"I didn't do it for you. I was promised a hefty sum for delivering this today. You just happened to be the recipient." I moved on, running my hand over the fine fabric he had set out. They were soft against my scared hands. From the corner of my eye I watched as he stepped closely to my side.

"I feel like I haven't seen you in forever." He paused and watched as I inspected a green cloak. "I see you're still cutting your hair short." I snorted. Geran was one of the small group that knew my true identity and gender, having grown up around me.

"I've been shaving my head for over ten years now. Did you really expect me to stop?" I asked shortly, not really needing an answer.

"And I still miss your long hair every time I see you." I frowned at his words. Did hair really matter that much to people? I continued admiring the cloak, the color reminding me of the grass in spring time.

"Take it. Every pretty girl deserves something nice every now and then. Even ones with scars." He traced the white lines on the back of my hand. His touch and horrible attempt at a compliment made me recoil. I ripped my hand away.

"My coin is for things that are useful, not for things that are pretty." A part of me ached from the words. I would love to have beautiful clothes and jewelry, to be excited about a mans attempts at courting me. But thats just not how life is. Geran chuckled and moved back to the other side of his booth. He crossed his arms over his chest and eyed me.

"Not everything has to be so grim. There is joy in the world, Lorn. Not everything is life or death." My anger burst to life within me. I braced my hands on either side of me and glared at him in furry. The boyish grin across his lips vanished, his eyes widening slightly in fear.

Good. I though. *Be afraid of me, it will keep you from ever touching me again.*

"You've never had to fight to live, so I can see how you can believe that." I spat through gritted teeth. His eyes narrowed as he walked back to my side, stopping so close I could feel his breath on my cheek. He was angry, it flashed in his eyes. A small part of me sparked with excitement, eager to rip away that anger and throw it back in his face.

"We are both human. My life hasn't been easy and you know it." He snapped. I gave him a cruel smile, not one of humor but one filled with anger and deadly promises.

"That may be, but one of us has the luxury of seeing peace and joy in the world and it's not the one with a knife strapped to her hip." His cheeks reddened and his gaze dropped from mine. My blood still boiling within me, I stepped closer, my lips almost brushing his as I spoke softly to him. "Touch me again, and I'll give you scars to match mine." His faced paled. "We'll see how pretty you think they are then." I barred my teeth before turning and walking away.

The crowd had thickened, the excitement could almost be seen in the air surrounding the square. The queen must be coming soon, giving me not much time to make my exit. I shoved and weaved my way through, but just going a few feet was a battle. I was half way across the square when the happy voices died and were replaced with the sound of trumpets. Two royal guards stood at the northern entrance of the square, announcing the queens arrival.

The crowd was silent as a train of guards came through the entrance and surrounded the large stone dais at the front of the courtyard. I eagerly and desperately shoved past a few more people They craned their necks for a glimpse of the queen as she entered. A few more feet and I would be free. I wouldn't have to listen to anything that evil woman said. But sadly, my time to exit had run out.

An audible gasp came from the crowd is the queen stepped into the square. She shown like a beacon in the afternoon sun, it was almost too bright to look. Her magic visible and felt even from so far away. Not every witch or warlock was able to use the magic within them, most of the time it lays doormat for their whole lives. But Mortala was one of the few who could harness it, and wield it dangerously and powerfully. Her extravagant gown was the color of the sky on a clear day, embroidered from the finest of silks with small stones bordering the neckline and hem. Queen Mortala is gorgeous, any female wanted to be her. She stood tall and poised as she passed her subjects. Yes, she was beautiful, but her wings were remarkable. Each the size of a man, they billowed behind her demanding the attention of anyone nearby. The feathers perfectly straight and even, each in it's rightful place. They resemble those of a hawk, strong and powerful but silver like they were forged from the purest of metals. Even I envied how they complemented her pale, smooth skin.

I shook with rage. It swirled within me, violent and eager to break free. This woman is responsible for the life I had been given. All the pain, violence, loneliness and heartache I have had to endure, is her fault. She enjoyed the pain and suffering of humans and made it nearly impossible to experience anything but within her territory.

My hands curled into fists, my metal fingers slicing into my palms. As she sat atop her throne, my jaw clenched tightly.

Blinded by my rage, I hadn't noticed that I was the only one still standing. The rest of the crowd kneeled before her, even the few humans present. They adored her, celebrated her, but feared her above anything else. They coward in her presents, leaving the square a sea of kneeling rats. But I wouldn't let myself fear her. I gave into my rage, unable to flee from it and glared at the queen. Her eyes fell to me quickly, her face unreadable as she took me in. I was nothing to her. I remained standing, even as a witch pulled on my pant leg, silently begging me to kneel. Afraid she would feel Mortalas wrath along with me. I would rather die than kneel to that woman.

The queen leaned to the guard closest to her and whispered something to him. He grabbed the attention of two other guards and they started towards me. I allowed them to take me roughly through the crowd, my eyes never leaving the queens face. I was shoved to the foot of the dais, my hat falling to the ground. She was more breathtaking up close. She stared down her nose at me, watching me and waiting. I held my glare and straightened my spine. Finally, she spoke.

"You dare not bow to your queen?" Her voice was smooth, the ends sharp like a broken piece of glass. "What is your name?" When I did not respond a guard smacked me hard on the back of the head.

"Lorn." I growled painfully.

"You're a woman." Her brows rose at the sound of my voice. "And your sir name?" She wanted my family name. Probably to punish my non existent family along with me.

"I don't have one." I answered simply. The queen raised a brow.

"An orphan." She paused, assessing me again. "And how old are you, Lorn?" I snarled at the sound of my name on her lips.

"If I had to guess I would say around twenty."

She pursed her lips. "Guess?" I gritted my teeth.

"I was never told my birthday." Her brow furrowed as she glanced at my hands, blood from my palms soaking my metal finger tips. She leaned forward in her throne and took a deep breath through her nose, like she was smelling me.

"What are you?" I let my confusion show, not able to hide it. Can't she tell? I had no distinguishing marks or coloring of a witch and there was no sense of magic within my blood. I only tilted my head in response to her question. Something flickered behind her eyes, realization? Her features returning to an unreadable mask as she sighed deeply. She sat back in her throne and looked out at her subjects lazily. When she spoke, her voice was demanding, power coated every syllable. "Kill her."

Chapter 3

Panic flooded my veins, guards grabbed my arms
and pinned them painfully behind my back. The crowd
cheered as more guards circled me unsheathing their
swords. I looked at the guard to my left, he wore no
helmet, his battle weathered face exposed. His chest
revealed him as a high-ranking officer for all the shiny
metals pinned to it. Without hesitating, I slammed my
head into his, my forehead smashing into his nose with a
sickening crack. His hold on my arm released as I
grabbed the knife from my hip and drove it into the
throat of the guard to my right, showering me in his
blood. Free from the two of them, I turned to face the
others advancing toward me. The crowd behind began to
scream and run from the square not wanting to be caught
in the middle of the fight. With five guards heading for
me I threw myself into the rushing force of witches and
warlocks and quickly disappeared into the ocean of
bodies.

Shouts from the queen were drowned out by the
screaming and footsteps of the panicked crowed around
me. They were hiding me without realizing it. I shoved
and fought my way through the crowd stumbling and
breathing frantically. Blood pounding in my ears, my
boiling rage and adrenaline pushed me deeper into the
crowd. I looked over my shoulder, I could see four guards
closing in, forcing their way through frightened sorcerers
and humans. I darted between an apothecary and a

bakery, squeezing my way through the tight alley and took a sharp left at the end. I set off at a full sprint and leapt into the air latching onto the gutter of a nearby bookstore and hauled myself onto the roof.

The footsteps and shouts of officers echoed through the alleyway below as they followed. Dagger in hand I ran for the other end of the roof and jumped onto the next building. I made it just a few feet across before I was yanked back by the back of my waist coat, the worn fabric ripping under the force. I stumbled back into a body and a knife was placed against my throat. The guard crushed me to his chest, his hot breath hit my cheek in deep pants. I hissed as the blade sliced across my skin, blood trickling down to my collarbone. Before he could cut any deeper I quickly reached back and drove my knife into him blindly. His body went limp and fell to the ground behind me. He lay motionless, my blade hilt deep in his eye socket. My victory was short-lived as three more guards pulled themselves onto the rooftop. Their faces went from shocked to furious as they found their fallen comrade at my feet. I turned from them swiftly and dropped to the street below hitting the ground hard. Air rushed from my lungs. Gasping, I rolled to my feet and pushed my way into the nearest store, avoiding the still packed streets.

Inside there were glass cases displaying jewelry and precious stones. The cases created a maze on the floor. Mirrors lined the walls making the entire space look fragile. A worker behind one of the cases balked at my sudden entrance, taking in my blood covered hands and face. His blue, magically tinted skin paled as I jumped over a display filled with sparkling jewels. I turned towards the doors as three guards charged through them. One hurdled the first case and landed a kick right to the center of my chest sending me crashing through a display filled with ruby encrusted jewelry. I felt my ribs crack under his boot, my skin stung where the broken pieces of glass had punctured it.

I was lifted to my feet by the same guard, his hand snaked around my throat cutting off my airflow. I delivered a knee to his groin, releasing his hold on me. I grabbed two thick shards of glass from the floor and jammed one into the base of his neck, severing his spinal cord. His lifeless body fell to my feet and I turned to face the others. The madness of a fight finally took over, my blood pumping wildly. They jumped the barrier to help their fellow officer. Both with knives, they came at me. I blocked one of their jabs with my arm and sent my elbow into the face of the other. The former stabbed his knife forward, slicing into my leg as I tried to move out of the way. Using the glass in my hands I jammed one forward and missed as I aimed for the neck of an officer. A fist connected with my jaw, sending stars dancing across my vision. My anger pulsing through me forced me through the pain blossoming in my face.

I lunged toward the closest of the two and knocked him backwards into another display. He grunted as he landed in a pile of broken wood and glass. Before he could recover I lodged a shard of glass into his throat. His face twisted into a silent scream as his blood streamed onto the floor around him. Arms wrapped around my neck as the other officer pulled me to his chest squeezing. I struggled against his grasp but he was far stronger than I was. Desperate for air, my lungs already screaming in pain, I forced the last piece of glass deep into his thigh. Air filled my lungs as he cursed and fell. Gasping, I stumbled through the rest of the shop and out the back door. I sprinted through the grim alley, ignoring the pain in my chest and leg. I listened as guards shouted at one another along the streets, splitting up to find me.

Even with my extensive knowledge of this kingdom and its layout I couldn't hide forever. I needed to find a way out fast or I would be caught. My ribs ached painfully. I forced my legs to carry me further away from the Square. I ran through alleys and hid in the shadows. I took passages and short cuts that only few in the city knew about. It was dusk by the time I reached the city gates. The streets were now empty and quiet save for the entire royal guard. My body ached from hours of running and fighting. I crouched in the shadows behind a bar and eyed the gates. Six guards, all on horses, two with bows and the rest had swords drawn.

They were waiting for me. I sat in the shadows panting and too tired to come up with a plan. I breathed heavily, cursing the tight fabric around my chest. Over the years I had escaped thieves, rapists and killers. I have always found a way out. Found a way to live even when I shouldn't have been able to. But staring at those gates guarded by men who weren't hurt or had been running all afternoon, I couldn't find a way out. I was going to be caught and I would be hanged or worse. My anger had dissipated and was being replaced with exhaustion when a woman came running up to the guards. She was human and frantically telling them that I was just seen down the street. She began pleading for them to catch me as five of them rode away, leaving only one guard in front of the gates. My heart leapt. This is my chance, thanks to the stranger that thought they had seen me.

I pressed by back to the walls, staying within the shadows, I crept along and made my way towards the guard and now crying woman. I scooped up a large rock and held it firmly waiting to throw it. Ten feet from the guard, still encased by the shadows being gifted to me by the setting sun, I finally saw who the crying woman was. Her long gray hair was tied into its usual bun and her face was wet with tears. Miss Pennly stood in front of the loan guard holding his attention with her sobs and pleads for help.

This woman had practically raised me. Saved me and kept me as her own. She had seen me every day for the last 12 years. She knew me when she saw me. She had lied to those guards. She knew I was here and knew I needed to get out. And now was my chance. I launched the rock at the guards head, high atop his horse. It hit him right on the ear but he didn't fall. Instead his attention was drawn to me. He drew up his bow quickly, my figure already sprinting at him. He loosed a arrow that narrowly missed me. I jumped with every last ounce of strength I had and collided with him, taking him off his horse and to the hard ground below. Rolling to my feet I sent a jab to his throat and a left hook to his temple.

Penns arms were around me before his unconscious body crumpled to the ground. She pulled me to the horse, now empty of its rider. The blood coating my hands, some of it mine some of it not, left bright stains on her wrists as I held onto them. She faced me after looking down the roadways for incoming guards.

"Go. Don't stop until you're out of the territory. Until you're out of her reach." She placed her hand on my cheek as a tear slid down her own. "You deserved a better life than the one you were given." My eyes burned as she placed a kiss to my temple. "Go find a better one." My heart cracked, sorrow filling it's gaps. The sound of hooves and shouts snapped me back, drowning my sadness momentarily. I pulled myself up onto the horse as guards began approaching from both side roads. With one last look at Penn, I drew the horse through the gates and disappeared into the night, the sun finally setting.

I urged the horse faster and faster as the hoof beats behind me grew as their numbers did. The few looks I threw over my shoulder I could count at least a dozen royal guards racing after me. The ebony horse beneath me blended well with the night making it easy to melt into the darkness. After what felt like hours, I had finally been swallowed by the night and was rid of the following officers. Their horses no longer audible. I drove the horse blindly through the country side, not willing to stop or slow. My body ached the longer we rode. I wasn't used to being on a horse at all let alone such a long, hard period of time. But as my energy depleted, my horses did as well. Despite my orders, the beast below me slowed and continued to do so until it could no longer move at all. With me atop it, the horse collapsed to the ground, breathing heavily.

Barely able to move, I crawled away and sprawled out onto the ground. My heart still pounding violently in my chest. The horses shallow breath was the only sound filling the chilly night air. My body ached and screamed. My ribs were at least bruised if not broken, and my skin stung where I had been cut. Pain surged through my chest with every breath. The open cuts on my skin burned as I pulled up my sleeves to examine them. Dried blood coated my body so thickly it was impossible to even see where the cuts were located.

I let my eyes close, my blood calming. I ripped the cloth wrapping my chest off and threw it to the side. The cool summer breeze and softness of my shirt against my skin felt heavenly. The soft breeze across my face and the swishing of leaves was almost enough to put me to sleep. But I sat upright looking around me. Trees. A whole wall of them lay behind me. I then realized just how long I had been riding through the kingdom. I was at the edge of the territory. I lay at the edge of the forest surrounding the queens land. I had to have been on that horse for several hours to make it this far. To have made it to freedom. This is where Penn had told me to go, the edge of the territory.

New found energy filled my veins as I got to my feet. The Forest of the Damned. That's what the people of Willowmore called it. We were told stories about this place as children to make us behave. Most adults still believed the horror stories of this place. But I knew they were just tales threatening death and creatures made from nightmares. They were just stories created to keep the queens people from fleeing, to keep us under her rule. I would not be scared. Forgetting the horse, I entered the forest.

The temperature seemed to drop by twenty degrees. The soft movement of the leaves seemed to whisper sharply to each other. The canopy lay so thick above, it was like a blanket. The feeling of being watched only grew the deeper into the forest I walked. I soon found myself regretting entering the woods, but I knew that if I turned around I would never find my way back. I had to keep going and hope that I found a way out.

I walked and walked, stumbling through the darkness. Every noise made me flinch, the cold sinking deep below my skin. My exhaustion had almost convinced me to stop and rest when, I heard it. A noise that wasn't the wind or trees shifting. It was a footstep. Someone or something was here. And they knew I was too. I froze, straining to hear any other movement. My heart pounded loudly. How could I fight it off? I had no weapons, no energy. I was bruised and bloody and the perfect target for any creature that wanted to do me harm. My panic spiked as I heard another footstep, then another. Then they came rapidly. Whatever it was, was running.

The steps became louder, and I knew it was coming right for me. I took off, sprinting and pushing myself as hard as I could go. But even everything I had left wasn't enough. A solid mass smashed into my shoulder and knocked me to the ground, a heavy weight fell atop me. I began bucking and thrashing trying to throw it off. My panic finally taking over, I let out a scream. A hand clamped over my mouth. A *human* hand. I froze, my eyes adjusting and focusing. Pinning me to the ground was a man.

I couldn't make out his features but his grey eyes seemed to glow in the darkness.

"Get off me." I snarled, struggling to pull myself free from his grip and weight. His body held me firmly in place. His body tensed above me.

"You're a girl?" His voice was low and filled with shock. He sat back on his heels, leaving my torso free to move. I attempted to throw a punch but my body ached with the movement and he caught my wrist easily. He grabbed the other hand and pinned them to the ground above my head. Whoever he was, royal guard or commoner, he was going to turn me in. Is this really how I was to be caught? So close to freedom? I gritted my teeth and called on my anger to fuel me one last time. I called to the aching in my chest, called to the pain filling my body and let it burn within me. I smashed my head into his, blood squirted from his nose and onto my already bloody skin. I smiled weakly as he cursed, his bright eyes narrowing dangerously. Pain danced through my skull from where it connected with his. After a moment of anger, his teeth flashed in a bloody wicked smile as he brought his face back to mine.

"You're a fighter." His voice sent a shiver down my spine. My body too tired to panic, to fight or even be afraid, finally shut down. My vision went black.

Chapter 4

Light danced behind my eye lids, like the sun was playing hide and seek. My head pounded and my body ached. Muffled voices floated around me. Was I back at the inn? Did those voices belong to guests having dinner in the hall below? How did I get back to the inn? The last thing I remembered I was running through a forest when-

My eyes shot open and I straightened in the chair I sat in. My wrists and feet were bound with rope. My heart raced frantically. I was in the middle of a large room, the ceilings were high and a dozen lit lanterns hung high above, illuminating the space below. Bookshelves were carved into the walls, the entire room overflowing with more books than I had ever seen. Carvings to resemble tree roots wound through the groups of books like tentacles. Long tables stretched the length of the room, their surfaces covered with every weapon imaginable. Knifes and swords of every length sparkled in the light. Axes, daggers, flails and bows. They were all beautifully crafted, each one polished to perfection and sharpened to deadly points. There were no windows, I couldn't tell if it was day or night. How long had I been out? Was it still Prospers day?

Tables stacked with books and lanterns were placed throughout the room. A large fireplace blazed to life, filling the room with warmth. The floor was smooth grey stone, it's color complimenting the room well. It was a rather beautiful space, but I didn't stop to admire it for long. Spread throughout the room, some sitting and others standing, were seven men. All with their eyes on me. Leather chest plates were strapped tightly to their chests. Weapons hung from their belts. They were all huge, much larger than Geran or other men within the city. Large muscles bulged from under their clothes. They were obviously well fed and very dangerous.

I strained against the ropes binding me to the chair. One of the large men pulled a chair in front of me and sat. The chair was dwarfed by his size. I recognized him as the man who had tackled me in the woods by his unnaturally bright grey eyes. He was at least a foot taller than me with lean muscles layering his body. His chest plate fit the contours of his body perfectly. The line of his jaw was sharp and defined, his nose was crooked from being broken one to many times. Flecks of his dried blood from where I hit him earlier stained his skin. Even thought I knew I broke the bone of his nose, his face didn't seem hurt at all. No bruises or scratched skin to indicate where I had hit him. His black hair fell over his bright eyes as he watched me intensely. I felt magic flowing through him, different than the warlocks I was surrounded by in the city. It was stronger, far more powerful than anyone else I had met. Whatever magic lived within him, he wasn't a sorcerer. There was something dark within his gaze that sent a shiver down my spine. I returned his stare with a glare. The silence in the room was deafening as they all waited for me to speak.

"We just want to ask you some questions." The grey eyed man said, his voice soft and deep like velvet. I continued to glare, letting my anger slowly burn to life within me. "What's your name?" He asked calmly. I remained silent but my insides twisted with the urge to speak like if I didn't I would burst. A muscle ticked in his jaw. "What's your name?" Unable to restrain myself anymore, I answered him the pressure building within me releasing immediately.

"Lorn." I growled.

"Don't try and fight answering or it won't be pleasant for you." He was using magic. My eyes flashed with violent anger. I'll rip him to pieces for using magic against me. "What are you Lorn?" I snorted, his question absurd and insulting. Obviously they worked for the queen, asking the same question she had asked in the city square. They didn't look like royal guards though. I looked around the room as pressure built within me again waiting for an answer. Every set of eyes was serious and listening for me to speak. I raised an annoyed brow at the grey eyed man.

"I know the shaved head might be a little odd but if I'm the first woman you guys have seen you all really need to get out more." A young red headed boy standing by the fire suppressed a grin.

"That's not what I meant." The mans silver eyes narrowed as he snarled at me. His jaw flexed in irritation. I grinned, happy I pissed him off. If they wanted to question me or turn me in or kill me, I wasn't going to make it easy whatever it was that they had planned for me. "We know you aren't human or a witch so what are you?" I found nothing but confusion. They were obviously just as crazy as the queen. "I need you to say it." His voice sounded almost desperate.

"Not that I think you or your precious queen will believe me, but I have no idea what you are talking about." I didn't need the pressure to build from the spell before answering. Anger flashed across his face.

"We do not serve Mortala." The venom in his words sent a pang of fear through my chest. If they weren't royal guards, what did they want with me? "Now, don't lie or it won't be pleasant for you." His voice dropped dangerously low.

"I'm not lying, I have no idea what you're asking me. I am human!" I snapped. He leaned forward in his chair, his face just a few inches from mine. The muscles covering his body strained under his clothing.

"We know there is magic in your veins we just need to know what kind." I barred my teeth, my wrists pulled against the rough rope, aching to get ahold of the man in front of me.

"If I had access to magic I wouldn't be tied to this chair and you wouldn't be fucking breathing." I brought my forehead forward hard, smashing it against his nose once again. He sat back, his eyes screwed shut as blood ran down his face.

"Fuck!" He growled. I shook my head, trying to get rid of the pain erupting through my face. I looked at those around the room.

"Anybody else turned on?" I teased, several of the men's faces turned scarlet. I smiled at their discomfort and the pain I caused the grey eyed man. "No? Just me?" Grey eyes met mine fiercely, his mouth opened to speak, but a male with wild green hair placed a calming hand on his shoulder, silencing him. He had white eyes, void of all color. His face was wrinkled with age and his bright orange robes swirled around him. Magic hummed powerfully through his blood.

"Let me talk to her Caligan." The grey eyed man glowered at me, the bleeding now stopped. But he stood from the chair and the warlock took his place. I mocked a frown as I watched him walk away.

"Play time over already?"

"My name is Ciprian." He gave me a kind smile, stealing my attention.

"You're eyes are white." I had never seen such a thing on a warlock before. I was stunned by the haunting feature. Humor crinkled the skin around his eyes.

"And yours are brown." Stating the obvious like I had. "I apologize for the circumstances in which you were brought here," he gestured to the ropes at my hands and feet. "But we must be cautious." I eyed him.

"Cautious? Everyone in this room is twice the size of me, at least two of you have access to magic and by the feel of it, you're both very powerful. Am I really that threatening?" I asked dryly, my temper still rising. The old warlock nodded.

"Yes, you are." I furrowed my brow. "Tell me Lorn, how do you know someone is a sorcerer? Tell me how you identify them." My eyes darted to his vibrant green hair and ghostly eyes. "Yes, there are physical attributes. What else?" I shrugged, not knowing the purpose behind such a question.

"You can feel the magic in their blood." I nodded to the glowering grey eyed man apparently named Caligan. "I can feel his, but he's not a warlock. His blood is different." His white eyes smiled as the warlock nodded.

"You're very right. Caligan isn't a warlock." I gaped at him before looking back at the large mans towering figure.

"Then what are you?" I asked. Caligan growled but nobody answered my question. I snarled at him. Ciprian leaned forward in his chair. "I can feel the power within you. It grows with your temper." He was crazy, they all were. I have never shown any signs of magic, I've always been normal; been mundane. I've spent my whole life being attacked for being human and now this crazy old man wants to tell me I have magic within me? "To further prove my theory," His white eyes held mine steadily. "Humans can't feel magic." Definitely fucking crazy.

"You're mistaken." I gritted my teeth, my anger flaring.

"I saw you in the square today."

My fury sparked. "Celebrating Prospers day were you?" I snapped. How could all these other human men follow someone that celebrates their hatred? The wizard shook his head, a glare forming in his eyes.

"I will never celebrate something that condones the violence of another creature." I dropped my gaze, the truth in his words undeniable. "I was gathering some supplies, the crowd granted me coverage." He waved a hand in the air, his face reclaiming a calm peace. "I saw you with Mortala. She noticed your blood too. Noticed it was different. She knew you were a threat." My heart seemed to freeze as he spoke, my instinct was to trust him, but why? Was this another spell? The sorcerer leaned forward in his chair. "You genuinely believe you are human, don't you?" I nodded. The others shifted closer to the old male and me.

"Let me prove it to you." His blank eyes were kind and his smile was warm. "If I can't prove you have magic within you, then we will send you on your way with whatever supplies we can spare. Nobody will ever know you were here." I eyed him skeptically.

"And if by some miracle you can, what will you do with me then? Turn me into the queen? Use me for your own reasons?" My curiosity overshadowed my anger.

"Then you can still leave if that's what you want. But you can also stay here, and I can teach you how to harness and control your power. We are not Mortalas people, we aren't even in her territory anymore. We will not hold you or force you to do anything you don't want to." His offer seemed genuine, but why would he offer to help a stranger?

"What's in it for you?" I kept my voice even. "Nobody does anything for free in this world. Why would you want to help me?" Ciprians eyes seemed to look directly through me as he considered my question.

"Everyone needs help every now and then." His hand gripped my metal tipped fingers, his movements quick. I struggled to pull away but the ropes forbid me from moving. His gaze was curious as he inspected the bits of metal. He gave the one on my pointer finger a gentle tug.

"They wont come-" My voice died in my throat as the small bit of metal pulled free and rolled gently into his palm. My shock made my chest constrict. I had tried cutting, prying even melting those fucking pieces of metal but nothing had ever worked. And seemingly without any effort, he was able to pull it free? I looked to the old warlock with wide eyes. He gave me a small smile before pulling a small knife from within his robes and leaned forward. I tensed, panic pulsing through me. But he didn't move to harm me. Instead he began cutting away the ropes at my wrists.

"I don't know what life you have led, but based on the scars covering your skin it hasn't been an easy one." I watched as he released one hand and began working on the other. Caligan tensed behind him and placed a hand on the scythe hanging from his hip. I shot him a glare but remained still. Ciprian continued. "We are all here," he gestured to the group around us. "because we fled lives full of violence and darkness. Here we have found peace, safety, and freedom. And if you choose, magic or no magic, you can join us and perhaps find peace of your own."

I rubbed my raw wrists as I thought about his offer. Could he really just want to be kind? Or was he hiding his true motives? I glanced at the newly freed skin on the tip of my finger. The skin was sensitive and smooth. I looked back to the wizard, who lounged casually in the chair in front of me.

"They were placed there by a very powerful creature. Warlock, witch or whatever they were, placed them there to smother your power." Ciprian explained. "Whomever it was, was very powerful. And yes, I can remove the rest of them. But I will need time in between each, as this one," He held up the small bit of metal "drained quiet a bit of my power." His bright hair and eyes seemed to have dimmed since the removal, the magic in his veins now flowed dully. My curiosity was now peaked beyond the panic, fear and pain jolting through my body.

"If you are just planning to let me go, why bring me here?" The others shifted uncomfortably around the room, Caligan stood still and his head tilted as he watched me. I turned back to those ghostly white eyes. "And don't give me any bullshit about wanting to help me find peace." My face twisted into a deadly mask. "What do you want from me?' Ciprian opened his mouth but Caligan was the one to speak.

"Because the magic that lies within your veins, is the same that flows through mine." His grey eyes traced my face with angry curiosity. "And for the past two hundred years, I've been the only one left of our people."

Chapter 5

"And what are you? Besides annoyingly large and obviously repressed sexually?" I couldn't help myself from goading him. I smiled wildly at the angry snarl that spread across his full lips. Ciprian raised a hand, silencing whatever was about to come out of his mouth.

"Grady, please bring something for Lorn to eat." There was slight hesitation throughout the group of men, but a tall, lanky man with bright golden hair silently and slowly exited the room through a door that lay behind me. The others remained quiet. Caligan remained behind the warlock and stood quietly. "Are you familiar with this lands history? I believe Mortala claimed the name, *Forest of the Damned.*" The wizard asked. I crossed my arms and leaned back in the chair.

"Only spooky stories. We were told about the Forest of the Damned as children and its still talked about among adults." I rolled my eyes. "Even the elderly are afraid of this place." The grey eyed brute tensed. Ciprian remained calm.

"Do you not believe the tales told?"

I chuckled lightly. "No, like I said. They are spooky stories told to scare us all into submission."

"And what do you know of Mortalas marriage?" Caligans whole body went ridged at Ciprians words, rage rolled off of him. I did my best to ignore him.

"King Dolant had an affair with a human and when the queen," the group of men all spat at my words. "When she," I corrected "found out, she killed them and his entire race." The warlock shook his head.

"That's not how the stories are told." His eyes remained kind but the lines around his mouth tensed. "She damned his people." I nodded, irritated by his correction.

"Same thing."

"No its not." Caligan snarled. He walked to stand next to the warlock, his body hard with anger. "She sentenced them to an existence worse than death." He bent low and put his face directly in front of mine. His hands rested on the arms of the chair, caging me. Fear and a small pang of something else shifted through my chest. His lips curled in a cruel smile. "She took his entire race, and turned them into a horror story." I raised a brow, not letting him see the fear within me.

"Are you saying that his people are the creatures that supposedly haunt these woods?" My voice was dry and even despite my racing heart. He flashed his teeth.

"Not supposedly. That's exactly what they are." His eyes darkened viciously. "The most powerful race of magical creatures, reduced to mindless, killing beasts. Cursed with roaming a dead, rotting forest for the rest of time." His words were icy, his voice a growl within his chest.

"If she cursed his entire race, and you are somehow apart of the same, how are you still normal?" His eyes never left mine.

"Magic is very specific, the larger the spell the more particular you have to be. She was only able to curse those within the territory. I was outside of the kingdom at the time she cast the enchantment."

"What does this have to do with anything?" I asked through clenched teeth, angry with his proximity. His eyes narrowed.

"Are you really that stupid?" My anger spiked. I kicked up, sending my knee into his groin. He went to his knees, cursing through his teeth. I leapt from the chair and slid around the warlock sitting across from me and over to one of the tables covered in weapons. I grabbed the first blade I saw which was a dagger. The blade was sleek black metal, the handle matching in touch and color. I hurled around and found Caligan on his feet and charging for me.

I swung the blade which he easily dodged. None of the others in the room moved to stop me, a few of them actually loosed small laughs which only fueled the anger within me. He stuck out his foot and looped it around my ankle and pulled me to the ground. I went down, but used the momentum to bring the blade through the thick muscle of his thigh. With a growl of pain, he kicked the blade from my hand, sending the dagger across the room. His body covered mine, pinning me to the ground below him. His hand wrapped painfully around my wrist, his eyes pinned to my hand. His face twisted in a wicked smile as he brought his steely eyes to mine. The room filled with quiet gasps from the men around us.

"Still believe you're human?" I followed his stare back to my hand where violet flames danced across the tip of my freed finger and down my palm. I writhed frantically under Caligans weight as panic erupted in my chest but it soon faded. The flame didn't hurt, they actually felt soft and familiar. It was almost like seeing a old friend. I realized with a small gasp that those flames weren't anything but my own anger. The fury within me flickered gently on my skin.

"Enough!" Ciprian bellowed. "Off of her! Now!" Caligan gave me one last smile before he released me and got to his feet. The place where I cut his leg didn't bleed, the skin under his torn pants was smooth and untouched. My eyes remained on the beautiful flame. It kissed my skin gently and lightly as it flickered. My anger now gone, the fire slowly died, leaving my hand feeling cold. I turned back to the warlock who now stood above me. He knelt beside me, his soft hand encasing my own as he stared at me with wonder in his white eyes.

How was this possible? How had I never known what lay within me? My heart raced, my body feeling shaky. This entire day had been too much. My entire life had changed within a matter of hours. I was now wanted within the kingdom. The queen wanted me dead, I found myself kept in a room by a group of strange men. And I now possessed the ability to use magic that had always been within me. This all had to be just a very vivid, very fucked up dream.

My heart beat rapidly, my body still aching and hurting from today's events. Panic, fear, and confusion clouded my mind, the room felt like it was tilting and spinning. The men around me faded into nothing as I stumbled through the room blindly. I pushed open the door on the far wall and tripped as I scaled a small staircase. I burst through the door at the top, the night swallowing me whole. I could hear footstep and shouts from behind me. Panic roared in my ears and filled my chest. I took off for the tree line across the dark open field I found myself in.

I fell back into the thick of the forest. Darkness swarmed me as my mind raced and my heart thundered. This was all a bad dream, none of this was real. It couldn't be. I stumbled and fell to the dry, hard ground. Footsteps closed in behind me. I turned, expecting to find one of the large behemoths that had taken me, but I was wrong. So terribly, dreadfully wrong. What stood before me wasn't a man, it wasn't even human.

The creature before me stood tall. Its skin thick and leathery, stretched tightly over a grotesquely thin body. Long, sharp claws protruded from long, boney hands. Sharp fangs dripped with slime. Its black eyes focused on my cowering figure on the ground. I had never known true panic until this moment. This was a thing of nightmares. A thing from hell. This was a creature of the

Damned. I scrambled back, a scream dying in my throat. The creature released a screeching roar as it lunged at me. I curled in on myself, awaiting the dreadful end I had been given. A painful ending, to a painful life.

The attack never came. Sharp claws didn't shred though me, and no fangs claimed my flesh. I peaked through a gap in my arms to find the creature dead on the ground, black inky blood seeping from the wide gash in its chest. Caligan stood above the Damned, chest heaving, black blood peppering his skin. His grey eyes glowed with fury as he looked down at the beast that was once one of his own. He hung his blood soaked scythe between his shoulders and knelt at my side.

He placed a hand on my shoulder, his mouth moving but I couldn't understand what he was saying. Darkness swirled around me. My body sagged, the shock and panic of everything too much. My vision swam as my emotions took over. I began to shut down, my mind and body too tired to fight, too tired to think. My head hit the hard ground and I was swallowed up and fell into nothingness.

Chapter 6

I awoke to the smell of lavender and leather. My body was cushioned and encased by soft, fluffy blankets and pillows that felt like they were stuffed with clouds. My body still ached and demanded more sleep. Instead of the sounds of voices and city streets that I was used to waking up to, the tranquil, summer sweet songs of birds flitted into the room around me. I didn't know it was possible to wake up so peacefully. The tired fog surrounding my mind cleared sharply and quickly as the memories of the night before came rushing back. The queen, the forest, my captures, and the creature of the Damned.

I sat up quickly, a sharp pain pulsed through my temple. I found myself in a large bed. Thick, fluffy blankets and pillows surrounded me like a nest. The room was painted a pale yellow, the sunlight coming in from windows cast the room in a warm, sweet light. Shelves filled with jars containing different plants and flowers, powders and liquids lined the walls. Two small end tables sat on either side of me, books covered their surfaces. A work table was pushed against the far wall, covered in notebooks and measuring tools. The space was clean, the air fresh with summer.

A bolt of fury went through me as I realized my skin was clean from the gore that covered it the night before. Scrapes and bruises bloomed violently over my body. A shirt, that wasn't mine, hung loosely from my shoulders and pooled around my hips. My legs were bare.

One of those fuckers had cleaned and dressed me. I leapt from the bed, anger burning hot within me. The shirt fell almost to my knees, it obviously belonged to one of those neanderthals that tied me to the chair last night. I looked for my boots and pants but didn't find them anywhere. My little golden watch was gone as well.

A chest lay at the foot of the bed, its wood heavy and smooth. I flipped the lid open to find neatly stacked piles of clothes. I pulled out a pair of pants, their length much to long for me but I would have to make them work. I rolled the legs several times before I could actually see my feet and had to use a belt I found within the chest to tie them around my waist. I would have to go barefoot, there wasn't anything I was able to do about that. There was nothing within the room I could use as a weapon, everything probably cleared out on purpose. I huffed angrily and threw open the door. My eyes widened at the beauty that lay before me.

A wooden porch surrounded the small cottage I had just left. The wooden structure was constructed by pale soft wood, pale yellows shutters were thrown open to welcome the soft summer breeze. Wooden bridges connected several other cottages, varying in color from blue to green to red. It was like a tiny village, but the most extraordinary part of the sight, was what it was held by. Enormous tree branches snaked through the air, holding the cottages gracefully and securely. I peered over the edge of the small balcony. We were several dozen feet in the air. The branches fell gracefully and connected with a tree trunk larger than any house I had ever seen. These men may be strange and infuriating, but they lived beautifully.

I made my way across the wooden bridges, hoping I would find a way down from the small town I found myself in. I trailed my hand lazily across the wooden railings lining the bridges. Down below was a large circular pasture with small buildings and a large garden dotting the green carpet. A few rows of lively, lush trees surrounded the opening, but beyond the forest lay dark, rotted, and dead in a vast expanse that sent chills down my spine. I really was in the Forest of the Damned. My stomach dropped. There was no hope of me escaping the group of strange men through there without boots, weapons or provisions.

I continued along the connecting bridges and cottages until they led me to a winding staircase leading to the ground far below. It wrapped around the massive trunk, the railings twisted vines. I walked down tentatively, my muscles and body aching and screaming from the damage done to them yesterday. I rubbed my single freed finger tip across my palm where my angry flames had flickered to life last night. My heart raced and my anger sparked inside of me once more the closer I reached the ground below. My goal was to find something to use to cut whoever it was that washed and clothed me while I was unconscious. Then find my boots and get the hell out of this forest.

The grass was soft and tickled my feet. I don't think I had ever walked through grass without shoes on. A small pang of sadness hit my chest at the thought. Something so small seemed like such a sweet thing. I stared at the blades of the greenery poking between my toes, the sight rather odd but felt weirdly free. Voices from across the clearing broke me out of my trance. The blonde man, Grady, from last night stood by the large garden with the green haired wizard. I squared my shoulders and strolled over to them, my anger simmering just below the surface.

The two were laughing and talking, Grady's sleeves were rolled up, his tan forearms on display. His belt was full of knives, a whip lay coiled through one of the loops. Ciprian was dressed in long, yellow robes. They glowed softly in the sunlight. They both turned to me as I approached, a wide smile on the warlocks face.

"Good morning Lorn." He squinted up at the bright sun. "Or should I say afternoon." Grady smiled kindly and offered me his dirt stained hand.

"I'm Grady. Sorry I didn't get a chance to introduce myself last night." I ignored his outstretched hand.

"Yeah it was kind of hard to have a proper introduction with being tied to a chair and all." I replied dryly. His hand dropped, but his smile remained and grew.

"I can see why Caligan likes her." The warlock chuckled and I glared at both of them.

"How did you sleep? I hope Caligans room was comfortable enough." My hands curled into fists, the metal of my fingers dug painfully into my palms. I stepped closer to the blonde man, craning my neck to keep eye contact. I snarled at him, my anger bubbling and rising within me.

"Is he the pervert that washed me and dressed me?" My teeth clenched painfully together. Gradys smile widened even further, stoking the flames within me. I lunged, teeth bared and flames sparking to life along my finger and palm. He jumped away from my reach but not before my violent flames touched his skin. I fell to the ground and turned to watch him dance out of my reach cursing loudly as he gripped his burned forearm. I smiled triumphantly as the rest of his strange group came running out of the few buildings dotting the clearing. Grady continued to curse and yell as our small group grew. I lounged back on my hands, my fingers sinking softly into the dirt of the garden underneath of me. Caligan took hold of Grady's burned arm and shot a glare at me. I smiled sweetly and turned to inspect the dirt under my nails.

"What did you do?" The annoying giant growled.

"I think its pretty obvious what she did." A man with a wild mess of brown hair said after looking at the red, bubbling burn on Grady. Caligan turned his glare at him and the red headed boy laughing silently at his side.

"I can see what she did," he returned his grey eyes to me and began stalking towards me "But why?" He demanded. I cocked my head and returned his angry stare.

"You couldn't have really expected me to be happy and grateful upon waking up, knowing you not only undressed me last night, but bathed me." He laughed then, they all did, except Grady who continued to hiss in pain. Caligan continued to prowl closer, his movements like a predator.

"Its called magic, sweetheart. I didn't touch or see anything." He gave me that same wicked grin he flashed me last night. A pang of embarrassment hit me as he spoke. I narrowed my eyes at him as my cheeks began to redden.

"How do I know if you're telling the truth?" I challenged. "I was unconscious, so who knows what kind of fucked up things you did or didn't do." The red headed boy grinned wildly at me while the others did their best to stifle their laughs and grins. Caligan placed his hands on his hips. His forearms were bare, scars decorated his skin like mine.

"After you blacked out, I used magic to get all that blood off of you and then to get rid of those clothes because they were torn and smelled like shit. I then carried you to bed and left." His voice was strong, no hint of untruth underlying his words. I climbed to my feet and crossed my arms.

"You're a dick. And don't call me sweetheart." His grin remained as he moved his hands to his belt. Two small black scythes hung from each hip and several small throwing knives were tucked between them. "Where are my boots?" I asked, my toes curling around the soft grass.

"Being cleaned." Ciprian said with a small smile. "I'll have them returned to you when they are done." I eyed the warlock. No warlock or witch had ever spoken to me with such kindness or gone out of their way to help me. He gestured to the wooden structure behind the large group. "Shall we sit? Talk about some things? We can answer any questions you may have." He said gently. I looked between the men around me.

"Am I a prisoner?" I questioned, my voice steady.

"No." Cirprian said at the same time Caligan shrugged and answered "Kind of." My body tensed as my gaze shot between the warlock and the annoying large man.

"How can you kind of be a prisoner?" I asked annoyed.

"We're not going to chain you up or force you to do anything," the man with the brown curly hair said, "but you can't leave. At least not yet." The group nodded. I glared at the one who spoke. He gave me a small smile and raised a hand in greeting. "I'm Lagan by the way."

"Pleasure." I replied with an eye roll. I returned my gaze to those glowing grey eyes. "Why can't I leave? If you're worried about me running and telling somebody about your little secret hide out, don't worry. I have no desire to let anyone know I had anything to do with any of this." I gestured to the odd group in front of me. A man with black hair and honey colored eyes that lifted at the edges spoke next, his voice gruff and hard.

"We aren't worried about that, nobody will believe you that there are people living in this forest anyway."

I glared at him. "Then why keep me? I'm obviously more of a burden than anything." I gestured to Gradys burnt arm. I shrugged. "It will just be easier on everyone if you let me go." Caligan waved his hand and the bubbling, bleeding burn on Gradys arm vanished without a trace of the gruesome injury. I gapped at the ease in which he had healed him.

"It would be easier," He agreed. "but I'm not too keen on letting the only other one of my race walk through that forest and get ripped to pieces." Sadness flickered through my heart. I finally had a chance to be free and find peace and immediately I find myself trapped. Caligans grin now completely vanished and his brow furrowed as he watched me. I let my anger burn the sadness away for the second time today.

"Let's all take a seat and we can talk more." Ciprian said again and began walking in the other direction. The group slowly turned and followed. Caligan was the last to turn. I was left alone by the garden. I had the perfect opportunity to run, boots or no boots. I could make a weapon once in the forest. But I wouldn't make it far. If last night was any indication, what awaited me in the trees would definitely require something more than weapons made of sticks. I followed the odd group.

I came up to an outdoor kitchen made of stone and polished wood. A roof was made from logs and the side remained open. A long dining table sat in the center of the space next to a large fire pit. A small barn sat next to the outdoor eating area, the windows thrown open. Inside I could see another kitchen and eating area, probably used in the colder months and when there was bad weather. The group sat around the table and waited for me to join. I took the only empty seat at the end of the table.

"So, as Caligan had kind of explained, you are not technically a prisoner but we are hesitant on letting go the only other of his kind still alive." Ciprian said softly. My body went ridged, what exactly were they planning to do with me?

"Are you wanting to use me to reproduce so your race doesn't go extinct?" My voice was filled with icy venom as I turned to Caligan who only smirked at my anger and fear.

"First off, its *our* race. And second, only if you say please." My hands curled into fists so tight I could feel the metal cut through my skin, drawing blood. The table held back laughs. "But that's not the plan. I just need to figure a few things out about you before you leave." He sat back in his chair.

"Like what?" I crossed my arms across my chest relief flooding through me. Not that I would be able to repopulate an entire breed of magic, but they didn't need to know that. They don't need to know anything about me or my life. The man with honey colored eyes answered.

"Like how it's possible you are what you are." The table nodded.

"I told you last night, for two hundred years I've been the only one left." Caligan said with dry coolness. My frustration started to grow larger and larger within me.

"How long will it take you to figure that out?" He shrugged. "So what am I supposed to do in the mean time?" It was Ciprian who answered then.

"You make yourself at home." He gestured to the space around us. The sun was warm and lovely overhead and the birds sang beautifully. "We only have one rule, that we all do our part for the clan. We take care of ourselves while also taking care of everyone else." They all turned their eyes on me. This was all way too good to be true.

"That can't be it."

"It is." A man with rich, mocha skin said. "We will find what job best suits your talents and interests, and one you can do to help everyone out. We all have our own jobs and do our part. I'm our blacksmith." He pointed to the red headed boy next to him. "Silas here, is our bomb maker. The things he creates help us keep our home here safe."

"During your time here, we will teach you how to properly fight and defend yourself." Lagan added.

"And how to properly use and control your power." Ciprian said finally. I considered their words carefully. Could that really be it?

"So what you're saying is, you're going to find out how its possible for me to be like you," I pointed at Caligan. "And then you'll let me go?" They all nodded.

"Unless, you choose to stay. And if that is the case, we will gladly welcome you to stay." These strange men were offering me a place to stay, train and grow my power, with virtually nothing in return. Maybe while I was here I could locate a place for me to go to after they got whatever information they wanted from me. A place far from Willowmore, where I could start over. Free from persecution and violence. A place I could find peace. Of course I can't trust these men, but much like the deals I had made in Willowmore, I could use this to my advantage. I sat back in my chair.

"Do I at least get my own room?"

The blacksmith, who introduced himself as Asher, showed me back up the spiral staircase to where my quarters will be. We began crossing several bridges, I followed quietly behind him, watching the others go back to whatever they had been doing before I burned Grady. The warlock remained at the dining table while Grady began preparing a meal in the kitchen behind him. Asher caught me looking down at the beautiful pasture and addressed me from over his shoulder.

"We don't know why, but its the only place within the forest that isn't touched by the rot and decay that effects the rest of it." We kept walking. A knife hung loosely from the back of his hip, glinting in the sunlight. I faked tripping, bumbling into him briefly.

"Sorry, I'm not used to not wearing shoes." I grumbled my apology and slipped the stolen knife into the back of my waist band. The blade rested against my back, the cold steal smooth against my skin. I felt more at ease with a weapon on hand. We stopped in front of a small outage with warn wood walls and a red roof. The door and open shutters matching the roofs red hue. Asher waved a hand in front of it.

"Nobody will be able to get in without being invited. But, you don't have to be afraid of us." His brown eyes were warm, I found no untruth to his words but some people were very good liars. I allowed myself to nod even though I still wasn't about to let my guard down. "At the base of the trunk, there is a stone staircase leading to a series of warm springs. Hang a shirt or something at the top so we know you're there and wont walk in on you." The idea of a warm bath had me eager to climb back down the large staircase. Asher then turned and started back across the bridge we had crossed.

The small house was quaint, with a small porch out front. It reminded me of what I imagined my own house would look like when I was a child. Another pang of sadness hit my heart at the innocent thoughts my mind used to have. I pushed the door open and instantly cursed myself for immediately loving the small home. The room inside was spacious with a large bed centered on the far wall. Fluffy and plump pillows and blankets beckoned to me welcomingly. Two small end tables sat on either side, an oil lamp placed atop one of them. Book shelves covered the walls, they lay empty but full of promise. I suddenly missed my vast collection back at the inn.

A desk and a long counter took up the rest of the wall space. The open windows allowed the light breeze to flow through the space peacefully. Peace. That's what this tiny home made me think as soon as I crossed the threshold. I turned and quickly stepped back outside, shutting the door softly behind me. I can't let myself think that way. This place was temporary, I can't go falling in love with my new little home no matter how perfect it was.

I stood with my back against the door for several moments before walking back in. On one of the shelves was a towel, some soap and a few stacks of clothes. I grabbed what I needed and began hunting for the warm springs Asher had told me about. At the base of the trunk, I left one of the shirts I had grabbed hanging on a branch before following the stone path down a hill, lush with beautiful plants and flowers. I walked for a while, distracted by the scenery when I finally came up on the mouth of a small cave. Small, glowing lanterns lit the walkway. A few feet into the cave, I audibly gasped.

It opened into a large cavern, the stone walls were smooth and glistened and sparkled as its surface shifted in iridescent colors. A large pool of water lay in the center, continually replenished by a steady stream coming from the far wall. It was breathtaking, the most beautiful space I think I had ever seen. This entire place, these odd men called home was like something from a dream. I eagerly stripped from the much too large clothes and sunk into the warm water. Its warmth was heavenly against my injured and aching body. I took my time cleaning my skin. even though Caligan had already washed it clean with his magic, I took joy in the feeling of the warm water.

I had never enjoyed a bath more. The multicolored walls sent tiny rainbows and sprays of color over my scared and bruised skin. When I finally pulled myself from the water and climbed back to the top of the hill, the sun was setting. The others had gathered around the dining table and kitchen but I didn't join them. I didn't feel like eating after the past couple of days events. Lanterns varying in size, shape and color lit and grew brighter the farther the sun fell in the sky. When I finally reached my cottage, the sky was dark but the trees around me and the ground beneath was lit with bright, colorful life.

I could hear the small group of men talking and laughing together while they ate. I realized, standing just outside the door, that the room I had woken up in, was across the connecting bridge. Great. I was neighbors with Caligan. I rolled my eyes and entered my temporary home. I laid the clothes I had stolen, when I awoke, in a pile on the desk and placed the stolen knife on the bedside table. Even though I had woken up just a few hours prior, I found myself exhausted. My body still ached from the trauma done to it yesterday and from the stress that followed. I pushed the heavy wooden desk in front of the door and locked it.

My mind told me I needed to stay awake and alert as long as possible, but I was too tired to do anything but crawl under the pile of cozy blankets. Almost as soon as my head hit the pillow, sleep found me. The sounds of night my lullaby.

Chapter 7

A loud banging woke me hours later. Sunlight streamed in brightly through the open windows. A few silent seconds passed before another loud knock came from outside the door. I grasped the dagger on the nightstand tightly and climbed from the cozy cocoon of blankets. I unlatched the door and shoved the desk out of the way. I glowered at Caligans towering figure as I opened the door. The morning sun stung my eyes.

"What?" I asked harshly, my voice thick with sleep. My body ached, my muscles still sore and stiff but they weren't as bad as they were the day before. His eyes traced my disheveled clothes. They hung from my thin frame and the pant legs had come untucked in my sleep and pooled around my ankles. The clothes left in my room are still too big, but not as big on me as Caligans had been.

"It's morning." He growled, his jaw flexing in irritation. I continued to glare.

"No shit." I felt as if I had just fallen asleep, how was the sun already up? His eyes narrowed.

"Breakfast will be served soon. Either hurry up or you wont eat until dinner." I rolled my eyes and moved to shut the door but his large hand slammed into its surface, stopping it from closing further. I gripped the knife behind my back tighter. "You have something of Ashers and he wants it back." He growled. So he finally noticed.

Why didn't he come take it back himself? Were they all really that afraid of me? Of my power? I hoped they feared me. With a small smile I stabbed the knife into the door where his hand rested. He pulled away quickly before I sliced through his flesh. His face twisted into anger and his mouth opened to say something but I slammed the door in his face, silencing him.

I rerolled the legs of my pants and sleeves before opening the door once more. Caligan was gone and the morning sun was already warm against my face, the air still and calm. Birds chirped merrily and sang within the trees. I climbed down from the small village in the branches and walked across the clearing to the kitchen area. The fire burned brightly within the pit and the table was crowded with sleepy men. Silas gave me a bright smile, his cheeks dimpling. Grady stood from his chair and offered it to me. I sat, giving him a small nod in thanks. I took an apple from a bowl in the center of the table and bit into it. The skin was sweet, juice dribbled down my chin.

Silas turned to me and began moving his hands before him, forming them into different shapes and then set them back atop the table. I looked at him with confusion, not understanding what he had just done. Lagan sat across the table, his thick brown hair stuck out in crazy angles. He spoke, breaking the silence between us.

"He can't speak." His voice was light and cheerful despite the drowsiness covering his features. That explains why he had been the only to not say anything since my arrival. "He uses his hands to make signs to communicate. He just said, good morning." He ran a hand through his messy hair. I turned to the red haired boy, his young face lit brightly with a smile. He seemed to be at least six years younger than the rest of the men, probably in his early teen years. I returned his smile with a small one of my own.

"Good morning." I paused. "It's Silas right?" I asked. His smile grew and he nodded before turning back to his bowl of chopped fruit. Lagan stood and collected his dirty dishes. He nodded to Asher who sat next to him.

"You've been introduced to Asher and Grady." He nodded to the dark haired man on the other side of Silas. His eyes were heavy with sleep as he slowly ate a bowl of porridge. "That's Elias." I felt like a child, the men surrounding me were all so much larger than me, their muscled bodies noticeable even through their clothes. They all took up too much space. They all towered above me, all capable of doing great damage. The eating area slowly emptied as they all stood and walked to the buildings on the other side of the clearing before disappearing into them. I remained, not knowing what to do. Eventually Caligan and I were the only ones left at the table. I finished my apple quietly as he ate a bowl of porridge. The summer breeze glided against my face gently. I closed my eyes as it drifted along, the songs of the birds flitting through the air beautifully.

Ciprian swept across the clearing half an hour after everyone had left. His robes were a deep blue and swished lightly around his ankles as he walked. He gave me a warm smile and poured himself a cup of coffee. His green hair was vibrant and wild, sticking out in all directions. His white eyes were wide with excitement. At least one of us was ready for today. He took a sip from his cup and gestured for me to stand.

"Good morning. How did you sleep?" He asked kindly as we walked to the fire pit. I shrugged, my muscles aching with the movement.

"Fine." I said quietly. He gave a small wave of his hand and three plush arm chairs appeared next to the fire. Caligan and Ciprian sat. The warlock gestured for me to join them. I could feel Caligans grey eyes on me as I sat and waited for the warlock. I could feel his stare on my skin like a gentle touch. I shivered and struggled to keep my eyes on the wizard in front of me. He drank heavily from his cup. I waited silently for him to finish. I started to get irritated the longer it took for him to finish his cup. Finally, he drained his drink and turned his attention to me.

"Tell me about yourself." He said, folding his hands in his lap. A spark of anger flared within me. I crossed my arms over my chest and glowered at him.

"You don't need to get to know me." I snapped. Caligan tensed at the acid in my words but Ciprian remained calm as he studied me. After a long pause he rose and stood before me. My body tensed as he reached for my hand, taking it gently. His hands were warm and delicate. They reminded me of thin glass or paper. I felt as if he would shatter if I used any amount of pressure.

He studied the metal on my fingers with intense curiosity. He flipped my hand over and then back again, tracing the lines the iron marked in my skin. He lightly grabbed the casing on my middle finger and pulled gently. It took longer than it had last time, but only slightly. The casing pulled free and rolled softly in his hand.

"Do you know who placed those on you?" He asked breathlessly. I shook my head and stared at the freshly freed skin.

"I have no memory without them. I always assumed it was someone's idea of a sick joke." I frowned, lightly touching the sensitive skin.

"I don't think it was done maliciously." My gaze snapped to his. "They were placed there with a powerful spell, very powerful magic was used to seal them to you." He wiped a bead of sweat from his forehead. "It took quite a bit out of me to remove just one. Whoever placed the spell was very powerful indeed." They had been put there with magic? I inspected him. His eyes seemed to have dulled along with his hair. The green wild locks seemed to have fallen and their color dampened. His skin was pale and clammy. If Ciprian was as old as he seemed to be, his power must be great. Sorcerers were known to live hundreds of years and age very slowly, for his age to be showing so much he must have been around far longer than me or any of the others here. The fact that such great power was used for something as insignificant as me seemed silly. A waste.

I rose from my chair and poured the weak male a glass of water. He accepted the glass with shaking hands and drank from it greedily. I felt guilty for how weak he had become, the magic thrumming through his veins was barely noticeable now. He finished the last of his water and leaned back in his chair. I returned to my seat and waited for him to speak.

"Thank you." He said pointing to the now empty cup. I gave him a small nod and held up my hand lightly.

"Thank you." I rubbed the tip again, finding the sensation odd.

"I can remove the rest but it will take time for me to recuperate. I might ask Caligan here for his help, I don't know if I'm strong enough to remove all of them." The young grey eyed man shifted in his char beside him. Ciprian gave me a weak smile. My heart sunk a little at his words. If I wanted him to finish with them I would have to stay, even if Caligan got the information he wanted. "Now, tell me about yourself." I frowned, frustrated yet again by the demand.

"You don't need to know me in order to get the information you want." I said dryly. He took a deep breath and folded his hands gently in his lap.

"Actually we do." The warlock replied. I raised a brow not buying it. "Magic always has a source. Something that powers it. Sorcerers rely on the earth for their power, we draw from it. Other creatures like ogres, rely on sunlight. Caligan and you, rely on emotion. You can draw from it, feel it, see it." He gestured to the man beside him. "When our source is blocked, so is our power. What we draw from will dictate how strong our power is in that moment." I gaped at him.

"Have you ever met an ogre?" My curiosity heightened. He chuckled softly. Caligan snorted and I shot him a deadly glare.

"Yes, and many other creatures." Caligan cut in. "But unfortunately, most have fled since Mortalas reign. Those that remained were executed at one point or another." My hatred for the queen grew. I admired the grey eyed man suddenly, for always calling her by her name instead of title. "I want to get to know you because I want to find what emotions are your strongest source. I can feel it sharpen when your mood changes, I just can't zero in on which ones are more potent for you."

I still doubted his words, but since the warlock removed another one of my metal casing, it made me feel like I owed them some cooperation. I cleared my throat and met his eyes steadily.

"What would you like to know?" I asked evenly. I didn't like talking about my life or the things I have had to go through. But if it got me out of here and on my way faster, I could manage a few stories. He tilted his head in thought.

"Why do you wear your hair so short?" He asked after a few quiet moments. My jaw clenched at the question and the memory it brought up. Anger sparked within me. I shook my head. I was not about to talk about that with strangers.

"Pick a different one." The warlock and grey eyed man remained silent, not budging. I sighed, obviously not going to convince them to change their mind on the question. I took in a large breath before speaking again.

"When I was young, a man attacked me and - " Ciprian raised a hand into the air, silencing me.

"Detail. Don't rush through it. Feel every moment of the memory." My temper flared. I didn't want to feel it. I didn't want to talk about it. It was obvious I didn't like the topic of conversation he had picked, and he wanted me to reminisce? I glared at him, my anger burning within me.

"When I was a young girl," I began again. "maybe ten or eleven I was sent to the market to pick up an order for the woman that employed me. On my way back I took a short cut through a series of alleys that I knew. I was a few blocks from the inn when a warlock with," I swallowed. The memory crawled across my skin making me flinch in disgust. "green skin came out of nowhere and grabbed me by the hair." My body shook with the rage that filled me as I thought of the mans face, thought of his horrid breath on my skin as he threw me to the ground.

"What did he do Lorn?" Ciprian said, his soft voice fed the furious flames within me. They swirled and fought to be released. I stood, facing the two males before me. The fire burned hot beneath my skin.

"Nothing." I snarled, lying between gritted teeth. "He did nothing to me."

No way was I going to talk about what that monster truly did to me. "I pulled myself away. He ripped chunks of hair out of my skull trying to hold onto me. When I finally broke free and made it home I shaved it and have done it ever since. I never let it grow long enough to pull or be used against me." My chest rose rapidly as I fought back my exasperation. "Every part of my life has been about survival so whatever else you want to know about me, whatever questions you have, let me answer all of them at once." I rolled up the sleeves of my shirt to expose the many scars decorating my skin.

"I've spent my whole life as a target and I am leaving this dreadful place behind. I could have been miles away if that brute," I pointed at Caligans glaring figure. "hadn't brought me here. You say that whoever cursed me with these," I held up my hands, the metal of my finger tips glinting in the sunlight. "Didn't do it out of cruelty. But if I hadn't have lived my whole life with them, I would have had access to the magic within me. I wouldn't have had to fight so hard to live. I would have been able to have a life that I could find peace in." My skin flushed with anger, my chest heaved. Ciprian didn't look at me, his gaze fell to my hands at my sides. Caligan held my gaze steadily.

"Are you satisfied?" I snapped. His eyes flared with anger but I turned my focus to Ciprian. "Can I go now?" I didn't care if he was possibly the only one who could remove the metal casings, I didn't care what lay within that dreadful forest, I didn't want to stay another minute here. The two exchanged a small glance, before returning their attention to me. My burning anger exploded, burning hotter and brighter as I watched them sit so calmly and quietly before me. Before I could yell or scream at them, Ciprian pointed a delicate finger at my hand before finally meeting my gaze.

"Your power feeds from your pain and anger. They are obviously your most potent emotions." His voice was sad and low. I looked down at my hand, the familiar flicker of flames danced across my fingers and palms once more. I couldn't think of anything to say to refute his claim. I could feel the anger and pain that swirled within me everyday, fighting violently within me. These guys may be weird and annoying, but they could read me like a damn book.

Chapter 8

I sank back into my chair and watched the flame slowly die as sadness filled my heart instead of the anger that flared to life so quickly. Despite the warm sunlight and the peaceful chirping of birds, I felt nothing but heavy sadness and fear weighing on me.

"Extraordinary." Ciprian whispered. I shook my head, a million questions running through my mind. Caligan had relaxed, his eyes shadowed in confusion and wrinkling his brow. I swallowed the lump in my throat. Ciprian leaned forward and took my hand in his and looked at the remaining metal casings glistening in the morning sun. He tapped one lightly.

"Who-ever placed these, knew what you are and wanted to protect you from it." I frowned as I thought about his words.

"Or they wanted to make sure I couldn't use it. You said they were powerful, maybe they just didn't want my magic to exist at all." I suggested but he shook his head.

"If they wanted to get rid of the power they would have just killed you, not try and give you a way to live with it." He rubbed the back of my hand gently. My eyes found Caligans steely gaze.

"Caligan," My voice cracked. Fear sparked in my chest. "What am I?" My heart raced as I waited for his response. Was I ready to hear it? My entire world had changed in a matter of hours. Would I be able to handle knowing what kind of creature I was? I was both relieved and frustrated by his response.

"An Empath. I can teach you and show you everything about them." My eyes rose up to meet Ciprians. His snowy eyes were gentle as he looked at me.

"And I will remove the rest of these." He tapped the metal on my fingers. "And we will teach to use your magic, how to control it." He waited quietly for me to answer. I sat quietly trying to get my thoughts in order. I could sense no evil from either of them, nothing to make me question their motives. Could I trust the warlock? Caligan? Could I trust the others they live with? I took a shaking breath and watched the grass move between my toes.

"I don't really have a choice." I said quietly. He stood, opening his arms wide to the space around him, his robes danced in the breeze.

"You always have a choice. This life can be whatever you want it to be. You can choose to see it as a prison, or as a new opportunity." His smile was small and kind. "Our king and government are long gone so we fall under no ones rule." I tapped my thumb on my collarbone as I thought over his offer. This all sounded too good to be true. "You can choose to keep fighting, or you can simply live." His words sent a pang through my heart. "Would you like a tour?" He asked. Maybe that could help me decide. I nodded. He turned to Caligan and began to say something but he was gone. He had been sitting there only a second ago, but he had simply vanished. The warlock shrugged and whistled in the direction of the garden. A blonde curly haired head popped out from behind an apple tree and Grady began jogging in our direction. The gardener quickly joined us, a smile spread over his lips. His clothes and boots were thick with dirt and grass stains.

"You can always walk over to me instead of whistling for me like a dog." Grady said cheerfully as he stood with us by the fire. Ciprian chuckled lightly.

"I know but that's too much work." He gestured to me. "I would like you to give Lorn a tour. Show her our home and explain what it's like here. Then she can help you prepare dinner tonight." Grady raised his brows and looked from me back to Ciprian.

"I can't cook." I said hurriedly. Grady smiled, a dimple appearing on either side of his lips.

"I can. Don't worry, ill do most of the work." When I didn't argue, he nodded and held out a hand, beckoning me to follow. I turned to Ciprian. His face was pale but his eyes seemed to have regained some of their lost brightness.

"Thank you." He gave me a small nod and I followed Grady across the grassy clearing. The morning sun cast the land in soft light, the scene becoming almost heavenly. This place was truly beautiful in every way. A small part of me didn't want to leave, but I shoved those thoughts aside quickly. The sun cast streaks of light throughout the branches of trees surrounding the small field. Wild flowers grew along the outer edge, their sweet scent flowing in the breeze. Three wooden and stone buildings were placed throughout the clearing. Curls of smoke rose from their chimneys.

"This place," my attention snapped to Grady. He stared out at the pasture, his golden hair glinted in the sun light. The sharp lines of his jaw exaggerated by the flattering light. "Is like our own little slice of heaven." I couldn't remember what the forest looked like last night when I had first entered. It had been too dark for me to notice any details about the woods around me, but he was right this place was truly heavenly. Grady began walking in the direction of the closest building. I jogged to keep up with his long stride.

"So are the creatures in the forest all so terrible?" I asked. His jaw tightened, a long scar along its edge shifting with the movement.

"If they weren't, why would we arm ourselves so heavily?" He gestured to his leather chest plate, matching the ones the group of men wore most of the time I saw them. Several knives were strapped to the front of the plate and his whip hung at his hip. "We are at war against the evil in this forest everyday. They used to be human, but now they truly are creatures from hell." We remained silent the rest of the walk, my mind spinning with the images of grotesque, violent creatures. The peace my surroundings had blessed me with suddenly evaporated.

As we neared the wooden building a loud banging rose from within followed by loud shouts and curses. Chuckling, Grady opened the door. A cloud of smoke barreled out of the open doorway, the inside slowly clearing out. Silas and Lagan were revealed covered in black powder. The two stood behind a large work bench. The table was covered in jars, all containing multicolored powders, pieces of metal varying in size, screws and bolts. Tools of every kind lay scattered around the room. Sketches and drawings of machines and weapons concealed the wooden walls almost completely. Contraptions made of metal and wood hung from the ceiling and sat along shelves. A large cabinet against the far wall was filled with bottles of different liquids, powders and strange concoctions.

Lagan began coughing as Silas waved at Grady and I with a wild grin. He pointed excitedly at a small metal cylinder laying on the table in front of him. It's center was cracked with black residue covering its jagged edges. I stepped closer to examine it.

"What is it?" Grady asked curiously. Lagan stopped coughing and shot a glare at the red headed boy.

"He decided to test out his new smoke bomb," he rubbed soot from his eyes. "Inside!" He yelled angrily. Silas only shrugged, his happiness untouched by Lagan's anger. He was obviously satisfied with the results.

"Silas is our bomb maker." Grady said to me. "As you can probably tell, he enjoys his job very much." He grinned at the young boy. "And Lagan is the poor bastard stuck sharing a work space with him." He added with a chuckle. I let out a small laugh as Lagan glared fiercely at Grady. I stifled it quickly as the three males all turned to stare at me. Desperate to take the attention off of me, I pointed to a drawing that was tacked to the wall.

"Is there a large need for bombs here in the forest?" I asked. Silas nodded.

"We use them to destroy Damned nests." Lagan Said. My blood chilled. More images of the creature flashed through my mind. How was Caligan so okay with killing what used to be his people?

"Are all of these bombs?" The drawing in front of me depicted an orb with jagged blades around the sides.

"No, some are ideas for weapons and other devices." Lagan answered as he brushed black soot from his muscled body. "My work doesn't explode and almost kill my partner." He snapped at Silas who then replied by making more shapes with is hands. Lagans eyes widened, his anger growing by whatever the boy had said. "You think my inventions are boring, do you?" Lagan yelled.

Deciding it was time for us to exit, Grady grabbed me gently by the elbow and pulled me from the workshop. Lagan's loud curses followed us. I walked behind Grady as he headed towards the garden. When we made it to the edge of the plot, finally out of earshot of Lagan's outburst, Grady turned and pointed at the stone building next to the workshop we had just left.

"That's where Asher works. He is our blacksmith, so his forge is located in there." He moved to the next little building made of old, weathered wood. "That is where Caligan makes all of our leather gear." He rapped his knuckles on his chest plate. "He also works on remedies and medicines as well. Elias is somewhere around the perimeter. He is on watch during the day and then Caligan takes over at night. He'll sometimes patrol or he will just hold up wards instead. Very rarely is there a sighting during the day but we like to be cautious." There was a edge to his voice. "The place you woke up in, with all the weapons and books is our armory. And no, I will not be showing you where that is located." The intrigue and hope that sparked within me soon died with his words. He turned and gestured to the vast garden behind us. "And this, is mine. I am in charge of growing the food and preparing meals."

He picked up a large wicker basket from the ground and handed it to me. He knelt in the dark soil and I sat in the grass next to him. He began showing me which plants were weeds and instructed me to pull them and toss them to the side. The birds in the trees above us sang sweetly in the warm morning air as we worked quietly together.

"Everyone has a job here." His voice was soft as he relaxed surrounded by his plants. "Each one is something we enjoy doing but it also benefits the clan as a whole. Plus it keeps us busy. When we get bored there tends to be a lot of fights." He smiled, his green eyes brightening fondly. "So while you are here staying with us, we will find a job that fits your talents and interests, but will also contribute to everyone. And if you decide to stay permanently, the job could change or remain. That would be up to you." Another long silence followed as we worked our way through the garden. It wasn't until mid day that I spoke again.

"How long have you been here?" I asked as we walked back to the other end of the garden. He stopped and shrugged before answering.

"Couple centuries." I balked at him. I couldn't feel any magic within him, so how was it possible for him to be that old, alive, and look so young? He knelt next to a bunch of tomato plants, picking and handing me the ones that were ripe and ready to be picked. I laid them gently into the basket he had handed me earlier. "The six of us met when we were kids. All of us were orphans so we were the only family we had. Caligan being as powerful as he is, bonded us all through magic and these," He pulled a leather cord out from under his shirt. Hanging around his neck was a small circle that glittered like crystal in the sun. "We are all connected. He lives, so do we." His voice grew sad and soft. So the rest of them were all human. "We all had pretty terrible starts in life. This way, we can make up for the time that was stolen from us." We moved onto a row of onions, he continued to pick while I carried. "We met Cip when we were young. Caligan has always been good at reading people, even as a child. He knew from the beginning that Ciprian was good and would take care of us." I listened quietly as he thought back on the early years of his life.

"Ciprian always thought all creatures should be treated equally, warlock, human, whatever you may be. He was ridiculed and hated by most for treating everyone equally and with kindness. So when he found Caligan, starving and badly beaten, he offered to take him in. But he only said yes if we could come with. We've all been together ever since."

"How did you all meet?" He turned to me then stopping his harvest. His expression was light as he shrugged.

"We met on the streets. All of us escaped a life alone." He shrugged. "Our pain and loneliness led us to one another." His answer was simple, his respect for his brothers and their lives showing. We spent the rest of the time in the garden in silence, enjoying the warm air and peace. When our basket was full, we made our way back to the outdoor kitchen to prepare dinner. Grady tasked me with washing and cutting the produce into small pieces. I was surprised he had trusted me with a knife considering how cautious they had been the night before. He stood next to me at the large counter and sliced a slab of meat into small cubes. When we had both finished he placed everything into a large pan and placed it on the stove. The smell swirled deliciously through the room around us.

I set the tables as everyone began filing in from their workshops. Asher, Silas and Lagan entered together, laughing loudly. Elias followed shortly after. They all scrubbed their hands clean from soot and grime from the days work. They all took their seats and began conversing quietly as Grady finished the meal. Caligan trudged from his workshop as the pan was set carefully in the center of the table. Grady took the seat beside me as we waited for Ciprian. Lagan told the others about Silas' testing of his new bomb this morning, now laughing along with everyone. My stomach growled loudly as the old warlock swept down from the village above, his robes flowing behind him.

"Please forgive me for being late, I was just finishing something up." The color had returned to his cheeks and his blood thrummed beneath his skin. He sat at the head of the table and drank deeply from his glass of wine.

"Well Cip, you're not forgiven. No dinner for you." Lagan teased as he scooped a generous portion of the beef and vegetable mixture onto his plate. One by one the pan was passed around the table, everyone eagerly filing their plates. A bottle of wine was also passed around the table. I poured myself a small glass after piling my plate high with the mouth watering medley. We ate in silence, all of us too hungry to converse. After we had all finished, except Silas and Asher who claimed seconds, we sat back in our chairs, bellies full. Ciprian cleared his throat and folded his hands on the table in front of him.

"So has it always only been you guys or has there been more of you?" I asked, the table fell silent, everyone surprised by my desire to speak.

"There have been a few others." Grady said simply. "They are no longer with us for different reasons."

"Like what?"

"We don't harm one another." Caligans deep voice rumbled down the table. His grey eyes held mine as he drank from his cup. "If one is to harm another, its taken to a vote to decide their punishment." The table remained quiet as I stared at the dark haired man.

"And that's happened?" My curiosity too much to be ignored. Caligan nodded once, his jaw flexing. "What happened to him?" The men around me stiffened, the air becoming heavy. Caligans gaze hardened.

"We killed him." A small ball of fear formed in my gut, but if he had tried to hurt one of them I understand the punishment. I wanted to ask what he had done to deserve their wrath, but Lagan spoke, my question being forgotten.

"It's not as straight forward as it seems. We get into fights and sometimes need a punch or two to feel better or to straighten out." The men around the table chuckled. "And we spar and train together, but there is a difference between practice or an argument and actually wanting to do harm or kill." I nodded and poured myself another glass of wine.

"What will my job be?" I went through the checklist of questions I wanted answered in my head. They all exchanged glances, thinking of possibilities for me. Lagan finally spoke.

"What did you do in the city?" I took a large drink from my cup, the wine bitter on my tongue.

"I worked at the inn I lived in, busting tables, taking orders and reservations and then I became a messenger." I paused. "Amongst other things." I said recalling the illegal dealings I had been involved in. I waited for them to curse me for working for the royal messenger service, but none of them did.

"What did your parents do?" Asher asked, finally done with his meal. I shrugged and took another drink.

"Don't know. I never knew them." The table was still as they all racked their minds for my place within their life. Silas tapped Lagan on the shoulder and signed a short message before looking down at his empty plate. "What did he say?" Based on the looks being passed around the table, I was the only one who didn't understand the freckle faced boy. Elias cleared his throat.

"He said you could do the cleaning and laundry." I glared at Silas, his hazel eyes widened with fear.

"I'm not a fucking house wife." I growled. The boy grinned wildly at me before making more signs. Lagan chuckled quietly.

"He says he likes you." He explained. My anger withered as I looked at the boys crooked grin.

"What do you do for fun? What do you enjoy?" Asher asked.

"I've never really had time for fun. I like to read, but that's pretty much all I've ever done besides work." I could feel a ball of sadness tightening in my chest. Its stupid, but it hurt that I had never had the luxury of having a true hobby.

"What we could do is have you spend a few days working with each of us and see if you take to anything, or if we discover something else you're good at." Ciprian suggested. "Maybe the more we work on your power and control, we will find a way to utilize those gifts." I frowned. Was this his goal? Use me for my magic? But nothing about him or their life style suggested anything like that. Nothing about these men seemed to be a lie or anything other than what they had shown me. I folded my arms across my chest.

"And what if after being here for awhile I decide I want to leave?"

"Nobody will force you to stay or do anything you don't want to. You may leave whenever you like once Caligan is finished finding out what he needs to know." Ciprian replied gently. "But if you choose to stay, indefinitely, we would love to welcome you into our clan." I scanned the faces around me, the men all nodded, agreeing with Ciprians offer. Caligan did not, his eyes met mine evenly as his gaze darkened. "But you don't have to rush your decision. Please take a couple hours, days, months; however long you need." Ciprians voice was gentle.

I considered his words. I could stay, have Ciprian remove the rest of the casings and help me develop my magic. A part of me wanted to leave now, find a new life far away from Mortala and her kingdom. But another part of me, didn't want to leave the peaceful home, not ruled by anyone, around people who seemed as damaged as I was. There was one question I had left that needed a answer. I gulped down the last of my wine and gave the warlock a stormy look. The setting sun behind us cast the group in a soft light.

"Can I have a weapon?" Grady was the first to respond.

"Absolutely not. Ive seen what you can do with your bare hands! I don't want to know what you can do with a blade." I couldn't help myself, I smiled at his words.

Chapter 9

Ciprian stood from the dining table and offered me his arm. My trust in the warlock had grown just a tad from this morning and how gently he had talked to me even with flame flickering in my palm. I refused his arm, but let him guide me up the long staircase and to my cottage. I let him in and watched in awe as he waved his hand and a large wooden box appeared on the long counter. I pulled several pairs of clothes out from it and held them up. They looked smaller than the others I had worn.

"I took in some of the boys clothes," a smile tugged at the corners of my lips as he referred to the five grown men as 'boys'. "I hope they fit alright." His voice was sheepish, he was worried I wouldn't like them or the beautiful white curtains he had sewn that also sat in the box. Everything they had gifted me with for my stay was far nicer and cozier than the room I had back in the city. I gave him a wide smile.

"Thank you. It's wonderful." I had never had someone go through so much trouble for me just to feel comfortable. Not even Penn. He smiled widely and patted me on the shoulder.

"Welcome home, Lorn." Something in my chest tightened at his words. He left me alone and I smiled to myself, enjoying the details of my room. Maybe this could be home. Maybe. I locked the door behind him. I turned back to the room to find the clothes and curtains in a neat pile and the large box gone. Laying on the counter in its place was a small dagger. I smiled softly and reminded myself to thank him tomorrow. I shrugged off my pants and crawled into bed, the mattress was light and soft. It felt like a cloud as I burrowed under the thick blankets. I fell asleep easily and quickly, too tired to fight my heavy eyelids.

I was awoken the next morning by the light of the morning sun coming in through the open windows, exploding the room in a brilliant light. I silently cursed the beautiful morning light for the wake up call and peeled myself from bed. I looked through the clothes I was gifted and slipped on a grey button up shirt and dark pants. The shirt was somewhat tight in the chest but fit rather well otherwise. The pants were nearly perfect, the length being just a tad too long for my short frame. I tucked the small dagger into my belt, immediately feeling more like myself. I was given a new cloak as well, it was black with a dark red trim. I hung it by the door and walked into the morning air. My boots lay by the door on the small porch, clean and polished. I was surprised by the slight disappointment that flitted through me at the sight of them. I had enjoyed being barefoot in the soft grass of the pasture. I plucked the boots from the floor and tossed them gently inside before heading down the stairs.

Ciprian sat by the fire pit, enjoying a cup of coffee and reading from a warn leather bound book. The dining table was occupied by the rest of the group, their faces drawn with drowsiness. I poured myself a cup of coffee and took a seat next to Grady, who greeted me with a sleepy smile. Caligan sat to my left, his face stained with black flecks. The same color stained his hands.

"How are you this morning, Lorn?" His velvet, sleepy voice asked. I gaped at him, shock and something that felt like happiness springing to life within me. He raised a dark brow. I shook my head, clearing my thoughts.

"I've never had someone ask me that." My cheeks heated as I spoke quietly so only he could hear.

"Nobody has asked how you are?" I shook my head. But a small smile spread over my lips. It felt nice to be asked. It felt like he was actually interested in my presence. Not even Penn, the woman who had raised me, had ever asked how I was. Just how work had been, or how much money I had made that day.

"I'm good." And I meant it. I don't know why, but that word seemed to fit how I felt this morning. He gave me a quizzical look before turning back to his breakfast. Asher finished the apple he had been eating and addressed the table.

"This morning we will all be taking turns sparring with Lorn." I raised my brows, the rest of the table exchanged glances. "If you are going to stay we need to make sure you're prepared to protect yourself." I shot him a withering look as he addressed me directly. "You may have fought in the city, but what we deal with out here is different. I want to get an idea of your fighting style and how we can improve it." Caligan rose from his seat but stopped when Asher placed a hand on his shoulder. "You're not exempt, Cal." His grey eyes flashed and glared dangerously at his brother as he returned to his seat. I hoped I faced him first, he deserved a punch or two.

When we had all finished eating, the eight of us made our way to the center of the clearing. Ciprian trailed us eagerly, excited for this mornings events. A very tired Caligan trudged after the rest of us. He must have patrolled all night. We gathered in the open section of grass between Grady's garden and the workshops. Ciprian conjured an arm chair with a wave of his hand and settled in to watch. Asher produced a large roll of leather and unrolled it in the grass. The leather revealed dozens of weapons. Swords in various sizes, knives, daggers, hatchets, brass knuckles; A scythe resembling the ones hanging from Caligans hips and a whip like the one at Gradys.

"Alright who's first?" Asher asked rubbing his hands together. Silas eagerly stepped forward, his hand raised in the air. He jogged to the other end of the designated fighting area and faced me. He unclipped the quiver of arrows strapped to his hip and tossed them and the bow strung across his shoulders to the ground. He waited patiently as I turned to select my weapons. I chose a dagger and two small knives. I tucked one into my belt and held the others tightly as I took my place opposite Silas. I set my bare feet steadily in the soft grass and waited to begin. My blood hummed excitedly, eager to relieve some anger. Ready to cause some pain.

"No killing or serious damage, once defeat has been made clear, the fight is over. Go easy on her Silas, she doesn't have any leathers." Ashers voice called, my blood boiled with rage. I bared my teeth in a snarl.

"Don't you dare." I growled. I didn't want to be given a win, I wanted to earn it. To show them what I'm capable of. To show them I'm not useless or helpless. The group behind me exchanged low chuckles. With a shrug, Silas started forward. He slid a dagger from his chest plate as he neared me. I let the rush of the fight take over, driving me and pulling me into a trance. Striking before he had the chance to, I threw a left hook at his ribs which he blocked with a cheeky grin. I grabbed the wrist he used to block and twisted, using the momentum to throw his weight over my shoulder. I pressed my knee to his chest after he hit the ground and stepped down on his wrist with my other. The dagger in his hand fell to the ground from the pressure I applied. The clearing fell deadly quiet as I pressed the blade of my knife to his throat, defeating him.

Silas lay wide eyed under me, cheeks flushing. Ciprians booming laugh filled he air, breaking the silence. The others joined him as I helped the boy to his feet. He brushed the dirt from his pants and shook my hand with a grin. Retrieving his fallen dagger, bow and quiver, he joined the others. Lagan pushed through the small group and walked toward me, declaring it his turn. He picked up a sword from the roll and handed it to me as he made his way to the other end of the fighting area. He set his feet and drew his own sword from his hip as he waited to begin. I tossed the knife and dagger in my hands to the dirt and readied myself for his attack.

We circled each other slowly, watching each other's movements carefully. Finally he moved to strike at my left side, but I blocked it easily. He quickly changed directions and sent another attempt to the opposite side. I blocked it, but was throw off balance. He noticed and threw his shoulder into my chest sending me to my back. The wind rushed from my lungs painfully. He smiled widely as he looked down at me, the others laughed behind us. Clenching my teeth I called to my anger, letting it rage within me and rolled to my feet.

In a flurry of movements we exchanged strikes each blocking the other. He brought his sword down in an over head stroke. Using all my weight I blocked it and pushed my body flush to his. I released my grip on the sword with one hand and pulled the knife stuck in my belt. I pressed it to his abdomen, the blade slicing through the top layers of his leathers. His body froze in surrender, slowly dropping his sword to his side. I was once again the winner. Ciprian laughed loudly again and clapped at my performance.

Grady was next, cradling his whip as he took his place. In the blink of an eye he sent the end of the rough rope curling around my ankles and yanked me to my back. I heard Caligan and Asher howl in approval fueling the anger blazing within me. I grabbed my knife and launched it at him. As he ducked to avoid it, I sliced through his whip with my sword. His eyes went wide as I sprinted across the small distance between us. Just before I crashed into him, I dropped to the ground and slid between his feet. Popping up behind him I pressed the sword to his skin, the sharp tip digging into the base of his neck. His hands rose in surrender.

Asher swapped out my sword and knife for two hatchets and faced me, flail in hand. It didn't take long for the fight to end, this time claiming me as the loser. Using the chain of his flail, he tripped me as I came at him and brought the heavy spiked ball into the ground right by my head; the perfect kill shot. He grinned triumphantly and walked back to his brothers. Caligan took his place, his two small scythes ready.

Angry from my loss, I made the first move. He blocked my upper strike easily and kicked his legs back to avoid another. As I swung another hit, one of his blades sliced through the the skin on my cheek. Blood trickled down my chin and neck. With a new fury I began cutting my way through the air. He was barely able to keep up and began giving up ground. I kept pushing until his back slammed into a tree. I spun on my heel and smashed the blade of the axe into the bark less than an inch from his face.

Panting, I glared into his stormy eyes. I pulled the blade free, splinters flying out with it. I gave him a wink, his features darkened as he strode back to the sidelines. Elias dropped his weapons to the ground and motioned for me to do the same. With nothing but our fists, we closed the distance and began our hand to hand combat. I dodged a jab and threw one of my own but it didn't land either. I faked another jab and threw a left hook instead, connecting with his jaw. Recovering quickly he hit me in the nose with a loud crack. My eyes began to water, blurring my vision. As I tried to blink away the tears as pain shot through my skull, he landed a shot to my ribs. The air rushed from me. I attempted to throw an elbow but caught another blow to my jaw, sending stars dancing across my vision. A foot to the chest sent me to the ground.

I lay on my back breathless as Asher shouted, calling the match. Elias stood over me, a vicious glare on his face. I hauled myself to my feet and met his glare evenly. The rest of the group joined us, ending our stare down with grins on their faces. Caligan addressed me, a smirk playing on his lips.

"Certainly not a house wife." He said lightly. I gave him a tired grin, pride blooming in my chest.

Chapter 10

"Your feet are shifting way too far forward." Caligan corrected my stance. We stood in the center of the large clearing. He had taken it upon himself to be in charge of my fighting lessons. Much to my dismay. He kicked at my toes. I shuffled back. The sun was high in the sky, its bright rays beat down on us. My body was drenched with sweat, my tongue dry as the dirt beneath my feet. The heat, plus the annoying critiques from Caligan, did nothing but feed my annoyance.

"You're also dropping your elbow when you punch." I snarled at him. His hair was damp with sweat, his shirt clung to him with moisture. "Don't get angry, just correct it." I glared at him and gripped the hilt of the sword I was given tighter.

"Stop talking and I wont get angry." He tilted his head, his grey eyes shining brightly in the afternoon sun.

"Control it." He snarled as he swung his own sword in a large arch that I side stepped and blocked easily. I responded with my own swing, which he barely moved to avoid the blade. The cocky smirk on his lips burned hot within me.

"Control what?" I growled. We began a series of jabs and swipes, the clash of steel rang through the loud opening of grass.

"Your anger." He blocked one of my strikes and brought his body flush to mine, our connecting blades crossed between us. I could see the droplets of sweat glistening on his brow. The light dusting of freckles across his nose from years of sun exposer. "Tell me, what makes you angry Lorn?" I snarled at my name on his lips and the slight shiver it sent through my body. I didn't have to consider his question, I had known the answer for most of my life.

"Everything." I slammed my shoulder into his, separating us. I swung, whirled and ducked. I used the weapon clumsily, but I met each of his blows with my own. The way he moved, the graceful movements of his body only fueled my anger more.

"Control it!" His deep voice echoed through the clearing as sparks of violet flame erupted from my finger tips.

"Fuck you!" I slipped my hand free and pressed my blazing palm to his chest. The outcome I was hoping for, did not come. His face twisted into icy fury as my palm sizzled against his flesh, but the flame went out. His hand wrapped around my wrist and his other dropped the sword at our feet. He swung my body, his empty hand cradled the back of my head, spinning and slamming my back into the trunk of a tree. His large body caged me in, keeping me utterly incapable of moving. The contact on my scalp sent panic and fear flooding through my veins. Images of green skin, memories of my hair being ripped away flashed in my mind.

"Control it, before it controls you." His face pressed dangerously close to mine, his teeth bared in anger. "If you don't learn control, this power. This flame," He held my wrist up painfully. "will consume you, until you are nothing but dust and ash." His voice was icy. His chest brushed mine. The smell of lavender and sweat filled my nostrils. The panic within me writhed and swirled frantically. In a moment of pure desperation, I reached out and bit the bridge of his nose. The coppery tang of his blood filled my mouth as he growled and released my body.

I stumbled to the ground, bile rising in my throat as more memories flooded my mind. I emptied my stomach painfully onto the ground. My hand wiped at my head, hoping I could wipe away the feeling my memories brought back. After my stomach settled I stood, turning to an ashen faced, bleeding Caligan. I glared at him, my eyes promising more than just a small bite.

"I'm sorry," Blood ran down his lips and chin. "I forgot." I didn't want his pity. He knew why I kept my hair short and he touched me anyway. I palmed the dagger from my waist band and charged. I kicked at his knee and sent an elbow to his ribs. The air whooshed from him in a loud *hmph.* He came down to his knees and I tangled my hands in his wet hair. I brought his eyes up to meet mine, hoping he could see the fire, the anger, the hatred in my eyes. I leaned into the wild rush of a fight. I let myself bleed into the craziness.

"Let this be a reminder," I dragged my tongue across his chin and lips, smearing my mouth with his blood. His eyes flashed, his eyes wide. I hoped it was fear. I hoped he feared me.

I hoped they *all* feared me. I kicked him back to the hard ground. He fell to his back, his eyes widening further as I climbed on top of him. My head still swam with the grotesque memories that haunted me. "To keep your hands away from where they aren't supposed to be." I gripped his wrist and slammed the dagger through his palm. I felt the skin, muscle and scrape of bone as the blade embedded into the ground beneath it.

His jaw flexed, his teeth grinding together as he held in a howl of pain. I licked my lips clean of his blood and smiled at his sweating face. I could feel the anger within him, rolling from him like waves in the ocean. I pulled myself from him and started walking back across the clearing to the winding staircase at the large tree trunk. My body shook with the fear still pulsing through me. I knew Caligan would heal quickly, but I smiled slightly knowing I had at least hurt him.

He wanted to get to know me, to ask me question to try and answer whatever ones he had. He was right, I needed to control my anger. But he was wrong about one thing. I was already consumed by the flame. I had been reduced to nothing a long time ago.

Chapter 11

The next few days I spent the morning hours working with Ciprian on developing control over my magic. We sat by the fire and attempted to cause a reaction using different emotions but so far the only one that will show results is anger. Every time I let go of my temper, bright violet flames would erupt across my palms. Ciprian had regained enough strength to remove one other metal casing, freeing both of my index fingers now. I tried not to show my frustration with the slow progress of their removal or the slow growth of controlling my power. I could see how much it drained the kind warlock to help me.

I spent the early afternoon hours sparring and working on my fighting technique with Asher and Grady. Caligan decided to hand over the job after our last training session. He sometimes would show up to watch or give obnoxious tips, but he never got into combat with me. The rest of my day was spent with Grady in his garden, learning about all the different kinds of food he grew. He was very passionate about his work and eager to talk about it. I mostly listened, hardly ever getting the chance to squeeze in a word during his "lessons." I didn't mind being silent, I was used to being quiet most of my life. I helped him prepare dinner every evening, only aloud to chop vegetables or occasionally mixing while it cooked on the stove. While I do that, he seasons and pours proper measurements of ingredients. Most of my free time in the evening was spent with Grady, Lagan and Silas.

Silas had taken the opportunity to teach me a few of his signs, with translation help from the others. We had covered some basics: hello, good morning and the alphabet. He had also taught me to say 'up top" which is what they called the area of green pastures, and 'the den' that was the area below with their hoard of weaponry. The latter I discovered is always locked and impossible to break into. Caligan caught me trying to find a way in on my fourth night here. The entrance was somewhere at the base of the large tree holding our homes in the sky. Despite the annoying grey eyed man, I found myself looking forward to my days, enjoying the place these men call home.

One evening we all sat at the table, talking quietly after dinner. Lagan had just finished telling us all about a idea he had for a new canteen that would keep water fresher and colder for longer than the ones they use now. Ciprian rose from his seat after Lagan's description of the new contraption and asked me if I would accompany him to his quarters. I agreed quickly, his presence becoming a comforting one to have around. I took his arm and we walked silently up to the small village in the trees to the small, circular, light green cottage that he called his own. Inside the room was covered with overflowing bookshelves, reaching from the ceiling all the way to the floor, not a single wall was bare. A small bed covered with lush, brightly colored cushions and pillows lay in the center of the room, surrounded by more stacks of books.

"You mentioned the other day that you like reading, so I thought I would give you some of my favorites." He gave me a small smile and raised his right hand. He pointed to one of the shelves and a small leather book flew from its place and landed gently in his outstretched palm. He handed it to me and I recognized the title as one he had been reading my first morning here. I gave him a wide grin and watched as he pointed to another shelf, this one closer to the ceiling, releasing a green book from its grasp.

I watched with awe as book after book danced through the air, gliding around me as if they were hummingbirds searching for a sweet treat. The books piled themselves together in a neat stack at Ciprians feet. When the last book found its place with the others, the warlock bent low into a dramatic bow as I laughed and clapped at his performance.

"I've never seen magic used so beautifully." I said as he stepped to my side. He gave me a warm smile and placed a hand over his heart.

"Thank you, darling girl." I was shocked at the gentleness of his voice and the kind words he used. His smile faded as he thought for a moment. "Most of my kind use their power for selfish and cruel reasons." His forehead creased in thought. "But I've always wanted to help people, not hurt them. Which is why I came here," he gestured to the home around us. "I use my gifts to provide for others and nourish life instead of hurting or killing it." I gave him a weak smile.

"Ive never met a sorcerer like you. Which is a good thing," I added quickly. "I don't like any that I've met, except you." I could feel my cheeks reddening at the admission. But it was true, I liked Ciprian. His bright smile lit his face once again and he wrapped me into a hug. I had only been hugged a few times in my life, all from Penn. It felt strange to be hugged so tightly and warmly. Something in my heart seemed to warm at the small act of kindness gifted to me by the warlock. Patting my back, he swept a hand toward the stack of books.

"Take them. They're yours." I shook my head.

"I can't take these, they belong to you. You said they were your favorites." He scoffed and scooped them from the floor before dropping them into my arms.

"I am the only one that reads them and I have read these several hundred times. Besides, your room is pitifully empty." He teased, directing me to the door. "Come and take more whenever you like." He opened the door for me. I gave him a small smile, thanking him as I left.

As I made my way down the series of bridges to my small cottage, I scanned the titles I held before me. My attention elsewhere I hadn't been watching my surroundings or where I was walking. I slammed into something solid, the books falling to the wood at my feet. One fell over the edge, another coming dangerously close.

I stumbled and two strong hands caught my waist, steadying me. Caligan smirked down at me, my cheeks heated as I became too aware of his hands on my body. A silent moment passed between us before he spoke.

"You're blushing, Lorn." He said quietly sending a shiver over my skin. I shot him a glare and shoved against his chest, separating us. I tried not to think about how solid his muscles had felt as I bent to retrieve my fallen books.

"How are you?" He asked. The same feeling went through me as the first time he had asked me that. Warmth blossomed in my chest, the small question bringing me a bit of happiness. He knelt beside me and scooped most of the books into his arms before straightening back to his full height. With a snap of his fingers the one that fell over the edge appeared back atop the stack.

"I'm good." I went to take them from him but he swerved out of my reach. He jerked his chin forward and I rolled my eyes and led the rest of the way to my quarters.

He set the stacks on my small desk and glanced around, taking in my room. I slid next to him, adding the three books I carried to his pile. I turned to look at him and found his eyes already on me. He tilted his head to the side, his black hair falling into his eyes.

"You don't talk much do you? Unless you're pissed off that is." It was more of an observation rather than a question. I shrugged and met his gaze coolly.

"I'm not used to talking." I frowned. "I'm not used to being around so many people all the time." I suddenly felt embarrassed of how lonely my life had been. Better off lonely than dead. Thankfully, he didn't comment on the sadness in my voice.

"Talkative or not, you've definitely won the guys over. Especially Silas." I smiled fondly at the boys name.

"He's very funny."

"He is." Cal agreed. "But for someone that can't talk, the kid never shuts up." I laughed at the truth behind his words but silenced it quickly. His thick brows rose in surprise as a small grin curved his full lips. My breath caught in my chest at the sight. "That's the first time I've heard you laugh." I rolled my eyes, heat creeping back into my cheeks. I scrambled to change the subject.

"Shouldn't you be out patrolling?" I asked, desperate for the flush in my cheeks to vanish. He shook his head.

"I'm just putting up wards tonight." He tilted his head to the side again, the sharp lines of his jaw clenching. "Besides we need to celebrate, I made you laugh!" He joked. I shook my head.

"It was a pity laugh." I lied. He took a step closer leaving barely a foot between us. I craned my head back to keep eye contact.

"You're not capable of lying Lorn, so don't even try." That was one of the few times he had called me by my name. I silently scolded myself for liking the sound of it on his lips.

"You'd be surprised to know what I'm capable of." The truth is, I'm an excellent liar. I just never found the point in it, its easier and better to just tell the truth. His eyes darkened. The air seemed to thicken around us. I took a step back, the room suddenly feeling too small. He turned to leave but faced me once more as he reached the door.

"I'de love to find out." His grey eyes shown bright, his gaze intense. A small thrum went through my blood at his words. He turned to leave, shutting the door softly behind him. I found myself releasing a large breath. I leaned against the table and replayed the encounter in my head. That was the first time I had talked to the grey eyed brute without wanting to kill him. He seemed less angry and annoying. Something about the conversation seemed different than those I had had with the others. It felt different to be so close to him than when I was with Grady or Silas. Pushing it from my mind, I began placing my new books onto my empty shelves.

I was running. Panicked and frantically trying to find a way out of the dark room I found myself trapped in. A sharp pain tore through my stomach as I was knocked to the ground by a invisible force. Fierce and intense pain racked my body. Screams forced from my lips as my skin felt like it was being shredded and torn by talons and claws. Blood soaked through my clothes and onto the ground around me. My screams and cries for help were drowned by the sound of laughter, high and cruel from the darkness around me.

I bolted upright, a scream dying in my throat. My heart raced. My shirt clung to my skin with sweat. It took a moment for me to realize I was in my room, in my bed, safe. *I'm safe.* I told myself over and over trying to calm my rapid heart. I jumped as a hard pounding came against my door, followed by loud shouts. I threw off the covers and threw the door open wide.

Seven men greeted me, panic and anger hardening their faces., weapons in hand. Ciprian was in a long green night shirt, the rest of them were naked from the waist up. Their muscled bodies tense, expecting danger. The night air was cool and still.

"What's wrong?" Asher asked quickly, his voice harsh and low.

"Are you hurt?" Lagan added. I shook my head, heat rising to my clammy cheeks. I had woken them up by screaming in my sleep. I felt like a child, waking their parents after a bad dream. I ran a hand down my face, wiping away sweat as I did so.

"No I'm fine. Nothing happened, it was just-" I trialed off, not wanting to admit what had frightened me. Their bodies relaxed as relief flooded through them, replacing the fear and panic. Lowering their weapons, Asher spoke quietly, their faces becoming drawn and tired.

"Was it a nightmare?" No mockery or humor was found in his words, only concern. I nodded, looking down at my bare feet. After a quiet moment he added, "Try and get some sleep." And he and the others trudged sleepily back to their rooms. Only Caligan remained. My eyes scanned his scared chest. My skin heated as my gaze lingered on the low rise of his pants and the deep muscles they revealed.

"You shouldn't feel embarrassed." His voice was low and soft. I looked into his eyes, his gaze firm and steady. "We all have them. You have to remember, you're not alone." His eyes dropped to my chest where my shirt clung to my breasts. He quickly turned to leave, the muscles in his jaw flexing. "You're not the only one who has seen the horrors of this world."

"Cal," I said in a low whisper. His body froze. I suddenly regretted using the nickname without his permission. "Thank you." He gave me a small nod and made his way back across the bridge, scythe in hand. I watched the muscles in his back move as he walked. I admired how the low light of the lanterns made the scars on his skin appear almost silver. I locked the door behind me and crawled back into bed. I slept fitfully the rest of the night. My dreams were filled with images of scars and a black scythe.

Chapter 12

Nobody mentioned the events of earlier this morning at breakfast. Thanks to Caligan, I now knew I wasn't the only one who awoke in the night afraid. I averted my gaze from him as we ate, not allowing myself the opportunity to picture his naked chest and the images it filled my dreams with. I told myself that my moment of admiration of his body was due to the delirious state I found myself in after waking from such a terrible nightmare. I told myself this, even though I knew it was bullshit. Asher and Cal ate quickly before disappearing into their workshops. Grady stood and placed his dirty dishes in the sink. He stood behind Silas and Lagan and addressed me.

"After you are done with Cip," He slapped the two on their backs, causing Lagan to spill his porridge onto the table in surprise. "you'll start assisting the destruction twins." I grinned at the accuracy of the nickname. At least once a day an explosion could be heard from within their workshop followed by Lagan cursing or his triumphant shouts. "Don't blow her up on her first day, try to return her all in one piece." Grady looked down at his brothers. Silas grinned widely and Lagan pretended to be contemplating what Grady had said. The table was soon clear and Ciprian and I sat in the grass, far away from Gradys garden and the workshops.

"Today is going to be a little different." He began. "I am going to tell you a story and I want you to concentrate on the emotions I'm feeling and see if you can distinguish them." I nodded and turned my full attention to the old warlock beside me. He had kicked off his own shoes and wiggled his toes in the grass beside me. "I grew up in Willowmore, a long time ago. I loved it. I loved the city and the people. It was beautiful and calm and a wonderful place to live. Creatures of all kinds lived together, worked together in peace. But when Mortala took power there was always a disconnect between warlocks, empaths, and humans; not as bad as it is now, but it was still not how it should be. Even after her barbaric ways took place I still treated everyone as my equal. I treated everyone with kindness. Right after she took power I faced tremendous ridicule for my beliefs and actions so I quickly became an outcast within Mortalas kingdom, even to my own people." He cleared his throat before continuing. "I was tired of living among such hateful creatures so I packed up my things and set out to find a new home. Hopefully one where it's people lived in harmony." I tried to focus on how he was feeling but his face revealed nothing.

"I found the pasture up top one day and decided it would be a good place to stay. Away from rulers and people." He shrugged. "Because who knows what other kingdoms would be like. I wasn't too eager to try and find one in hopes it would be different. So I created this," He waved his hands to the space around us. I found myself relating largely with his hope and desire of a new life. "I stayed here, only venturing to the city every now and then for supplies I couldn't grow or make myself. A couple years went by, and I went to fetch some new fabric for clothes when I found a small boy. He was so much smaller than he should have been.

"His clothes were practically rags and they hung from him. He obviously hadn't been fed properly in quite some time. He was dirty and bleeding heavily from fresh wounds. I found him huddled in an alley." Ciprian winced at the memory. "He was terrified. I asked him where his mother was and he told me she was dead. He was so small." He shook his head, his eyes far away. "I scooped him into my arms and carried him home. He slept most of the way, when he was awake he just stared at me, his eyes wide but so full of sadness.

"I made him a room and fed him. It took several meals before he was able to keep all of it down. He ate more than any grown man I had ever seen." He chuckled softly. "He asked me if he could stay, and of course I said yes. After a few days he asked if his brothers could come and stay with us. I took him to the city to help retrieve them, but he said he wanted to find them on his own. So I let him go and told him to meet me back at a coffee shop when he was done. He came back with five boys that looked nothing like him, it was obvious they weren't related by blood, but I never questioned it." His eyes were lined with tears as he looked at me.

"They've been with me ever since, became the family I never had the opportunity to have within the kingdom." Something in my chest constricted. Ciprian had saved the boys and raised them as his own. Showing them kindness and love. Despite the small smile he wore, the air around him had thickened and darkened. A violet haze drifted around him and flowed down his shoulders. I furrowed my brow.

"You're angry." He nodded. "Why?" The story was about how he gained his family, why would he be so angry?

"These boys are my children. They're the only family I have had in centuries." Tears spilled down his cheeks as the haze around him shifted to a deep grey. "Knowing that their start in life was filled with violence and sorrow instead of love and happiness makes me angry and so sad." Grey must mean sadness. "I hate the thought of them ever being in pain or receiving something less than they deserve." My heart ached. I wished I had someone in my life to be that angry at my pain. Ciprian cleared his throat and wiped his cheeks.

"You were able to find my emotions." He stated, changing the subject from him to me. I nodded. "How?" He asked, the grey haze around him lightening.

"It floats around you. It was purple when you were angry."

He nodded. "Like your flames."

"It turned grey with your sadness." My voice was quiet. He gave me a small smile, his eyes distant and foggy as his past floated through his mind.

"See what other colors you can find." His eyes remained unfocused as he settled deeper into the grass. I took that as my cue to leave. I climbed to my feet unsure if I should leave him or not, but based on the colors floating around him, he wanted to be left alone. I waved to Grady as I passed his garden. He was covered in dirt and grinned at me. I knocked on the door of Silas and Lagans workshop before stepping inside. They both sat behind the work bench, bent over bits and pieces of wood chips and multicolored powders. I rolled up my sleeves and took a seat opposite them.

I watched as the two worked on a small contraption, wooden and small in stature. It reminded me of a music box. They spent the rest of the morning placing small amounts of powders and liquids, their names and purposes unknown to me, into the small box. I watched and listened to Lagans comments and laughed at their silent bickering. Lagan placed a lid on top of the box when the sun had reached its peak in the sky. The sunlight reminded me of the color that seemed to permanently hang on Silas's shoulders; bright and golden. I decided that color must mean happiness. Silas grinned eagerly at me before using his hands to sign to me, spelling out the word *Ready?*

"For what?" I asked as Lagan gestured to the open door. Silas shouldered his bow and hung his quiver from his belt before leaving the building. Lagan guided me to the side of the building and pressed a finger to his lips, telling me to be quiet. He disappeared around the corner with Silas. I waited for a few moments alone until Asher, Caligan and Lagan returned, joining me on the side of the workshop. Lagan pointed across the pasture to where Silas was stalking toward Grady as he worked in his garden.

Silas placed the tiny box next to Gradys feet in the grass and backed away silently. Oblivious to whatever the young boy was planning, Grady continued plucking weeds from the brown earth. Finally Silas rejoined our group. He slung off his bow and knocked an arrow.

"He's not going to hurt him." Lagan whispered in my ear. My body had tensed as Silas drew back the arrow, but was relived by Lagans words. We waited as Silas locked in on the tiny box hidden in the grass. Releasing his arrow, we held our breath in anticipation. Half a second later, the tiny box made a loud popping noise and a large cloud of pale blue smoke enveloped the golden haired male. We waited quietly as the smoke cleared, revealing his limp form in a pile in the dirt, asleep. His chest rose and fell evenly. Our small group of onlookers erupted and howled with laughter and toppled into the grass. Silas raised a fist into the air triumphantly as silent laughs racked his chest.

"What was that?" I asked gasping between laughs. Lagan wiped a tear from his grinning face.

"Something new we came up with. It knocks anyone out within a ten foot radius." He began laughing again, holding his side as he rolled in the grass.

"How long does it last?" Asher asked as we finally collected ourselves. Silas shrugged.

"We will find out when he wakes up." Lagan answered, grinning wickedly. The small group was swarmed with the bright golden light. I found even myself, wrapped in the soft golden light. Asher started to walk back to his forge, a small smile still wide on his lips. Lagan sprawled out in the grass, his muscles stretching and bulging under his clothes. He began counting, waiting for Grady to wake up. Cal climbed to his feet as Silas tapped me on the shoulder. He made several movements with his hands that I had yet to learn. I gave him a quizzical look.

"He says you look pretty when you smile." Caligans velvet voice translated, his jaw and shoulders tense as the golden light around him began to fade into a light purple. He strode away to his workshop. I gave Silas a small smile and joined Lagan in the countdown.

After dinner we all sat next to the fire pit talking quietly. The moon shown brightly over head and the stars twinkled like polished jewels. Elias spoke with Caligan, telling him about a den of the damned that he had tried to find today, unsuccessfully. I sat in the soft grass playing a game of cards with Asher. Ciprian cleared his throat, calling for our attention. His yellow robes seemed to glow in the firelight. He took a sip of his wine and waved a hand at Asher. Asher stood and retrieved a a small leather bundle from the kitchen counter. He laid it on the ground in front of me. He unrolled it, revealing four knives, their blades made from the same black metal as Caligans scythes. Their hilts made from a dark red stone with flecks of black snaking throughout.

A pair of brass knuckles lay beside them but my eyes widened at the two axes laying in the center of the roll. They're handles and blades matching the knives. I studied them and the craftsmanship, never having seen such beautiful weaponry.

"They're yours, Lorn." Asher said softly. My eyes snapped to his. He gave me an encouraging grin and pushed the roll closer to me. I carefully lifted one of the hatchets, the weapon heavy and smooth in my grasp. I felt as if I touched them too roughly I would scratch them, ruin them. But they weren't made for decoration or for looking at, they were made for hurting. Slicing and gutting. They were made for war. Made for me. "Based on your fighting style and how well you used them last week, I thought they would be a good fit for you." I set the axe down and gave him a wide smile.

"Thank you, they're beautiful." My cheeks heated at the generous gift. He gave me a grin and a small nod. Caligan cleared his throat, stealing my attention. In his hands he held a leather chest plate matching the ones on the others around the fire and two leather blade coverings. After a moment of admiration, I realized that they too, were for me. I climbed to my feet, eyes wide. He carefully strapped the plate around my shoulders and waist. His scent of leather and lavender surrounded me as he bent low to tighten the straps. My pulse quickened at his nearness. His fingers grazed my sides, my skin sparked under his touch. The air around him turned golden and bright and softly faded to pink, a tiny mixture of black swirled within. When he finished he told me to take off my belt and he re-looped it adding the coverings for my axes so they rested above each hip.

Asher rose from the floor and held my weapons for me as I slid each of them into their designated sleeves, woven within the leather of my chest plate before placing the two axes through my belt. I twisted my torso, giving the leathers a feel. They fit like a glove.

"They're perfect." I said looking up at Caligan. "How did you know what size to make them?" Grady snorted at my question. I frowned at him.

"Well with the amount of time he spends staring at you, it wouldn't be that hard to figure out your measurements." He said suppressing a smile. The others shared knowing looks as I returned my gaze back to Caligan, my eyebrows raised and cheeks reddening. He shot Grady a glare, his colors darkening. But it was Elias who spoke next.

"She's the first woman any of us have seen in months." His eyes trailed down my body. I resisted the urge to cover myself with my arms. "Of course we are going to look." Deep violet smoke swirled around

Caligans shoulders and shot a dangerous glare at his brother who met his eyes evenly. His words made me feel dirty, like a piece of meat in a cage with an animal. My skin began to crawl. Memories of all the men that have made comments like that or forceful advances towards me over the years flooded through my mind. I pushed my way through the group of men and headed to the winding staircase.

I had never considered myself to be pretty or beautiful like the girls I had grown up around. They all had long hair, wore pretty dresses and didn't have scars covering their skin. Is that how they all saw me? As just another female, walking around for their enjoyment? A small part of me wanted to be happy about the fact Caligan had spent time watching me. But most of me just felt sick because of Elias's words. I spent the rest of the evening alone in my quarters.

Chapter 13

My muscles ached in protest with each step I took up the winding staircase. My sparring session with Asher and Grady was longer than usual. Ciprian had canceled my morning lessons for the time being, assigning me with focusing on reading emotions from the others within the clan. Because my mornings were now free, the blacksmith and gardener decided that time will now be added to my fight training. Not that I didn't enjoy it, I loved the action and rush that a fight gave me. They both had given me great advice on my technique and taught me a lot. But my body didn't like it as much as my brain. My muscles were sore from the constant movement and brutality of my daily activities.

The sun had set a few hours earlier and the multi colored lamps hanging from the branches around me cast the small village and bridges in a whimsical glow. The sky was clear above, the stars and moon glowed brightly in the peaceful night. Asher, Elias and Grady were still down by the fire pit, laughing and talking loudly. Silas and Lagan had disappeared back into their workshop after dinner, wicked grins on their faces. I knew whatever the two were up to, was going to be interesting to witness in action. I hoped that their next test victim was Elias. His gross comment from the other night still stung and slithered through my mind whenever I saw him.

The village in the sky was quiet. Ciprians home was dark. Light poured from Caligans open windows but no sound other than the hooting of owls rang through the night. I pushed open my door, eager to crawl into bed bu I froze just inside the threshold. A small creature flew through the air around my small home. Its whole body could have fit in the palm of my hand. Its body was covered in black fur. The wings sprouting from its tiny back had streaks of white through the black and twin white spikes sticking from the very edge.

At the sight of my entry, the small creature descended and landed lightly onto my unmade bed. Its eyes were large and the brightest shade of green I had ever seen. Small white horns curled from the top of its head, matching the shade of the fur on its chin making it look like a tiny beard. His round belly and chest were the same shade of white. I backed slowly out of the room. What was this thing? Was it dangerous? This was the Forest of the Damned after all, and all I had ever heard of was that everything here was deadly. I stepped out onto the small porch outside my door, my eyes still on the tiny creature. My back hit something solid, making me jump.

I turned to find Caligan, his brow raised and small grin hiding on his lips.

"Whatcha doing?" I must have looked pretty strange backing out of my own home like I was. I grabbed his arm and pulled him in front of the doorway.

"What is that?" I whispered and pointed at the small black animal, still sitting on my bed. The grin on Caligans face spread wide as he walked deeper into the room. I tensed as I watched him near the animal with an outstretched hand. He made a tiny clicking noise with his tongue, stealing the creatures attention. Large green eyes tracked Cals movements with joyful curiosity. The tiny creature leapt into his outstretched palm. Cals smile widened, stealing the breath from my throat. When he turned his grey eyes to me, I could have sworn the world stopped.

"Its a dragon." His words broke me from my trance. I walked to his side slowly, still unsure of the tiny beast.

"I thought dragons were huge." Its green eyes turned to me, I could have sworn the little thing was smiling at me. Tiny teeth poked out from its inky fur. Cal traced a finger down its furry body.

"You also thought you were human." His velvet voice teased. I couldn't help but smile. He was right, there was so much about this world I didn't know, that I had been blind about and kept from my whole life. I reached out to touch the dragon. "Careful, they do breath fire. That part of the legend is true." I grinned wider and brought my eyes closer to the dragon.

"Its okay," I told it. "So do I." Caligan chuckled deeply beside me. I ran a finger down the animals spine, down to the tip of its tail. Its large green eyes closed and a soft purr rumbled through its small chest.

"I think he likes you." I met Cals grey eyes. They were bright, his colors a soft gold.

"How do you know its a he?"

"Only the males have horns." I turned back to those large green eyes. I straightened to my proper height. The male dragons head tilted and then his spiked wings spread wide. He jumped from Caligans hand and landed softly on my shoulder. His tiny head rubbed softly against my cheek, another purr forming in its throat.

"Have you ever seen one?" I asked, smiling at the softness of the fur tickling my skin.

"Once." Cal stepped closer, his eyes on the creature on my shoulder. "In the forest of Norkin." I frowned.

"Where?"

His grey eyes met mine then. He stood very close, having come within a breaths length away to study the tiny dragon. "It's an elven kingdom on the southern part of the continent." I gaped at him. His brow furrowed.

"There is an elven kingdom? And you've met them? Seen them?" A small grin twitched his lips as he nodded. A million questions swept through my mind.

"What are they like? What's their land like? How far away are they? What other species and races have you met?" A laugh racked his chest, the sound sent gold light through the air and wrapped itself around me. I decided that I liked the sound.

"With the amount you read, I'm surprised you don't know everything about them." I shrugged, my eyes falling back to the dragon, now climbing down my arm.

"There isn't any information of any land besides Willowmore within the kingdom. No maps, no books. I think its Mortalas doing. Wanting to keep her kingdom in darkness to what the rest of the world holds." Sadness wove into the air around me. A silent moment passed between us as we both watched the happy little dragon as it scaled my arm.

"Come with me. I think I have something you'll appreciate." His warm hand grasped my own, sending a small jolt down my arm. The dragon leapt into the air and perched himself onto Cals shoulder as he pulled me from my room. I did my best to ignore the feeling of his callouses pressing against mine as he led me across the various bridges and down the winding stairs. Our new friend sat happily atop his broad shoulders.

At the base of the large tree, where I knew the armory was held, Cal touched a piece of bark and opened a door that seamlessly blended in with the rest of the tree. How he knew exactly where the door was, I had no idea. He went in before me, holding the door while I stepped inside behind him. Torches lit a small staircase, leading deep into the earth. At the end Cal pushed open another door. Inside was the room I had first woken up in when I had arrived in the forest. Tables of weapons were still piled high, the book shelves overflowing just like I remembered. With a wave of his hand, a roaring fire burst to life within the hearth. I wondered what the true extent of his power was.

He walked to the far side of the room and began pulling books, seemingly at random, from the shelves and stacking them in his hands. When his arms were full, he set the stack on the floor in front of the fire and sat. I joined him sitting across from him as he began looking through the titles for the one he wanted. The tiny dragon jumped from his shoulder and plopped onto the rug beside us.

"There are hundreds more, but these are just a few about the other kingdoms that surround Willowmore." Excitement and curiosity sparked within me. I leaned forward, eager to take the stack from him and uncover what their bindings held. He pulled the one he wanted from the large stack and flicked through the pages. He placed the open book in front of me, a map spread across its pages. I was instantly mesmerized by the detailed drawing of the world that I was so blind to. Cal pressed a finger to a large portion of the map.

"That's Willowmore," His finger circled the map where a thick black circle surrounded the kingdom. "This is the forest." His finger traveled to the lowest part of the map. "This is Norkin." The land was huge, larger than Willowmores territory. He traveled to the east. "This is predominantly ogre territory." I balked at him. His shoulders lifted in a shrug. "Their kind isn't the nicest." I wanted to ask about them more, but he moved on. "Here is Veletin." They lay at the top of the map to the north. "This is where fairies and sirens originated. Their palaces are extraordinary. Some under water, others floating high in the sky."

My heart and mind exploded in wonder. I had never known this much lay outside of Willowmore. I had never known all of these races and creatures still existed, let alone where their land was.

"This is incredible. I never knew there was so much in the world."

"Mortala has done a great job of keeping her people in the dark and afraid to travel outside her reign."

I nodded, his words couldn't have been more true. "So Willowmore used to be Empath territory right?" He nodded, a muscle in his jaw flexing. "Where were you taken when the curse was cast?" I realized I still knew so little about my own people and their history. He pointed back to the elven territory. "Why did you come back?" His body went ridged with anger, violet pulsed around him.

"I was taken by slave traders passing through the northern part of the territory. They brought me back and sold me off when I was a kid." My heart ached at the sorrow and anger in his voice. I knew not to tell him I was sorry, those words didn't seem right to speak.

"You found Ciprian and the others though." A small smile twitched his lips. He nodded as he picked up the tiny dragon.

"Yeah. I never would have met them if I hadn't been taken." He paused, his colors conflicting together. "I am glad you're here." His body tensed as he waited for me to respond. My heart stopped in my chest. He had never said something like that to me, it was always teasing or correcting my fighting techniques. Besides, why would he be happy about my presence? I was an asshole and nothing special. I was more of a burden than anything.

"Why?" My confusion obviously confused him as well. His grey eyes narrowed, his brow furrowed.

"You're like me. In more ways than one." Is he talking about the magic we shared? "It's just nice not being alone anymore." His voice dripped with sadness, the air around him dulling to grey. I could understand that. Being surrounded by people all the time, but not having anyone there to relate to or truly see you was lonely. I knew that pain.

"I hate being a prisoner," My heart raced at the truth laying on my lips. "But I enjoy it here." Cals colors brightened quickly and fiercely. His was surrounded by a hopeful soft light. I cleared my throat, averting my gaze from his, I could feel him watching me. I needed to change the subject, talking about feelings and myself was never my favorite. I patted the dragon on the end, his green eyes sleepy as he laid in Cals hand.

"What shall we name him?" His colors were reluctant, but his eyes eventually fell to the tiny beast. He held out his hand and carefully dropped the drowsy dragon into my hands.

"Zigmund."

I laughed at his name suggestion. "That's terrible!" His bright grey eyes twinkled as he grinned at my criticism.

"It is, but that was the name of an old friend of mine. He went by Ziggy." I thought about that, looking at the now sleeping dragon.

"I like Ziggy."

Cal carried the stack of books up to my room while I cradled Ziggy in my arms. The tiny dragon slept soundly through the walk and spent the night asleep on my chest. His fuzzy body and steady breathing a comforting presence while I settled in for bed. As I lay in the darkness of my room, the cool night air blowing in from the open windows, I couldn't help but smile. My evening with Cal had been enjoyable, the information he had gifted me something exciting to look forward to. The memory of his deep laughter soothed me into a deep sleep, my colors a soft gold around me.

Chapter 14

I have decided, I hate summertime. The afternoon sun beat down hard on the small group of us within the pasture in the forest. Sweat dripped from my body and soaked my clothes so they clung to my skin. Asher, Grady and the destruction twins stood around me, all half dressed with weapons in hand as we took turns facing off. They had the luxury of being able to remove their shirts in an attempt to cool off, but they still were drenched with sweat. It was Lagans turn to try and disarm me. We circled one another, both breathing heavily.

I struck, swinging my axe toward his stomach, my dagger aiming for his throat. He danced back, his footing graceful as he dodged my attack. His sword darted for my legs, I stumbled back trying to avoid the blow but his blade sliced through the leg of my pants. I stopped, surprised by my own stupidity. I held up my hand, Lagan stopped, the tip of his sword resting in the grass.

I bent low, and brought the blade of my axe to the middle of my thigh. I slid the sharp blade along the fabric, cutting through the thick material smoothly. I did the same to my other leg. I tossed the use to be pant legs to the side, the air now freely touching my legs feeling amazing on my too hot body. I grinned wildly at the small group, pride of my thinking blooming in my chest. Ashers gaze widened and his eyes dropped to the grass. Grady and Lagans faces turned a shade of red I didn't know was even possible for the human skin to achieve. Silas's eyes blew wide and he smacked a hand over them. I rolled my eyes.

"They're just legs. You all are standing here half clothed, and you don't see me blushing." Gradys eyes lifted to the pale sky above us.

"Yeah, but you're a girl. It's different." Lagan said, his eyes still on my bare legs. I glared at him. Even in a forest of crazy hermits, there was a different standard. I lunged, swiping my blade low at Lagans gut. He jumped back and stumbled into the dirt.

"Come on Lagan, you wouldn't want to be beat by a girl dressed so unseemly." I grinned wickedly as the others chuckled behind me. Lagan clambered back in the grass, attempting to get up but fell once again when his eyes met my legs. I couldn't help myself from giggling at how skin affected these men. Each one capable of tearing me to shreds, but became completely helpless at the sight of a woman's body. I slid my axe and dagger into their sheaths and held out my hand to help the large man up. He shook his head and fell onto his back, his arm thrown over his eyes. I shook my head.

I turned to find the others walking to the shade the outside kitchen provided. I placed my hands on my hips.

"You're all ridiculous." I giggled. Ziggy came swooping through the summery air and landed softly on my shoulder. His fuzzy head rubbed against my cheek in greeting, a little purr in his chest. I scratched him lightly behind his horns, happy my new friend came to find me.

"Is this the dragon I've heard so much about?" Lagan asked as he climbed to his feet. Ziggy purred and wiggled happily at the attention of a new friend.

"Aren't you all supposed to be training?" Elias called as he began walking our way from the edge of the forest. He pointed at me, his honey eyes bright in the sunlight. "Show me what you've learned." I handed Ziggy over to Lagan and turned back to Elias. I set my feet, hands grasping my axes tightly. His eyes tracked the movement and flashed viciously as he approached. With surprising speed, he swept into a roll, the blade of his knife slicing across the exposed skin of my thigh. Blood welled and trickled down my skin.

I hissed at the stinging pain, but let it drive me. I dodged his next few strikes and landed a few of my own, his skin bleeding and torn in places. He caught my wrist after a swing and bent it painfully back, something popping inside making my axe fall to my feet. I yelped at the aching he caused, but the pain was quickly out shadowed. His other hand drug a knife across my other hand, freeing my other blade from my grasp. This isn't how I sparred with the others, we would make it clear what damage would have been done, but never draw this much blood.

I shook myself free of his grasp and took a step back, inspecting the blood welling across my palm. I thought we were done when my hands lay empty, my weapons disarmed and on the ground. But Elias wasn't done. Before I could even register the movement, his fist connected with my jaw. I fell back in the dirt, my wrist screamed as I landed on it. My chest ached and pounded with intense pain as Elias' boot connected with a hard kick.

"Elias!" Grady screamed.

"Stop!" Ashers voice rose.

"The fights over!" Lagan added. I looked up to find Elias throwing Lagan off and to the ground, the others running our way. His eyes filled with violent promises. What the fuck is his problem? He bent low and hit me again, my eye swelling almost immediately. I scrambled back in the dirt, trying to put space between us. I wasn't quick enough. He sent an uppercut to my jaw and climbed on top of me when I fell back into the grass. I waited for the next blow to come, but instead I heard a body crumple to the ground, his weight lifted from me.

Elias squirmed and writhed as if in pain on the grassy field. Veins popped from his neck as he floundered. Tears spilled down his cheeks, his mouth open in a silent scream. The others stood around him, watching as he flailed in pain. What was happening? What did they do to him? I realized quickly that it wasn't anything they had done, but what Caligan had done. He came stalking across the pasture, his eyes trained on Elias. His grey eyes glowed and sparked with anger, his body ridged. Ziggy jumped from my arms and sprang onto Elias's chest. A small spark of flame erupted from his tiny mouth and smoldered the leather of his chest plate.

Anger swarmed me then, at the uncalled for violence Elias had thrown at me. I climbed to my feet and spat a mouth full of blood onto the ground. I let my anger swirl within me, driving me to close the distance between me and his body, still on the ground. Fire erupted to life along my fingertips as I let my anger go, not wanting to contain it. My anger only built as Cal scooped up the tiny dragon and threw me over his shoulder before I could step any closer.

"Put me down you brute!" I yelled, my eyes never leaving Elias. I pounded against the hardness of Cals back, desperate to get my hands on the figure on the ground. His body had stilled, pain no longer raging through him.

"He will be dealt with." Cals voice was deep and gruff, anger tainting his words. I ignored the sparks that went though my body where his hands touched my bare skin. I now regretted cutting away so much fabric.

"Let me do the honors." I growled as he carried me back to the winding staircase.

"I don't really feel like burying anybody today so, no." I fumed silently as Cal carried me up to his home in the sky. My heart and blood still raced and thundered through me, my anger still spiked. Cal dropped my onto his bed, Ziggy bounced to my side. His green eyes sad as he watched blood drip from my mouth and above my swollen eye.

Cal grabbed a small jar of a blue cream and knelt before me, his colors raging around him. I sat still, teeth clenched as he spread the blue substance onto my cut and swollen skin. When he was done he replaced the lid and eyed me.

"What happened?"

"He wanted a turn sparring with me. He cut open my hand, twisted my wrist and then when I thought it was over, fucking jumped me!" I stood and began pacing, my fury still great. "What the fuck was his problem?" Cal stood to his full height, his arms crossing over his chest.

"Elias has a temper. He tends to get angry during a fight, sparing or real." I rolled my eyes.

"So do I, but that?" I pointed out his window to the ground below. "That was excessive and ridiculous!" His colors sparked, his eyes dangerous.

"I know, and I'm sorry. Like I said, he will be dealt with." I whirled at him.

"You wanted me to come here, to stay. You promised me safety, not underserved beatings!" His eyes darkened, his colors swirled with violet and grey. I threw open his door, my blood roaring in my ears as I walked across the bridge to my own home. Ziggy flew behind me, his fuzzy body brushing the skin of my cheek as I closed us into my room. How could a creature with a legend of great destruction and violence be better company than a human man?

Chapter 15

My hands were bound as guards dragged me to the center of the square. The queen sat upon her throne, an eager grin across her beautiful face. I screamed for help. I screamed for Caligan, pleading for the clan to help me. The crowd of warlocks and witches cheered in approval as a noose was thrown around my neck. They screamed my name triumphantly.

"Lorn!"

They had finally caught me, were finally getting rid of another ungrateful human. I yelled once more, my voice soon cut off as the rope pulled taunt and hauled me into the air.

"Lorn!"

"Lorn!" A voice yelled snapping my eyes open. I struggled against the grip tight around my wrists, my heart racing. Panic blurred my vision as I frantically clawed at my attacker. "Lorn!" The voice yelled again, deep and familiar. "Lorn!" The voice slowly brought me back to reality.

"Cal." I whispered, my throat sore. His hands held my arms firmly, his eyes wide as they searched my face. I closed my eyes as relief hit me. "It was just a dream." I whispered to myself. He slowly released me from his hold, my hands fell limply to my sides. His colors started fading from a panicked red, his fear pulsing visibly through the air around him. I wiped sweat from my brow, my shirt completely soaked through. He sighed heavily next to me as I tried to catch my breath. Ziggy sat next to me, his body ridged, sensing my fear. I rubbed his head gently.

"At least you're not ignoring me anymore." He said quietly. I had spent the last week that followed the day Elias attacked me avoiding the men I lived with. Taking meals in my small cottage and spending my days with Ciprian. Elias's anger still potent in my mind. Thanks to whatever Caligan had spread over my wounds I healed quickly and without scaring.

"I wasn't ignoring you." I sighed.

"Yes you were." He countered. I sat up to face him.

"I just can't get Elias out of my head. His anger and hitting me and what he said the other night-"

"Fuck what he said." He cut me off, his colors darkened around him into a furious purple. "He's full of shit. We've seen, been around, and been with plenty of women in our lifetimes." A spark of jealousy brightened within me. I stomped it out quickly. "We don't stare at you because you're a girl or because we've been alone for too long." He rolled his eyes at what Elias had been implying. "We stare because we've never seen another woman like you before." His voice was gruff, thick with irritation and something else. Something darker. I raised a brow.

"Meaning I'm the only female you've ever seen with a shaved head?" I asked dryly.

"Meaning, you're effortlessly beautiful and not only do you not know it, but you also couldn't give a shit less about looks." His words made my stomach tighten. The colors around him eased, they stopped swirling so violently. He thought I was beautiful? Or was he just saying that to make me feel better?

"And he has been punished for what he did the other day." I wished I was the one to deliver his punishment, but I'm sure Cal did a better job than I could have. I tore my eyes from his gaze, my skin feeling too hot. I squinted at my door. It hung at a odd angle, broken off its hinges.

"You broke my door." I looked back at him. He shrugged, a small smile tugging on his lips. He looked down at his calloused hands.

"You wouldn't answer." His smile faded. "I'll fix it." He promised.

"I thought you had to be invited in?" I challenged. He gave me a sheepish smile.

"All magic has a loophole. Every spell, every potion, every incantation. Some are easier to find than others, and me, being the one who created the spell to block intruders, I know where to find the loophole." I always thought magic was final. I never knew here was a way to reverse it.

"Were you the only one I woke up?" I asked noticing the lack of the others. Maybe I hadn't yelled out loudly like I had last time. Maybe Caligan had been the only one to hear me. He shook his head, embarrassment heating my checks. I tapped my collarbone with my metal thumb.

"But I was the only one you called out for." His gaze was steady, his grey eyes bright. He was shirtless again, fresh, bright red scratch marks painted his chest. Without thinking I reached out and gently touched them. His skin was soft and warm. The contact sparked against my uncovered finger tips. Caligans colors darkened, as did mine.

"Did I do that?" His muscles jumped under my touch. His silence was answer enough. I could feel my colors starting to dull to a grey. I had not only screamed out for him waking the whole clan, but I had clawed him in my panic. My eyes burned. He placed a calloused finger under my chin and brought my gaze to his.

"It's okay. Honestly I probably deserved it." He said with a small smile. His throat bobbed as his eyes darted to my lips. His colors around him dulled slightly. "Was I the one hurting you? Is that why you called out for me?" My tears ached to fall, my mind almost too exhausted to hold them back. I shook my head, the tension in his shoulders finally releasing.

"I was yelling for you to help me." I admitted, blinking away my tears.

"Did I?"

I shrugged. "You woke me up. So I guess in a way, yes." Several long moments passed between us. His grey eyes were bright as his colors shifted and swirled quickly around him.

"Try and go back to sleep." He stood, the bed shifting under the absence of his weight. He grabbed his large scythe from the floor and walked to the door. With a wave of his hand it fixed itself back into place and he shut it quietly behind him, the lock clicking into place. I curled up under the blankets, relishing the feeling of his skin on mine as I found sleep once again, Ziggys tiny body curled against my throat. My sleep was dreamless and peaceful the rest of the night.

Chapter 16

I spent the following week working with Silas and Lagan. Ciprian canceling our lessons once again.. Caligan hasn't tried to steal anymore of my time to ask me questions, he says he's been reading up on a few things. I know I should be annoyed and focused on getting out of here as soon as possible, but something about this place has kept me enthralled and eager to see another day. The bomb maker and inventor were excited to have me back in their workshop everyday. Silas had me measuring out powders and liquids for different explosives while Lagan allowed me to help him assemble some of his devices and machines. Silas had also taken most of the morning to teach me more signs to further our communication.

This morning I took a seat at the table next to a very tired Caligan who greeted me with a small smile. I poured myself a warm cup of coffee and waited quietly while the others ate. Ziggy zoomed happily through the air, gaining smiles from everybody except Elias who glared darkly. Silas chopped a selection of fruit into tiny pieces and piled them together before offering them to the tiny dragon. His black and white fuzzy tail wiggled happily as he ate the juicy fruit. Lagan turned to me after serving himself a second helping of eggs.

"Why do you not eat breakfast?" He asked me. I wasn't riled by the random question, but it felt nice to have someone interested in anything about me.

"Most of my life was spent with eating very little not very often. So I guess I'm kind of used to not eating." The colors shifted angrily around the men at the table. Asher opened his mouth to speak but Elias cut him off, addressing me directly for the first time in two weeks.

"Today will be your last day with the destruction twins." Silas grinned at the nickname. Despite his happy smile, his bright golden colors dulled to a soft grey. I nudged him with my foot under the table.

"Don't be sad. I may not be working with you but I'm not going anywhere." He smiled widely, the golden light returning. The rest of the table exchanged looks at my words, their colors brightening as well.

"Awh, she likes us." Grady teased, his face wide with a grin. I took a sip of coffee and glowered at them from over the brim of my cup.

"I'm liking you a little less right now." Truth is, I did like them. They were funny and kind and didn't seem to be wanting to use me for any ulterior motives other than just curiosity and being protective over Cals people. The colors in the air remained bright, Caligans shown the most. I scolded myself. I should choose my words more carefully, I didn't want to give any of them false hope of me staying if I still wasn't sure if I was going to. Elias cleared his throat before continuing.

"Starting tomorrow, you'll be working with me." Cal shot him a dangerous glare. "And Caligan." Elias added quickly. Caligans colors darkened, his breakfast forgotten in front of him. The violence in his stare sent chills of fear down my spine. Lagan got to his feet and slapped me on the back disrupting the tense moment passing between Caligan and Elias.

"Better get a move on, we have a lot to do today." I joined him and Silas. Grady shot us all a glare from his seat.

"I better not become your surprise test dummy for whatever it is you fuckers have planed." He growled, obviously still upset over being knocked unconscious. I giggled and Silas and Lagan exchanged a look.

"We'll see." Lagan said with a shrug. Grady leapt to his feet, anger heating his cheeks and hanging heavily over his shoulders in thick purple clouds. The three of us ran for the workshop laughing as he cursed at us, Ziggy flying after us. The sky was dark overhead, clouds hiding the morning sunlight promising a storm. When we entered the workshop, Silas made a beeline for his supply cabinet. He gathered bottles and jars into his arms, all containing different powders. I sat atop one of the stools and watched them work. I wasn't allowed to help do any of the measurements today. The ingredients apparently too delicate for inexperienced hands. I rolled my eyes at their reasoning. Silas blew something up at least once a day, if anyone shouldn't be handling dangerous mixtures, its him.

"Today," Lagan began, separating and sorting through the various jars and bottles. "We are making stink bombs." Silas grinned widely, his eyes full of excitement and mischief. "They are vey easy to make and very effective. Days like today are proof that Silas blows stuff up on purpose even though he claims they are accidents because he has never set one of these off inside the workshop." Lagan shot the grinning boy a glare. The latter responded with a vulgar hand gesture earning a small laugh from me. Lagan shook his head at his brother. "When we are done putting them together, we will give you a demonstration." It was my turn to grin.

"And by demonstration do you mean Grady is getting another surprise today?" I couldn't hide the eagerness in my voice. The two smiled devilishly.

"Everyone is getting a surprise today." My smile widened and the air glowed brighter. It took us a few hours to make half a dozen stink bombs. Ziggy explored the nooks and crannies of the workshop while I watched, allowed only to seal the tiny capsules with hot wax after they carefully assembled the powders and activators inside. Once we finished, we each took two and chose our targets. I picked Caligan and Elias. Elias, so I could finally get back at him for being an ass. And Caligan just because. Lagan chose Asher and Ciprian and Silas decided to designate both of his for Grady.

The sky had finally broken loose, rain fell heavily to the ground. I felt myself getting annoyed by the rain, but stomped out the feeling quickly. While living in the city, rain meant being wet while also being angry for the day ahead. But here, I didn't have a reason to dread it. I closed my eyes and relished the feeling of the cool droplets on my skin. My bare feet squished lightly in the muddy grass. Ziggy climbed inside the pocket of my shirt, his white horns barely visible from the top as he curled into the warmth and dry coverage I granted the tiny beast. Lagan and Silas joined me in the wet grass outside the workshop.

Asher and Elias were in the center of the pasture sparring. Rain soaked through their clothes and their hair clung to their faces. Asher wielded a battle axe and Elias used a sword. They circled each other, lunging back and forth to strike or block in a violent dance. It was mesmerizing, watching them move their weapons as an extension of their bodies. Lagan and I exchanged a glance, stink bombs in hand. With a grin I called for their attention.

"Excuse me gentlemen?" The two froze, their weapons raised as they turned their gazes to us. "Catch!" I yelled as Lagan and I released the small capsules into the air. As they landed at our targets feet, a loud popping noise filled the air and a plume of green smoke surrounded them. Emerging from the putrid cloud, Asher and Elias began coughing and gaging, weapons forgotten on the muddy ground.

The two evil geniuses beside me began jumping up and down in triumph. Lagan suddenly seemed as young as Silas despite the age difference. I laughed at their excitement and then laughed harder as Asher puked into the wet grass. Grady, who witnessed the assault, stood laughing on the other side of his plot. Silas threw off his bow and quiver and charged. Seeing the oncoming attack, Grady took off in the other direction, Silas hot on his heels.

They disappeared into the trees. After a short silence, another loud popping noise sounded, then another, followed by Grady's loud curses. Silas came sprinting back into view. Fist raised in the air in victory. I fell into the wet grass in a fit of laughter. Rain soaked through my clothes. Lagan fell to my side, pointing at Asher's still vomiting figure. The air around Elias blossomed into a purple fog. He began yelling curses and threats at us as we laughed.

The wind picked up suddenly, blowing fiercely through the clearing. The rain fell harder, lightning cracked across the sky. The sound of thunder was almost deafening. Silas pulled me from the ground, the wind almost knocking me back down. We all struggled across the pasture, trying to reach the long twisting staircase. Ziggy slept soundly against my chest, unbothered by our struggle. We fought desperately against the fierce wind and the harsh rain. Despite the annoyance surrounding the smelly group of men, I laughed. I laughed at their anger and at the vicious wind. I laughed as we stumbled over the bridges and past the open windows of Ciprians cottage. I laughed even harder as he poked his head out, his nose wrinkled in disgust.

"What the fuck is that smell?" I grinned, having never heard the gentle warlock use such fowl language. The words sounded funny coming from the male sitting within the warm shelter of his home. Grady, at the front of the small group stopped and shot Silas a glare.

"These three decided to ambush us with stink bombs!" He made a move for Silas, anger reddening his face. Both he and Lagan jumped behind me, using my body as a shield.

"You guys know she's smaller than you right?" Asher asked, shouting over the roar of the wind.

"Yes, but she kicked his ass once, she can do it again." Lagan replied, earning a laugh from all of us. Grady continued his advance, no humor on his face.

"That's enough." Demanded Ciprian. "Get inside before you all catch a cold." He retreated back into his home with a smile. We all trudged down the bridges, the thick tree branches offering us some harbor from the storm. Our feet squished underneath us, our feet leaving a muddy trail behind us. I fell behind the group and ran back into the window Ciprian had stuck his head out of. I handed him the stink bomb Lagan had designated for him. I snatched it from him when we fell to the ground laughing down below.

"Want to help me get Caligan?" His only reply was a wicked grin.

The storm continued to rage around us as night fell. Dinner was moved into the barn for the evening. I stood at the threshold, leaning against the wooden door frame, Ziggy resting on my shoulder. I watched the downpour of rain and the bright cracks of lighting that lit the sky and the earth below. Something about the storms rage was beautiful, peaceful even. I was surprised at the things I found myself distracted and enchanted by within the forest. Things I would have cursed or hated while living in the city, now seemed to take on a completely new life. My admiration of the stormy night faded as Ciprian and Caligan started making their way across the large pasture. The two seemed to be in a very passionate discussion.

Caligan had slept most of the day, tired and drained from holding up wards from the night before. The warlock wore a long red cloak, the hood pulled up tightly around his face to avoid the rain. Caligan however, wore no cloak. His clothes were soaked with the rain, the fabric clung to the grooves of his body and his hair lay flat against his forehead. But he didn't seem to mind the rain or the storm. I palmed the stink bomb and gave the pair a small smile.

"Good morning Caligan." I said as he met me at the entrance to the kitchen. Their conversation died quickly at the sight of me. I jumped in front of Caligan's towering figure and stopped him from going any further. Ciprian gave me a discrete wink before finding his way deeper into the room. Caligans face was drawn into a grimace, his colors and anger swirled around him. "Your boot is untied." I pointed to the loose laces on the ground. I knelt to the ground quickly, Caligan took a shocked step backwards. I craned my neck to meet his eyes as I tied the laces. Something flickered within the grey and black mixing through the air around him. I held his gaze as I retied the laces, making sure they were tight. I slowly stood, my eyes never leaving his.

"Thanks." His voice was clipped and low. A shiver went through me.

"You're wet." His mouth quirked up slightly at the edge. With a wave of his hand the water soaking his body disappeared leaving him dry and warm. I stepped to the side and waved a hand, allowing him access to the rest of the small building. He gave me a quizzical look before striding away. I thanked my pick pocketing skills I had gained while in the city while I slipped the stink bomb into his pocket without him even feeling me.

I joined Ciprian who sat by the large fireplace at the far end of the building. He watched the group of men talk loudly at the dining table, a small smile on his aged face. I sat on the floor by his feet and leaned back against his chair. I teased Ziggy with my finger and watched him chase it across the carpet, trying to look inconspicuous. The warlock poked my shoulder lightly and raised a questioning brow. I gave him a small smile before returning to my fury friend.

Several minutes later Grady announced dinner was ready. Ciprian started to get up when I stopped him by placing a hand on his arm. Together we waited, our eyes on Caligans large figure. We watched as Caligan took a seat, setting off the stink bomb. A cloud consumed the table and the rest of the clan. Ciprian and I fell into each other as we laughed.

"Motherfucker!" Grady shouted through the smoke. I didn't have to see the colors around him to know he was furious. I snorted, my laughing fit growing more intense. Ziggy danced excitedly around my feet, sensing the happiness swelling in my chest. Ciprian waved a hand through the air, the smoke and odor vanishing. The group around the table stared at the old warlock and I. We slowly collected ourselves and took our seats at the table. Nobody spoke, until Caligan began chuckling, the sound came deep from his chest. My colors glowed. The others joined in until we were all laughing together, save for Grady who sat in his chair fuming.

"How am I the only one that's pissed off?" He snarled.

"You should be happy," I giggled, wiping a tear from my eye. "I got Silas too." He shot me a glare. Ziggy flew to his side and rubbed his fuzzy head against the gardeners cheek. His anger quickly disappeared thanks to the gentle little animal, and he began serving himself a bowl of soup from the pot placed in the center of the table. Caligan raised his glass and tapped it gently against mine with a wide grin lighting his face.

After we had all finished eating, we cleared the table and Ciprian produced two bottles of wine. He poured us all a glass as Silas took out a deck of cards and began dealing to the group. Lagan produced a small cloth bundle from his pocket and passed it down the table to me.

"When we first brought you here, this was in your pocket but it was broke." I unwrapped the small bundle to find my watch. The smooth gold shell warm and familiar against my skin. I hadn't realized how much I missed it until now. I clicked the button, freeing the face from its cage. The hands ticked slowly and soundly. "I fixed it." Lagan added, his cheeks reddening. I smiled, the air around me almost as bright as the air around Silas.

"Thank you. I missed the stupid thing." I admitted as I tucked it into my pocket, its comforting weight settling in there. Lagan nodded, the redness of his face deepening. I collected my dealt cards.

"Can I ask you something Lorn?" Asher asked from across the table. I nodded.

"When Caligan found you in the woods-'

"You mean, when Caligan *tackled* me in the woods?" The table grinned.

"When he tackled you in the woods, and brought you back, you were dressed like a man. Waist coat and everything." I nodded, not understanding where he was going with his question. "Why?" I shrugged and took a drink of wine.

"Living in the city, being a human made me a target but being a woman, made it even worse." The table fell silent. "I dressed like a man so I wouldn't have to worry about being followed and attacked by other men." Silas frowned. He moved his hands quickly, too quickly for me to understand. I turned to Lagan for translation. His face turned a shade of scarlet I had never seen.

"He said that, shouldn't your-" He pointed at my chest. "Give you away?" I suppressed a laugh at his embarrassment.

"Breasts?" I asked. His red face nodded. I shook my head. "I would wrap cloth around my chest to make it flat." I paused for a moment, studying my cards. "Within Willowmore, its illegal for females to carry weapons. And with the jobs and other things I did to make money, I needed a weapon."

"What kind of jobs?" Elias asked.

"Well, like I told you I was a messenger but I wouldn't just deliver letters. I ran drugs, payments. I was paid a few times to rough up a few humans and warlocks who were in debt to the wrong people. I stole quiet often when I was younger too. That's how I got that watch." Silas grinned.

"So you were a criminal?" Grady asked. I nodded.

"And I was good at it."

"I'm assuming the hand I felt against my ass earlier was you placing that bomb in my pocket?" Silas choked and wine spilled from his nose. I nodded and drank greedily from my cup. The colors around Caligan were golden and tinged with a light pink, their brightness matching the gleam in his eyes. "One of your occupational skills?" I grinned. Asher won the hand and Silas collected the cards before dealing us each new cards.

"I thought your reaction was going to be more like Grady's." I admitted. He shrugged. Ziggy climbed onto Cals chest, the big brute pet the dragon gently.

"If it was any of these other assholes, it would have been worse than Grady's." He gestured to the men around the table. There was a moment of silence as we all studied our cards.

"It's nice to see you smiling and laughing, Lorn." Asher said as he rearranged his hand. Lagan groaned.

"First Silas and his royal highness," He gestured to Cal, who glared dangerously at the inventor for the nickname. "now you?" He pointed his wine glass at Asher down the table. "Are we all going to take turns flirting with her?" Silas punched him in the arm, trying hard to repress a smile. Asher shook his head.

"I'm not flirting with her." He turned his gaze to me, his brown eyes glimmered with warmth, his colors a steady grey around his shoulders. "You don't really talk or smile. You seem like a very angry person, so it's nice to see you happy." A lump formed in my throat at the honesty and truth behind his words. Its been easier to let go of my temper since coming here, I haven't been overwhelmed by my anger very much since I met the strange group of men. But it still raged within me, aching to be let out. I was always angry. I gulped down the rest of my wine and met his gaze evenly. My own colors swirled grey and purple around me.

"If you lived the life I have, you would be angry too."

Chapter 17

The table fell silent, our game forgotten.

"We've all lived rough lives." Asher said as he leaned forward in his chair, his muscular arms straining against his shirt. "Lagan grew up in an abusive orphanage. Caligan and Grady started their lives as slaves. They were starved and beaten regularly." Caligan shifted tensely in his chair. "We found Silas when he was five, his vocal cords had been cut and he had been throw in a ditch to bleed out." For once, the freckled faced boy didn't have a smile. "Elias escaped the sex trade when he was nine, and I," My gaze returned to Asher. "I watched as my father was killed by the royal guard and I was then hunted for being his son. I'm still wanted within the Willowmore kingdom to this day." A lump formed in my throat as I looked at the faces around me, drawn at the mention of their pasts. Their colors were dull and somber. Asher continued.

"We have all been through hell. We've all done terrible things to survive. But you seem to be the only one who refuses to leave their past behind." I glared at him, my anger flickering within me. Who is he to judge me for my past and what its done to me?

"What do you want from me Asher?" I growled. "You give me a bed and some warm meals and expect me to just be okay? To let go of all that has happened to me?" He remained silent, stoking the fire within me.

"What the fuck do you want?" I demanded. He met my glare coolly, his eyes remaining warm and kind as my anger grew. The others tensed as we stared at each other. Purple flames sparked to life along my finger tips. Cal laid a calming hand on my knee under the table in warning. *Control it.* His words rang through my mind. I clenched my fists, snuffing out the fire.

"I want to know you. We all do." The table stayed silent. "We want you to stay, Lorn. We want to help you find a new life. Help you leave the fucked up world you were born into and help you find a new one." Penns face flashed across my mind, his words very similar to the last ones she had said to me. "We can't help you escape something we don't understand or know about." He was right. They had taken me into their home, risked everything they had built for themselves to help a stranger. My whole life I had wanted a place I belonged. Not with people who needed my talents or services, or wanted whatever coin I could bring them. But these men had all been gifted a terrible life and they fought for a new one. The colors around Asher were pure and light. He wasn't trying to upset me, he was simply trying to make me understand. I filled my cup and drained it quickly before taking a deep breath.

"I grew up in an orphanage within the city." The men around me leaned forward as I began telling them about my life. Telling them about me. "The place was run by sorcerers, the witch in charge was the worst out of all of the workers there. She would beat us all the time, over stupid insignificant things." Elias actions rang a little too close to home the day he flipped out on me. "We would go days without food or water. We would have to fight over blankets in the winter time because she wouldn't give us enough for everyone. She hated humans more than Mortala does I think." I flinched at the memory of that terrible woman and the things she had done to me. The memory of her orange hair and sharp teeth made my skin crawl. I rested my hand over my stomach, where the jagged scar pierced my skin, gifted to me by that horrible witch. "Most didn't survive more than a few years. I was one of the few who did.

"I spent most of my childhood there. I managed to escape and I found an Inn on the other side of the city. I walked right up to the owner and demanded a job. Her name is Mrs. Pennly. She hired me and gave me a room as payment." I smiled at the memory of my friend. "A few years went by and I became a messenger and stopped working for her. I made enough to pay my rent and get me a meal most days. But I faced more violence on the streets than I ever did at the orphanage." The lump in my throat grew and my eyes burned. I tapped my thumb against my collarbone, the metal against my skin comforted my aching heart. Ziggy sat in front of me, his green eyes wide as he listened to me talk, as if he could understand me.

"I've been jumped, beaten, stabbed -" I shook my head, not wanting to allow certain memories to resurface. "I was more of a target that most." I ran a hand over my shaved head at the memory of the green skinned warlock. "Ive been an inch from death more times than I can count." Caligan refilled my glass as I scanned their faces. Tears fell freely from Ciprians snowy eyes. "These past few weeks I've spent with all of you, have been the only peace I've ever known." My cheeks were red by the admission. I drained my glass of wine, warmth spread through my body as the bittersweet liquid ran down my throat. I rapidly blinked away the tears from my eyes, not wanting them to see me cry. Asher drank deeply from his glass, his colors soft and calm.

"I guess now is probably the best time to tell you." Cal said, his voice low as he toyed with his glass. "You're free to go." My heart sped up, my emotions swirling confusingly within me. "If you choose to leave, we will keep our word and help you in any way we can." The table remained silent as they waited for me to say something. I could leave, I was free. I could go anywhere. I could travel to the elven kingdom in the south or travel to see an ogre. I should be happy, excited. But I wasn't. Sadness whirled around me, weighing heavily within me. I had found myself enjoying life here, enjoying seeing and spending time with the strange men seated around me these past few weeks. I looked at my glass.

"And if I'm not ready to leave yet?" Bright, hopeful colors burst into the room. Cals swirled frantically despite the calm position of his body. His grey eyes shown brightly.

"You may stay as long as you like." I nodded before draining my glass once more.

"Good. Cause I've got a few stacks of books left to read and I wont be able to carry them all on my own if I leave." Silas began moving his hands frantically, his eyes wide as he watched me, a wide smile on his lips. I turned to Lagan who grinned at his brother.

"He says we have a lot more books, so you should just stay until you've read them all." I couldn't help but smile at the young boy.

We played cards well into the night, the storm still raging on around us. I was asked no more questions, instead we laughed and joked. Ciprian was the first to head off to bed, but the others soon followed. I was the last to climb the rain soaked staircase to bed, shielding a sleeping Ziggy from the rain. I spent several long minutes squishing my toes in the soft mud and grass down below. I imagined that I looked rather child like, playing in the rain and mud. But I couldn't bring myself to care. Something about the act felt freeing, felt innocent. Felt like something I never would have been able to experience if I still lived within the kingdoms walls.

When my feet became cold I made my way to my small cottage. The rain fell softly, bolts of lighting still lit the sky in webs of light. I wiped my feet clean with a towel and climbed into bed, laying Ziggys tired form atop a pillow. I don't know when I had started to feel safe within the small village in the trees, but I didn't lock my door or even shut it. I left it open, so I could watch the rain fall and see the art created by the lighting from where I curled up in bed. The rain hitting my small wooden roof was the sweetest lullaby.

Well after the rest of the clan had fallen quiet, sleep taking them into the night I still lay awake, watching the night sky. With my door open wide, I had a direct view of the front of Caligans cottage. The lights were still on within, I could see his figure bent low over a table through the window. His brow was furrowed in concentration, his hand running mindlessly through his messy black hair. Almost as if I had called his name, his head turned and his stormy eyes met mine from across the bridge connecting us. My brain told me to look away, or to close my eyes, to act like I hadn't been watching him like a freak. But I held his stare. Shivers crept down my spine. The last thing I remember before falling asleep is how brightly his grey eyes shown.

Chapter 18

The grass down below was littered with broken
tree branches and pieces of roofing from the workshops.
Thankfully, the three buildings stood relatively unharmed
by the storm, as did our homes. Grady's beloved garden
however would need a lot of care. His crops lay in a
twisted, barbed heap. Broken stems and stocks stuck into
the air like broken bones piercing skin. Ciprian knelt in
the dirt beside a sullen Grady, helping repair the damage.
I helped Asher and Silas clear debris blown in by the
storm. Lagan climbed on top of Ashers forge to repair
the damage done to the roof. Ziggy zoomed around him,
curious about what the man was doing. We spent the
morning collecting the broken branches and stacking
them into a large pile next to the large fire pit to use as
firewood and kindling. After we cleared the pasture,
Caligan came out of his workshop and made his way over
to me.

"I need an extra pair of hands." His voice was
gruff, his colors a dark grey. Lagan had finished his work
on the roofs and he and Silas lounged in the grass. Ziggy
played in the grass between them, all three enjoying the
sunlight and cool breeze. Ciprian and Grady had
successfully healed most of the damaged produce, lifting
Grady's spirits significantly. Seeing that the work had
been completed, I gave Caligan a small nod and followed
him inside. He wasn't wearing his leather chest plate and
his large scythe wasn't strapped to his back. As we walked

I watched the muscles shift underneath his shirt, the fabric stretched tight over the hard plains.

I had never been inside his workplace and I wasn't surprised to find it just as clean and light as his small home. The walls were the same pale yellow and large cabinets and tables were placed throughout. Most of the shelves and counters were covered in jars containing flowers and different plants. Bottles with colorful liquids, bubbled teasingly. A small bed was placed in the corner and a small desk holding rolls of leather and cutting and staining tools lay upon it's surface. I perched myself atop the end of the large work table in the center of the room. Caligan rolled up the sleeves of his shirt, revealing his scared forearms, his muscles bulging with the motion of his hands.

"Take a small amount of each of these," he placed two jars in front of me. "and grind them together." He placed a mortar and pestle next to my knee, his finger grazing my leg. I ignored the spark it sent over my skin and focused on my task. Each jar held a different flower; one was a collection of small white buds, its petals folded together in a small spiral. The other was a light purple, its petals large and fanned. I did as he instructed while he carefully measured different liquids and powders and set them aside. We worked silently together until I finished grinding the flowers into a fine grit. He then took the mixture from me and began adding his powders and liquids before mixing them all together.

"What are we making?" I asked curiously, breaking the silence.

"A healing remedy for Damned bites."He said as he delicately poured a blue liquid into the mixture in hand.

"You're not into biting?" I said, trying to push him into reacting. Into talking, instead of suffering quietly in his grey cloud. His stormy eyes met mine, his glare dangerous as purple wove into the haze around his shoulders. He nodded to the bowl in his hands.

"Their bites are fatal if they aren't tended to properly and quickly." His emotions swirled violently around him.

"Have you ever lost someone to the damned?" His body tensed, his colors raged wildly around him. His silence was answer enough. I waited for him to continue, his jaw tensed as he ground his teeth together.

"We were young. It was the first time any of us had seen one." His mixing became rough as the memory of his late friend was brought to the surface. "His name was Daregg." His colors were dull and grey around him, sadness overtaking him.

"How many others have you lost?"

His eyes flashed. "Two, neither to the Damned. Mathick was two years younger than me. He was here only six months before he hung himself from a tree outside the clearing." Caligan shoulders slumped slightly. My heart ached for him, for the losses he has had to endure. "Sometimes it's not easy to leave the horrors behind you." His voice was rough and thick with emotion.

"And the other?" Cal dropped the bowl to the counter roughly, his eyes dark and his colors shifted to a dark violet around him.

"Why so many questions?" He demanded. I shrugged glaring at him.

"I just want to know more about you." I admitted. He placed his hands on the table, his knuckles turning white as anger pulsed through him.

"His name was Jordame. He tried to kill Silas when we were teenagers." Anger roared within me. The thought of someone trying to hurt that happy boy had my blood boiling. "Silas is the only one of us that's innocent. He never had to kill or fight his way through life." He shrugged, his expression dangerous. "Jordame resented him for it." His breathing became heavy, the air around him danced aggressively.

"What happened to him?"

"We took a vote. The others voted for exile, but I gave an executive order and chose."

I frowned. "What's an executive order?" His gaze was predatory, a small ball of fear formed in my gut. Caligan was attractive, no denying it, but that look made me scared to be near him. I held his gaze, swallowing the lump in my throat.

"We vote on major decisions. But I have the right to overrule."

"Just you?" He nodded.

"We are all equals, all equally responsible and in charge of our lives. But sometimes even we get blinded by our freedom. We need someone to take charge when that happens." His importance to this clan was bigger than I thought.

"What happened to Jordame?" My heart raced as his eyes traced my face and neck.

"I ripped him apart." He held my gaze for a silent moment before returning to the remedy in the bowl. His colors remained angry, grey fading in around the edges.

"I didn't mean to upset you."

"What makes you think I'm upset?" He asked sharply. I raised a brow.

"Maybe its the scowl on your face or the short, clipped way you're talking to me. Or its the fact that your colors are off." I said slightly annoyed. He stopped mixing and looked at me quizzically.

"My colors?"

I frowned. He and I had the same magic within us, didn't he see emotions too? "I can see what others feel. They are colors that float around you. You don't see them?" He stopped mixing and leaned against the table.

"I don't see them, I feel them." He shrugged. "It's different for each of our people." I liked the sound of that. *Our people.* "Each emotion has a different texture, different temperature." That's interesting. I wonder what each one feels like, would he tell me if I asked? "What are my colors?" He asked curiously, his hard gaze flickering. I eyed him carefully, hesitant to continue. I didn't know how he would feel about me being able to read him so easily, but then again, he can do the same to me. The thought made me slightly uncomfortable.

"They're violet and grey. Very dark. They're dancing around you angrily." His colors stilled as I spoke. "Grey means sadness and purple means anger." I finished analyzing his emotions, fearing his reaction. His glare remained and I met it steadily.

"What others have you discovered?" He pushed the bowl to me and motioned for me to continue mixing as I talked. I mixed slowly as I thought of all the colors and their meanings I had been able to piece together.

"Gold means happy, Silas is always glowing with it." I smiled softly. "Red is fear. I've seen pink, mostly around you." I gaged his reaction, his face still stoncy. "But I haven't figured out what that one means. You are also surrounded by black a lot, but I don't know about that one either. When someone is being honest," I thought back to Ashers words from the night before, his eagerness to help me as we talked around the table. "Its colorless but its pure and bright." I continued sitting silently as I waited for him to speak.

"What color is it when someone lies?"

"I don't know yet." I gave him a feline smile, my desire to lift his colors almost unbearable. "Lie to me." His eyes darkened, more black swirled into the air around him. My wonder behind the colors meaning intensified beyond belief. He thought for a moment, considering his lie.

"I despise your company." His colors sharpened violently, the air alerting me to his dishonesty. I repressed a grin. He enjoys my company? He never seems to want to be around me, especially the first week or so that I was here. My own colors turned soft and golden. "Did it work?" He raised a brow. I nodded with a smile, a blush ran up my neck. Why do I get so flustered by him? I feel like a stupid girl with a crush, the ones I would see in Willowmore acting like fools every time someone handsome was around. Caligans colors resumed their purple and grey haze.

"I'm angry that I have to be awake right now to make a remedy for something that is going to try and kill me tonight." His jaw flexed. "I'm angry I have to spend my evenings awake when I would much rather be up during the day." I guess I wasn't the only one who was angry most days.

"Why would you chose the job then? Everyone else seems to enjoy their essential tasks. Why not switch with Elias? You already do more than the others." I waved a hand to the remedy ingredients in front of me. The purple around him depend.

"I chose it because I would rather get killed than one of my brothers. Elias hates his job too, spends most of his days just wandering through the woods, he would hate it even more at night and wouldn't last past his first shift." His words were raw and honest. A tinge of sadness pinged against my heart. I felt sad that Caligan would lower his life's worth beneath everyone else's. It also made me sad I had never had anyone I would give my life to protect. How long has Caligans life been?

"Can I ask you something?" He raised a brow in response. "You said you've been alive for a long time, but you still look so young." He nodded, waiting for me to go on. "Why have I aged normally?"

"Those casings on your fingers have blocked your magic in every way. They didn't allow your body to age like it should. One year of our lives is equivalent to nine in mortal years." A small ball of fear settled in my stomach. The short life I had lived already had been filled with so much pain and loneliness, could I survive hundreds of years? I shook away the thoughts, not wanting to continue down that path. I changed the subject.

"How many times have you been bitten?" I asked as I passed back the bowl. He placed eight empty vials on the table before him and began filing them with the now completed remedy.

"More times than I can count." His colors swirled fiercely, seeping around him. I became desperate, aching to lighten the haze on his shoulders.

"I'm surprised you can count at all." I teased, trying my best to make my voice light. Relief spread through me as a small grin appeared on his lips, the grey and purple swirls fading into brightness.

"Aren't ladies supposed to be nice?" He asked, the smile on his lips trying to grow larger. "I've always thought it was unladylike to be rude to the men providing you with things like shelter and food." He shot back, throwing a small cork at me before sealing off a vial with another. I grinned wickedly.

"I think I've made it pretty clear I'm no lady. Besides," I said with a sigh. "It's so much more fun doing and saying whatever the fuck I want." He laughed then, the sound deep and lovely. The haze around him lightened further, a rosy pink working its way through the cloud.

"Such a dreadful mouth you have." He leaned against the table, his remedy now bottled and finished. "How do you ever expect to get a husband using such fowl language?" He taunted, a gleam in his stormy eyes. I shrugged, trying my best to twist my face into mock sadness.

"I have no idea. Although Silas thinks my smile is rather enjoyable, maybe if I smile while I curse nobody will notice." He shook his head and rolled his eyes skyward. "You don't agree? Do you not like my smile Cal?" I laughed. I meant it as a joke, but a small part of me was eager to hear his answer.

"Your smile is very pretty." Black swallowed the air around him, seeping as his dangerous eyes met mine. "But there is something about the way you glare at me that I find much more enticing."

Chapter 19

"I won!" I yelled throwing my cards onto the ground in front of me. Elias, Asher, Silas, Grady, Cal, Lagan and I sat together in front of the fire pit outside playing cards. Ziggy was having fun stealing our discarded cards and making a small nest of them at Cals feet. It had been two months since I first came to live with the strange clan. Playing cards had become our nightly routine. My fifth win in a row for the night had my opponents furious. Elias tossed his cards, his face red with anger.

"Cheater!"

"Am not!" I yelled back. Caligan snickered from his chair behind us. Truth is, I was cheating and Caligan knew it. I could see when the others where lying about which cards they held, their colors flashing with their deceitfulness. Caligan knew what I was doing, knew he didn't stand a chance of winning so he opted not to play. Silas smiled as Elias's anger grew. He leaned forward, his eyes hard, his colors dark and furious.

"Don't lie. You are cheating!"

"Prove it." I challenged. His hands curled at his sides, his knuckles turning white. Asher placed a calming hand on his brothers shoulder.

"Remember, she can literally set you on fire and Cal will beat you to a pulp, be careful with how you behave." I giggled at his warning, the anger in Elias eyes flashed. With a huff, he stood and began trudging across the pasture, his giant figure shaking with anger. Silas shrugged.

He doesn't like to lose. He signed. Elias door slammed from above, his anger echoing through the clearing. Lagan turned his eyes to me, his stare accusatory.

"Were you cheating?" I grinned, not hiding my guilt any longer. The group laughed deeply at my answer. "How?"

"Is a new power of yours the ability to see through things?" Asher chimed in, holding up the cards in his hand. Silas arched his brows, and moved his hands to his lap to cover himself. I rolled my eyes as Lagan flicked him on the forehead. "If she could see through things she wouldn't be wasting it looking at you, dipshit." I laughed.

"I can't see through things, but I can see when you're lying or telling the truth." Lagan and Silas's eyes widened while Ashers narrowed. I had done my best to keep the progress of my power hidden from my housemates. Caligan and Ciprian the only ones knowing what the true extent of my magic was.

"Liar."

"Try me." I shrugged. Asher thought for a moment, the others waited to see if my ability was real or not.

"My favorite color is orange." His colors flashed in warning. I smirked.

"Lie."

"Cucumbers are my favorite vegetable." Another flash.

"Lie."

"This is stuff any of us could have told her," Grady interrupted. "Test it on something none of us know." Asher took another minute to find the right question to ask, the one question to prove my power.

"The first woman I had sex with had a birthmark on her upper thigh in the shape of a flower." His colors were pure. Silas looked to me for confirmation, surprise on his face from the bluntness of Ashers statement.

"True." Asher smiled, validating my claim to see truth. Instantly the small group started saying outrageous, vulgar statements to play with the new toy of my abilities. Silas, to my surprise was the worst of the five men. The majority of his statements were almost enough to make me blush. They were almost enough to make any of the men blush. Caligan left soon after the little game had started, to go on patrol; a smile on his lips as he turned from his brothers. I retired a little while after, my heart and colors light as I left my friends by the fire and went to bed, Ziggy flying happily after me.

Chapter 20

Our homes in the sky were silent, peace filling the air as the small clan slept soundly. I had finally started to drift to sleep when a flurry of movement and shouts from the bridges outside shocked me upright in bed. I shot to my door and flung it open. Asher and Silas sprinted down the bridges to the staircase, shirtless with their weapons in hand. Lagan followed, his sword drawn, his colors bright red and alert.

"What's wrong?" I demanded, running after him. He pushed past me, his jaw clenched and his body tense.

"Go back to bed, Lorn." He ordered. He disappeared down the stairs. Elias came sprinting from his room, daggers clutched in his hands. I jumped in front of him, gripping his wrists. He freed himself from my grasp easily and shoved me into the banister of the bridge.

"What's wrong?"

"Caligan." Was all he said before vanishing into the night to help his friend. Panic surged through me, my own colors brightening with fear. I quickly grabbed my axes from inside my cottage before sprinting after the others. I bounded down the stairs and emerged into the night just after Elias. The grass was cold and damp beneath my bare feet but I ignored it and plunged into the night.

"Go back inside." He snapped as he swatted tree branches from his face as we entered the forest.

"You first, I'll meet you there." I bit out through gritted teeth. The woods whispered as we raced to Caligan. The air was frigid, autumns presence breathing down the neck of summer. I had no idea where Caligan was, or how they knew he was in trouble. There was no way they could have heard him yell or call out all the way in the safety of our quarters. I sent up a silent prayer, asking for him to be okay. For him to stay safe until we reached him. Our eyes adjusted to the darkness, a flash of movement caught our attention straight ahead. How did they know where he was? We broke through the trees and found the rest of the clan fighting along side Caligan. And I came face to face with the creatures of the Damned.

Their skin was dark and leathery like I remembered. I could count their ribs individually they were so thin. Their coal black eyes glittered with hunger as they snapped their gnarled fangs at my friends. They outnumbered us three to one. I bit back my fear and called to the anger constantly alive and burning within me before hurtling myself at the closest beast.

I sliced through thick skin, black blood sprayed from the wound. The creature let out a shriek as I cut into its gut. My body quickly became slick with its inky blood. I ripped my axe free and swung the blade clean through its throat, silencing it forever. A sharp pain ripped through my shoulder, tearing and ripping the skin and muscle as one of the creatures clawed me. I turned to face it, its hand raised high in the air with my blood coating its sharp talons. I ducked, narrowly missing another strike from its claws. I dug the sharpened edge into the flesh of its leg, earning me another hight pitched howl. It dodged the next swing of my axe and clamped its hand on my shoulder, digging its nails deep into my body. With surprising strength it lifted me from my feet and threw me backwards.

I crashed into another body and took us both to the ground. The wind rushed from my lungs. I scrambled to stand, Asher lay unconscious at my feet. The impact of my body being thrown into his knocked him completely vulnerable. I set my feet wide and stood protectively over the man I had grown to call my friend. I bared my teeth as two Damned charged me. I gave into the frenzy of the fight, let adrenaline and anger flow through me, guiding and taking control. I threw the hatchet in my left hand, the edge sinking deep into the skull of one of them. I ran at the other and rammed my shoulder into its gut, sending its body up and over mine to the ground. I drove my loan axe into is head, its body falling limp beneath me. I turned to the others. Grady and Silas were helping Lagan fend off three creatures. Caligan was finishing off one and Elias was backed into a corner.

He had a large gash in his forehead, and blood seeped quickly from a wound in his side. He stumbled backwards into a tree as a creature closed in on him. I wouldn't be able to reach him in time if I ran. I set my feet and launched my axe through the air and watched as it found its home in the brain of the Damned. Elias slid to the ground as the beast crumpled at his feet. His eyes were wide as he turned his gaze to mine. The world fell silent as the last of the creatures were finished off. I bent and retrieved my blade from the dead beast closest to me before making my way to Elias. I stepped over bloody corpses, their black blood oozed and pooled from their wounds and silent mouths. I stood before Elias, my chest rising and falling rapidly as I tried to catch my breath.

"I told you to go back inside." He panted, his face ashen and his colors a dull purple. I shrugged and held out my hand for him.

"We protect each other, right?" I threw their words back at him. They had told me that the first night I stayed here. At the time I found them cliché and I didn't believe they would take the promise seriously. But I had plunged into the unknown for Caligan. For all of them. I had decided without even realizing it that I would die protecting these men, as they would die for me.

Elias brought a weak hand into the air to grab mine, but it quickly fell limp back to his side. His eyes rolled back in his head and his body slumped to the earth. Caligan knelt to his side and wiped at the Damned blood caking his chest. A large bite mark bled steadily from his side. Caligans colors deepend and hovered calmly as he controlled his panic. He shouted for Grady and Lagan to bring Asher back home as he threw Elias's unconscious body over his shoulder.

Silas and I flanked them as we listened and watched for another attack. We made it back to the clearing and to the entrance of the kitchen and dining barn without another ambush. We rushed through the doorway, slipping on the trail of blood we created. Ciprian met us by the fire and conjured up a mat for Asher to be placed on. Ziggy, having seen me enter, flew from Cips shoulder and landed lightly in my hands. His green eyes wide, with what I swore was worry. I placed the dragon on my shoulder after placing a light kiss to his head and followed the others as Cal rushed Elias to his small home in the trees.

It was the first time I had ever seen it. Clothes, books and weapons covered every inch. Bones from various animals were thrown into piles, some having been carved and others simply collected. My nose wrinkled at the clutter and messiness the man lived in. Cal dropped Elias's body onto his bed and disappeared back through the door before returning with an armful of bottles and vials, one of which being the bite remedy he and I had made a few weeks ago. The green haired warlock quickly cleaned the wound with a wave of his hand and Caligan began spreading the bite remedy to the open wound generously. Grady and Lagan had left Asher in the barn and joined Silas and I in the doorway as we waited for the two to finish their work.

"He is going to be fine. We administered the antidote in time." Ciprian said to us finally after Cal was done spreading the mixture over the wound, finishing off the bottle. The men around me released held breaths at the good news of their brother. Ciprian placed his hand on Caligans shoulder and pushed him to the door. "He needs rest and you all have wounds that need tending to." He shut the door behind him gently and glided back to the barn. The brightness of our fear and panic now faded around us. The five of us trudged after him.

We took our turns waiting for Caligan and Ciprian to sew up and clean our wounds. We passed around a bottle of rum to help ease the pain coursing through all of us. I sat in front of Caligan, clutching my shirt to my chest as he sewed up the gashes in my back and shoulder. I could tell he was trying to be gentle, but I hissed as the needle pierced my skin painfully. I took a large gulp of rum, the amber liquid burning as it slid down my throat.

"How did they know you were in trouble?" I asked, trying to distract myself from the sting of the needle.

"I called for them." He replied quietly.

"There is no way they heard you all the way from the forest." I growled through the pain.

"Of course not. I called through the brand."

I tensed as he pulled the last of my wounds closed. "What brand?" I asked through gritted teeth. He finished closing the gash and knelt in front of me, holding out his upturned forearm. Just below his wrist was raised white flesh. Lines curved and intertwined in beautiful symmetry. I had to stop myself from reaching out to touch the lovely scar, cursing myself for the urge.

"We all have them. They connect us. We can tell when one of us is in danger or hurt. We can tell when one dies as well." His colors deepened at the thought of his lost brothers. I looked at the faces of the men around me. Asher was awake and talking, asking for details of the battle. Silas sat calmly in front of Ciprian as he sewed up his arm, the cut in it small but deep. Lagan and Grady replayed the most exciting parts of the fight to Asher with a wide grin, his colors golden despite the urgent red they had been a short while ago.

"Thank you. For protecting my brothers. And for helping me." Caligans grey eyes bore into mine as I pulled my shirt back over my head, careful not to expose my breasts. His colors swirled like the night sky around him. Bits of sparkling gold shimmered through a sea of velvet black. Something lit within me as I met his gaze. My own colors began fading darkly to match his. I tore my eyes from his, suddenly very aware of my body. My skin was layered in blood and mud. I probably looked terrible, no wonder Caligan had been staring.

I shook my head and stood abruptly. I left Ziggy in Cals care and left the barn quickly. Why am I letting myself get so frazzled? Why is it that every time I was around Caligan I seemed to completely lose myself and my thoughts? I tried to ignore the fire he had lit within me as I walked across the green pasture to take a bath.

Chapter 21

When I emerged from my bath, I found the clearing quiet, my house mates finding sleep and peace. I padded to the kitchen in the barn on bare feet, my colors too bright and lively for sleep. I poured myself a small glass of rum, hoping it would sooth my racing mind. Images of the Damned whipped by in blurred memories. They were truly terrifying, the stories and tales of their horrors seemed like fairy tales compared to the real thing. How did Caligan face those creatures every night? How did he get rid of the fear that they induce? I took a large gulp of rum, the liquid burned down my throat and eased my nerves slightly. I leaned against the counter, my eyes on the crackling hearth across the room.

How had all these men survived so long with these monsters? They were so strong and fast, how had they only lost one member to them? I found myself admiring their bravery, their loyalty to each other, to willingly throw themselves into the face of death. I downed the last of my drink, my body calming. The air around me turned thick and heavy, its weight pressing onto my skin. Red and purple colors swirled around me, thicker than I had ever seen them. I pressed the heels of my palms into my eyes, willing myself to calm down. I cursed myself to giving into my emotions so much. But my heart beat steadily within my chest, my mind and body warm and heavy with exhaustion and rum. These colors weren't mine.

I looked back at the violent swirls around me, they filled the air, trailing down from the village above. I followed, my curiosity and worry taking over. They grew dense and heavier the further up I climbed. The hanging houses were silent, making the colors seem even more dreadful. The trail led me to the door of Silas's home. I tentatively knocked but nobody came to answer. The air continued to swirl and thicken. I tried the handle and found it unlocked. I slowly pushed the door open and stepped through its threshold.

The oil lamps burned low, books and drawings covered the walls. Pieces of machines and bombs covered tables and desks. A small bed was pushed into the corner, and Silas lay atop it, thrashing violently in his sleep. His face was twisted as if in pain, as if he was calling out, but no sound left his lips. His colors swirled cruelly and painfully around him. He was having a nightmare. Sadness and panic flooded my heart as I crossed the room to him quickly.

"Silas!" I yelled as I placed my hands on his shoulders, trying to steady his panicked body.

"Silas!" The young boys eyes opened quickly and widened, fear still plastered across his face. Silas has always been so gentle and kind, I never knew he was capable of such strength and violence that he showed then. One second I was kneeling beside him, the next, my back was thrown against the wall with his hand wrapped around my throat. A knife pressed to my abdomen, his face contorted in an angry and panicked glare. Whatever it was that controlled his sleep, now controlled him. His past haunting him even with his eyes open.

My head throbbed where it had hit the wall, my throat ached under the pressure of his grip. I stood on the tips of my toes, desperate to ease the tension cutting off my air.

"Silas." I gasped, my voice rough. "Silas its me, its Lorn." His eyes remained unfocused and angry. I glared at his colors in frustration. I wanted to scream at them, beat them away from the sweet boy I knew Silas was. Something tugged within my chest, like a lock clicking into place as I watched his colors. I latched onto them with desperation, connecting with his pain and fear. I willed them to brighten and thin, giving back the Silas I had grown so fond of. I pleaded silently for them to lift, and to my surprise, they did. They slowly started to thin, his fear disappearing.

I stilled in Silas' grip and drew his anger and panic away, changing his colors to his usual soft gold. I could feel his violent emotions swirl inside me, replacing my own as I took them from him. My heart raced, my skin slick with sweat as I watched his eyes soften. My body shook as his fear, anger and panic flooded my veins. I wanted to scream, run and fight my way out of this room but I stayed still, taking his horrors from him until they were gone. His eyes widened as his mind finally cleared and he could see who I was and what he was doing to me. He released his hold on me and I slid down the wall to the floor gasping.

He knelt in front of me, his eyes pleading as he signed to me, *I'm Sorry I'm sorry*. I waved my hand and clambered to my feet, my mind racing with his fear.

"Its okay, I know it wasn't you. Try and get some sleep Silas." I stumbled past him and onto his small porch, shutting the door behind me. My breathing came rapid, my skin crawled and my blood ran cold. My body vibrated with his emotions, not knowing how to purge myself of them. I walked blindly, my vision blurring as I forced myself to walk. I needed help, I wanted to yell for help but my voice wouldn't work. As if on cue, Caligan's head popped out of his quarters on the other connecting bridge. I jumped at the sudden sight of him. His brows drew together as he looked me over. The low light of the lamps hanging from the branches cast his face in shadows, making his high cheekbones and sharp jaw look almost wolfish.

"Are you okay?" His voice was low, his colors unreadable. My body continued to shake.

"I took it." My voice was a whisper as I looked at my hands.

"What?" I kept walking until I stood just before him. His hair dripped with water, his skin clean from the blood and grime of earlier.

"I took it."

"Took what Lorn?"

"Silas. He was having a nightmare and I- I took his fear and pain." I stammered, the panic in my chest blooming larger and hotter. "I took it and I don't know what to do with it, I don't know how to get rid of it." The shaking proceeded to increase as my breathing became more and more rapid. I was panicking, badly. I shoved past Caligan and stormed into his small home. I don't know why I decided to come in, but I knew I needed help and he was the only one I would be okay with seeing me afraid since he's seen it before. I began to pace as he shut the door softly behind him.

"You took his fear?"

"Yes." I snapped. " I took it and replaced it with peace but now it's inside of me and I don't know how to get rid of it. I don't know how to get it out, Caligan." I sunk to the floor and wrapped my arms around myself, not knowing what to do. The panic in my chest ached and continued to swirl violently in my colors around me. Caligan knelt in front of me, his eyes calm as he placed his hands on either side of my face. They were warm and calloused, the touch sending tiny sparks down my spine. The fog around my thoughts seemed to still and clear a little bit.

"Focus, Lorn. Control your emotions." His voice was even, steady as he spoke. "Focus on the color, and will it to change. Make it change just like you did for Silas." My heart beat painfully against my chest. "Control it before it takes hold of you completely." He demanded. My eyes tracked the chaotic, panicked colors around me. They clutched me tightly, refusing to let go. I watched the red, but focused on Caligan's touch on my skin. I focused on the feel of his calloused, worn skin. He was warm, his presence anchoring me.

I watched the frightened air around me and imagined it lightening. I picture the red fading to a light pink and to my surprise, they did. The tightness in my chest eased as the colors began to fade. The air lightened, I imagined how the air had looked when I laughed with Silas, or found Caligan watching me as I trained. I thought of the bright warm glow that seemed to follow me most days. My colors soothed, the air pure and soft like the summer sun. I heaved a heavy sigh and closed my eyes as relief flooded through me.

"That was perfect, Lorn. Your control was amazing." I opened my eyes to meet that grey stare of his. Being so close to him allowed me to see the tiny freckles dotted across the bridge of his nose and the black flecks in his eyes. My heart raced, but no longer with panic or fear. His voice and gentle touch had focused me and calmed me. But now, his closeness was doing something else to me.

"Thank you." I said breathlessly. He shrugged.

"I didn't do anything. You did it all on your own. I didn't need to even help you change how you were feeling." His eyes searched mine, satisfied with the relief he found behind them, he pulled his hands away and sat in front of me. My skin felt cold where his hands had been. Ziggy popped his head over the corner of Cals bed, his green eyes wide as he watched me. I leaned over a rubbed the tuft of fur under is small chin, a purr rumble through him.

"Have you ever done that for the others? Taken away a feeling?" I asked softly. He nodded.

"Sometimes, things are just too hard or heavy to let go of."

I pulled my knees to my chest. "Have you ever taken anything from me?" His jaw flexed.

"Yes." No lies, no trying to avoid the question. I could tell he was worried about his answer. "Does that upset you?" I shrugged.

"Depends. When we take one emotion, is the emotion that replaces that not real? Is it something we create and force on the other?" His brows drew together as he shook his head.

"No, whatever emotion fills in that gap that we remove, it always true and authentic. The peace you brought Silas was his own, if he didn't want to feel that he wouldn't." Relief swept through me. I didn't want to control what others thought or felt, that would seem like such an invasion. Taking away pain or fear still didn't feel right, but I couldn't watch as Silas struggled with his past.

"Then no, I'm not upset." His body relaxed. "What did you take from me?" His colors became somber.

"You hold more pain, and anger than any crowd I've ever been in." My heart squeezed, my cheeks reddened with embarrassment. I hated that he could read me so well. But he probably felt the same about me. "I didn't take it all, but I eased it. It was so heavy," he shook his head, his eyes distant. "I don't know how you carried it all for so long."

"It's been easier." I swallowed the lump in my throat. "Coming here has made it easier." I stretched my legs out, my body too uncomfortable with where the conversation had gone. "Its pretty much impossible to be sad around Silas and Ziggy." He smiled at that. I stretched my arms, my breasts strained against my shirt. His colors shifted around him, changing to a swirling black as night.

"What are you thinking right now?" He raised a brow. "What are you thinking about? What are you feeling?" His eyes darkened, half hidden under thick lashes as his colors swirled smoothly. "Your colors are black and I still don't know what that means." He remained silent, his eyes tracing my face in the low light. I sighed impatiently, frustration flowing through me. "We're friends for fuck sake, just tell me." The words came out harsher than I meant them to. His colors darkened further.

He leaned in close, his lips almost brushing mine. His hands slid up my thighs smoothly before quickly grabbing my hips and pulling my body flush to his. My chest pressed against his, the beating of my heart increased to an almost painful speed. A powerful shock swept through my body. He had never touched me like this before, been close to me like this before. The air around him swirled violently, my own colors starting to darken to match his.

"I'm thinking about that dreadful mouth of yours. And what it must taste like." His glare bore into me, his words dancing across my skin like a tender caress. A burning formed in my stomach. "I'm wondering if you taste as good as you look." He bent his head low, his lips dragging lightly across the exposed skin of my throat. I bit my lip as his traveled lower, gliding across my collarbone. "And I feel like if I don't find out," His teeth scraped my skin, a small moan formed on my lips. "I'll lose my mind."

He pulled back so I could see his face. His pupils swallowed the grey. My colors now mixed with his, undistinguished from one another. I knew now what the color meant. Black was lust. It was hunger. And the color surrounded us both, swallowing us in our need for one another. My mind went hazy. I placed my hands tentatively on his chest and dragged them over his muscles until I reached his neck. I pushed myself closer, pulling him to me even more. I wound my hands through his black hair, relishing the feel of it between my fingers. His hold on my hips tightened. His jaw flexed, fueling the throbbing I felt between my legs.

Unable to control himself any longer, Caligan crushed his lips to mine. His lips felt like velvet as they moved fiercely with mine. His tongue slid between my lips and danced with my own. Every stroke and lick sent shocks of need through my body. Both breathless, he pulled away and laid his forehead against mine. My body thrummed with need. I was desperate for more. More of his mouth on mine. More of his hands on my skin. More of mine on him. I slid onto his lap, my legs on either side of his hips. I moaned as I felt his hard length under me, intensifying the burning within me. I slid my hands dow the plains of his chest and began fumbling with the buttons of his shirt and pulled his mouth back to mine.

I nipped at his lower lip with my teeth sending a growl rumbling through his chest. Undoing the last button of his shirt, I peeled it from him desperate to feel his skin. A low moan came from him as I dragged my few free nails over the scared muscles of his body. I had never wanted the rest of these casings removed more than I did in this moment. His hands tightened at my waist and felt their way up my chest. His hands gripped my breasts, their hard peaks sparked with pleasure as he dragged his hands over the thin fabric of my shirt. I loosed a quiet moan. He placed a hand on my cheek and tore his lips from me.

"I've never heard a sound more heavenly than that moan." His voice was thick with hunger. With his hand wrapped around my waist, he stood not taking his eyes from mine. He placed me gently on his bed and stood before me. His gaze was predatory. He dipped his head to my stomach, unbuttoning the bottom few bottoms and kissing the skin he exposed. His soft lips trailed light kisses over the deep scar across my abdomen.

"What's the story behind this one?" All desire fled from my veins and filled with fear as the memory flashed through my mind. I remembered that dark room, the pain, the blood, the cruel laughter. This was not a conversation I wanted to or was ready to have. My body tensed and he noticed. His colors shifted. "You don't have to talk about it. I didn't know it was one you-" I got to my feet and pushed past him.

"Forget it." His hand wrapped around my arm when I reached his door. His eyes were wide, his colors a mix of grey and purple. Anger flared within me. I didn't want his pity. I didn't want him to feel sorry for me. I just wanted out of this room. He opened his mouth to say something but I cut him off before he could. "Its nothing Caligan, its best we just forget this ever happened." I ripped my arm from his grasp and bolted into the night, Ziggy followed me. Cal didn't. Every step I took closer to my cottage, the harder it became to block those dreadful memories from my mind.

When I was finally in the safety and solitude of my room, I allowed myself to cry. Cry for my past. For the horrific things tainting my skin. I cried for the happiness and wholeness I felt under Caligan's touch. I cried for the choice I had made and the disappointment it had brought me. I cried for my broken heart and fractured soul. I let my tears clean those memories away and eventually, I let them put me to sleep.

Chapter 22

We all spent the next two days inside. Caligan
held wards up around the perimeter so we all had time to
heal. Elias was awake and getting better by the hour. The
rest of us were healing nicely and taking advantage of the
free time. I stayed in my room the majority of the couple
days, too exhausted to face Caligan. Nightmares had
flooded my dreams, leaving me unwilling to sleep for fear
of waking the others while they tried to heal. Silas still felt
guilty from hurting me the other night. He brought meals
to me with bunches of fresh flowers to try and make up
for it despite my assurance that I was okay. But the boy
still had managed to make me smile with every vase full.
Ziggy stayed by my side for most of my days, his tiny
warmth and big eyes a comfort.

I didn't see Caligan until our first day back down
below together at breakfast. He greeted me with a glare,
his colors the same purple and grey mix as they were
when I left him alone in his room. The table seemed
awake and ready for the day, each of them anxious to get
outside again.

"Are you excited for today Lorn?" Lagan asked
around a mouthful of eggs. I raised a brow.

"What should I be excited for?" The heads
around the table whipped to Caligan.

"I thought you were going to talk to her?" Asher
asked. Cal glared at his brothers and then at me.

"I didn't have time." He growled, his eyes never leaving mine. Ciprian scoffed.

"What have you been doing for the past two days?" The warlocks skin was pale and his eyes were dull. Holding the wards for two days having drained him completely it seemed. Caligan didn't reply, just continued to glare.

"Talk to me about what?"

"We found a job for you!" Grady answered with a grin. I raised my brows, eager to hear what my place will be within the clan. "A shadow!" A what? I looked to Asher for help.

"Its what we call Caligan, cause he spends his time in the dark and doesn't make any noise when he moves through he forest." I was going to be working with Caligan? I shot him a look down the table. He had finished his breakfast and sat back in his chair with his arms crossed over his chest. His gaze still hard and intense on mine.

"I'm going to be working with you?"

He shrugged. "You're a natural. You are quick on your feet and skilled with those axes of yours. You took down more Damned than all of us the other night. Its a perfect fit." His voice was low and even.

"And how do you feel about working with me?" My heart seemed to stop beating as I waited for his answer. His gaze didn't waver, there was no hesitation in his words.

"I need the help and you, like I said, are a natural." My colors glowed with pride. Finally a job I would enjoy. Maybe it will be a little awkward with Caligan, but hopefully it will give me a sense of duty and purpose within the group. The men around me waited for my response.

"When do we start?" The colors around the table glowed golden. My decision to accept the job obviously making the group happy.

"Now." Caligan rose and walked to the center of the clearing, his scythe strapped between his shoulders. The rest of us hurriedly cleared the table and walked together. I left Ziggy in the care of Ciprian, the warlock happy to have the company of the tiny creature. The sun was bright, the sky clear and a beautiful blue. My body thrummed with excitement but hopes that it wouldn't be weird with Caligan flitted through my mind. I didn't know what to expect being alone with him all day. Would he want to talk about what happened? We all stopped in the middle of the clearing as Caligan turned to address us.

"Thank you all for agreeing to help me with her training." Relief flooded through me, thankful I wouldn't be alone with him. "You guys will have it pretty easy." His gaze swept around the group then landed on me, his jaw set tightly. "You however, will not." Of course. Was he planning on punishing me for the other night? He pulled a black piece of cloth from his pocket and held it out to me. "Put this on." I scowled but did as I was told, tying the dark fabric around my eyes. "Now, the rest of you will go into the trees and find a place to hide. No further than half a mile in. It will be Lorns job to locate and disarm you without being detected. If she is spotted or overheard by any of you, she will find a new target while you re-hide."

I could hear their retreating footsteps after Caligan had finished explaining. After several minutes I pointed to the fabric over my eyes.

"Can I take this off or am I supposed to find them wearing it?" My tone was dry with annoyance. Caligan stepped behind me and untied it, careful not to touch the short hair of my scalp, before folding his arms across his chest.

"I didn't want you to know which way they went. You need to track them on your own." He growled. My blood heated with anger as he glared down at me.

"Why are you so angry?" I demanded. I truly didn't understand why he was so upset with me. He was the one who had asked questions he didn't want to know the answers to, asking questions I didn't want to answer. His gaze hardened.

"Go." He said through gritted teeth. I rolled my eyes and turned to the grass around me. Frost clung to the blades of grass, footsteps easily able to be found as the damp grass folded beneath their heavy feet. As soon as my feet left the lush pasture, the temperature dropped. Cold seeped into my bones. The peace drained from the air, leaving it heavy and dull. Ignoring the chill, I focused on the tracks. I followed the path of footprints and broken twigs and disturbed leaves, walking slowly and carefully.

Trying to be quiet I slowed my walk to almost a crawl. It was the better half of an hour until I hit a dead end. No more tracks or signs of life. I was about to turn back when a flash of bright red hair caught my eye. I crouched low behind a tree and found Silas laying in a tangle of bushes with his eyes closed. I stood up, no longer trying to be quiet as I approached the sleeping boy. I placed my boot on his chest and he awoke with a start, his eyes wide and his colors panicked as he reached for his knife. I lifted my axe and shook my head.

I helped him to his feet, his cheeks red with embarrassment from having been caught. He gave me a small wave before jogging back to the clearing. With a sigh, I made my way east looking for another path to follow. After an hour I finally came up on another set of prints. I followed it, keeping my footsteps light and silent. I crept up on Grady, his back to me as he kneeled behind a tree trunk. His shoulders were tense as he watched and listened for me. Quickly and without complication I slipped behind him and pressed the blade of my axe to his throat.

With a grunt, Grady set off back home. With him and Silas out, I had Asher, Lagan and Elias left. The sun was high in the sky by the time I found the next set of tracks. I squatted down next to a rotting tree, my nose wrinkled at the putrid smell. The Damned weren't the only horror of this forest, even the vegetation was disgusting. I scanned the forest floor, tracing the trail of footprints . They traveled about fifteen yards to my left before seamlessly disappearing. No trace of them continuing, I scanned upward. Sitting in the tree branches above, was Asher.

His arms were crossed over his chest and his head bobbed with drowsiness. I crouched down low and crawled painfully slowly towards the trunk of his tree. When I finally made my way below him I leapt to my feet and jumped into the air, lunging for his dangling foot. I latched onto it and yanked his large frame from the tree. He landed on his back, drawing his sword swiftly despite the groan of pain that came from him. I placed the blade of my axe to his stomach before he could raise it to defend himself. He rolled his eyes.

"You're supposed to disarm me." He said, arguing that I hadn't done what I was supposed to. I raised a brow and applied slight presser to the blade in my hand.

"I don't need to disarm you if I have already gutted you." I growled. He shrugged and replaced his sword. When he stood he gave me a mock bow and left me to the forest. I yawned and stretched my aching back. My throat was dry and my body tired. I was eager for this to be over. I walked another hour, unable to find another set of tracks. My colors began to darken to a deep violet the longer I wandered through the trees.

Finally, I heard movement up ahead. I replaced my axe and withdrew a knife before closing in on the moving figure. I was expecting to find Lagan or Elias on the other side of a thick tree trunk, tired and bored. I bet they're beginning to wonder if I had forgotten about them. They were both probably more eager than I was for this to be over. But what I found was not the inventor, nor Elias. It was a dark, thin body with leathery skin and sharp claws. I had tracked one of the Damned. Fear rolled through me and shown brightly in the air around me. The creature turned to me and snarled its pointed teeth before charging.

"Fuck!" I hissed as I jumped out of the way of its swinging claws. I slipped my hatchet from my side and discarded my knife. I leapt at the beast, swinging my axe at its side. It dodged my attack with surprising smoothness. It swiped a hand at me, catching me in the arm and slicing through my clothes and skin. I snarled at the beast and let the pain feed my anger. My colors now a violet so deep they were almost black. Grabbing my other axe, I began a series of jabs and strikes against the beast. I shredded through its thick skin, black blood sprayed and coated my skin in a gory layer. I growled at it's howls of pain, letting it burn hot within me. With one final swing, I brought the blade of my axe down and onto its neck, severing its head from its body.

Breathing heavily, I stared down at the lifeless creature at my feet. Dark blood flowed from its wounds like a river and pooled around my booted feet. My hands were slippery with it. My anger still clouded my mind. I wiped my blades clean on my pants, the cloth staining instantly. I turned and found Lagan, Asher and Grady all staring at me, weapons drawn and jaws dropped. I picked up the severed head of the creature, its eyes glassy and its teeth dripped with blood. I shoved my way past them without saying a word.

I made my way back to the clearing, the chill and fear of the forest left behind. Peace flowed over and through me, destroying the angry haze surrounding me. I glared at Caligan as I walked to him. His face icy and smooth as stone as he looked at the head in my blood stained hand. His colors flashed red and twisted with purple as I approached. I stopped in front of him and dropped the grotesque head at his feet. He met my glare with one of his own.

"I'm done." I snarled, declaring todays training over. I shoved my way past him and stormed up the stairs into the branches above.

Chapter 23

The next two weeks were filled with the same things. I spent the mornings finding the others throughout the forest and the afternoons sparring and fight training with Caligan. I enjoyed my lessons, but I could do without Caligans glares. He still wont talk to me other than correcting me on my fighting technique when I made a mistake; which apparently was often. My heart ached every time I saw him. With every glare and silent moment we shared I could feel our friendship slipping further away. His colors were always a dull grey around me and sometimes a vibrant purple. I had no idea what he was thinking when he was with me and it was slowly driving me crazy. I spent my days trying to decode his emotions and my nights replaying the memories of his hands on my skin and his mouth on mine.

I was awoken roughly by Caligan throwing my weapons belt and a cloak atop my sleeping figure before leaving the room. I scowled, hating the fact that he could get into my room whenever he wanted while I slipped from bed and got dressed. My eyes were heavy with sleep as I tugged on my boots and strapped my axes to my hips. My hair had grown out quiet a bit in the few months I had spent in the forest. The short length was longer than I had allowed it to be in years. A part of me didn't want to shave it, to cut it, but I reminded myself that I needed to. I silently reminded myself to shave it this evening. It couldn't have been longer than an inch of growth but it was still too much. Tired and annoyed, I gave Ziggy a kiss on his sleepy head. I trudged along the bridges and down the stairs, leaving the small dragon to sleep within my cottage. Summer was coming to an end, fall getting closer everyday. The air was crisper. It would probably feel like winter once inside the forest. I figured it was going to be the same routine today, but to my surprise the clan was packing supplies into packs when I met them in the kitchen inside the barn.

"What are we doing today?" I asked nobody in particular.

"We are all going to walk the forest today." Ciprian said as he placed a loaf of bread into the bag before him. "We are going to walk the paths we take when we venture to the city." My stomach dropped.

"We are going into Willowmore?" I asked. The warlock shook his head, his green hair flying crazily around him.

"No, we are simply going to the edge of the territory." The tension in my stomach relaxed.

"We want you to get a better feel of the land and where the boundaries are before you start patrolling." Elias said. His face was tired and dark circles marked under is eyes and his hair was wild from patrolling last night. He and Caligan had traded shifts so Cal could help me train during the day. Well, kind of traded shifts. Caligan still held wards up and Elias just sat within the clearing instead of going into the forest itself. Elias wasn't very happy about the trade but he didn't argue.

"Why is everyone going?" I glanced around the crowded kitchen of tired men.

"In case we run into any trouble. The further away one of us needs to travel, the more of us go with." Lagan explained as he sat back in his chair. "And since you need to travel all the way to Willowmores edge, we are all going."

"The further apart we are, the longer it takes for us to reach each other in case of emergency." Grady added yawning. I nodded, a small ball of anxiety still lay in my stomach. When everyone finished filling their packs and eating breakfast, we set off together. The sun had yet to rise but the stars twinkled brightly above. Ciprian and Caligan led the way while the rest of us trailed behind them. Our boots were quiet in the soft grass. I praised myself for putting on an extra layer of clothing as the temperature outside the clearing dropped significantly.

We walked silently for hours, our eyes and ears focused on the forest around us. I mentally marked our path, memorizing the odd tree trunks or large boulders we passed to help me remember the path. Caligan looked over his shoulder occasionally to check we were all still together. His eyes skimmed my face longer than the rest. The sun was starting to rise, barely breaking through the thick canopy over head when he stopped, body tense, holding up his hand for us to halt. We froze, listening carefully for what had raised his suspicions. He slowly unhooked his scythe from his back and took a few steps froward.

After a quiet moment, a creature of the Damned lunged out from behind a tree, claws outstretched. Instinctively my hand went to the axe at my waist and gripped the handle tightly. The rest of the group readied themselves to attack, but Cal swung his blade high into the air and brought it down through the creatures skull. Blood sprayed onto his face and chest plate, making him look dangerous and deadly. I pitied any creature that came anywhere near the powerful empath warrior. We remained still and silent for several minutes, listening for any other incoming ambushes but none came. Replacing his scythe between his shoulders, we continued on our way.

As the sun rose, I became distracted by the wood around me. Frost hung from branches and glittered in the morning light. Frozen water clung to the dark, rotted roots and limbs. The forest looked beautiful, peaceful even. I couldn't help but admire the contrast between the almost black trees and the crisp white frost. I was relieved I had left Ziggy back home, or I'm sure I would have lost him as his fur blended in perfectly with the rotting trees.

At mid day we finally reached the edge of the forest. We stayed a few feet within the trees with the open plains of Willowmore stretching out before us. The land I had crossed the night Caligan had found me. That day had been one of the scariest but also the most wonderful day of my life. It was the day I was set free and found my new home. A mental shock went through me as I referred to the clearing and hanging village as my home. But it felt right. Being here felt right.

This was the beginning of my new life. I smiled to myself as I scanned the grassy hills before me. I never had to go back to the life I had before. I now knew of a whole world, of whole civilizations that I could see. I would never be stuck again, never be trapped to live in pain and fear ever again. Something lifted within me, like something heavy being released into the clear sky above. I'm sure it would have been a peaceful scene if I didn't know what lay beyond those hills. If I didn't know the cruel kingdom and people residing within it's boundaries.

The men passed around flasks of water and cut bread and cheese into slices for each of us. I stood watching the birds flying overhead, their songs drifting through the cool air. I was about to turn back to the group behind me when something in the distance caught my eye. A strange structure was erect some eight hundred yards out into the green plains. Parts of it swayed with the gentle breeze, the other parts held firm.

"What's that?" I asked to nobody in particular, pointing to the discovery. "I don't think it was there when I arrived." I said as they crowded around me, inspecting the structure from afar. Silas shrugged, his brow furrowing as he squinted.

"No idea." Asher said. "And you're sure it wasn't there before?" He asked. I nodded. My curiosity getting the better of me, I asked if we could take a closer look.

They all exchanged glances. Ciprian studied me. I know its Mortalas territory, but the land was deserted except for us. If anyone ended up spotting us, we would have plenty of time to retreat back into the woods. The rest of my clan apparently came to the same conclusion I had, because they all silently pushed their way out of the trees. It took us several minutes to cross the space between us and the odd structure. When we were about twenty yards away, I finally realized what the construction was. My heart sank and my stomach twisted sickeningly as we neared the makeshift gallows. There were four figures hanging, their bodies stiff with death and decay.

We stopped ten yards away and silently took in the dreadful scene. Something about the hanging bodies were familiar, even with the weeks of death taking its toll. I stepped closer, away from the group of men to take a better look. The first body was a woman. Her dress was long and tattered, a small apron was tied around her waist. He hair was tied into a bun at the top of her head, strands of her grey hair flew around her rotting face. A wooden sign was hung around her neck. TRAITOR TO THE QUEEN was written in bold letters. I studied the woman for several minutes before a sickening, painful crack tore through my heart. Tears sprang into my eyes as I realized who the woman was. Mrs. Pennly hung before me, neck broken and body withering away.

My chest ached, my lungs seemed to have quit working as I looked to the man swaying gently next to her. His lean body moved with the breeze, his once handsome face was now twisted with rot and decomposition. Geran. The female next to him was a witch. The same witch that had tugged on my pant leg in the square those many weeks ago. Her light purple skin, now grey and cold. The final body was the guard from whom I stole his horse at the gates of the city. The same sign hung from all their necks. They were deemed traitors, because of me. They were innocent. But because they knew me, because of what I did, because of what I was, they now hung as a symbol. An example. No matter how briefly or insignificantly I had touched their lives, the queen punished them for it.

My knees buckled and tears clouded my vision. Anger and sadness fought violently within me. I felt other sadness, other pain as I sunk to the ground. It wasn't mine or the feelings of the clan around me. It was the emotions of the people that hung before me, tainting the ground around them. Their residual fear swarmed me, choking me, raging within me against my own pain. I could feel their fear, their pain, their sorrow.

My heart and soul shattered as the emotions battled within me. My finger tips burned, flames flickering across them and crawling up my palms. It was too much, all of it. My life before coming to the forest, the pain and violence that still controlled and haunted me. The heartbreak Caligan had unknowingly formed within my heart. And the knowledge that Geran and Penn, my only friend and the only mother I had ever known now hung because of me. It was all too much.

My flames burned hotter and brighter. My anger beating my sadness, finally became more than I could control. I screamed and tears slid down my cold cheeks. My anger and broken soul finally burst and engulfed me in flames. Why did it have to be me? Why did I have to be the one the queen wanted? Why did that wretched witch want me dead so badly? Want me to hurt so much? The fire licked my skin, blinding me from the world around me. Their heat did not burn me, it instead fueled and directed my hatred as it boiled and rolled from me. My ears began ringing as my voice cracked, my scream dying in my throat.

I heard something then, something faint but I heard it through the roar of my flame. It came again, this time louder and more clear but I still didn't understand what was being said. My fury continued to bubble and burst from me. I felt nothing but pain and anger. The sound came again, fighting through the fire and this time I understood what it was.

"Lorn!" A voice shouted through the roaring fire around me. I knew that name, I knew that voice. Only one person had ever been able to make my name sound lovely to my ears and only one person had a voice as soft as velvet. Caligan. An image of his face popped into my head, his grey eyes staring at me. Those eyes pulled me from the darkness I was enveloped in. The flames around me flickered, the flame slowly being snuffed out by the image of Cals face. The memory of his touch, of his smile of his laugh. The fire began retreating back into my

palms before fizzling out completely. I opened my eyes.
The ground around me was charred, the grass
underneath burned and dead. Caligan was crouching in
the grass a few feet away from me, away from where the
flames were. His eyes were wide and worried. His chest
heaved as he said my name again quietly.

"Lorn, are you okay?" I didn't respond, I couldn't.
My voice no longer worked. I looked to my hands. The
remaining metal casings lay cracked in the grass beside
me, the rest of my fingers now free. My pain set them
free. Set me free. But I didn't feel free. I could never be
free of the pain and trauma that followed me everywhere.
I felt caged and surrounded by the queens evil and
cruelty. I will never truly be free of her. Caligan asked me
something again, but I didn't hear him. My body began
to shut down as I stared at Penns decaying face. She
deserved better than this. My heart broke even more as I
wished that I had never met her, wishing I could have
saved her from this fate.

My body went limp as Caligan scooped me into
his arms, his familiar scent of leather surrounded me. We
passed the shocked faces of the others, the blood drained
from their skin as he took me back into the forest. He
cradled me gently to his chest as we made our way back
home. He didn't put me down once or take turns with
someone else. His thumb rubbed soothing circles on my
leg and he whispered to me but I didn't understand a
word of it. My mind felt clouded, like I wasn't seeing
anything even though my eyes were wide open. When we

finally returned home at dusk, Caligan set me gently in front of the fire within the barn before joining the other in the kitchen to talk quietly.

I stared at my hands. They felt sticky, unclean. Felt like they were covered in blood. Covered in the blood of those hanging, swinging in the fall air. My skin began to crawl, my whole body now felt thick with blood and gore. I got up from the chair on shaking legs and walked blindly to the caves on the other side of the clearing. I was desperate to wash my skin clean. The steaming water beckoned to me welcomingly as I undressed. My blades clattered loudly to the stone floor at my feet. I sank deep into the warm water and began scrubbing at my hands. I didn't even notice or take time to appreciate the rainbows splayed across the cavern. The sticky invisible gore wasn't coming off. My skin burned and stung as I clawed at it, frantically trying to clean myself from it. Hot tears ran down my cheeks as the water started to turn red.

Finally, it was coming off. If I scrubbed hard enough, I would be clean. I would feel better. I jumped, my heart hammering painfully in my chest as Caligan leapt into the water with me. His clothes still on, his blades and chest plate on the floor next to mine. He grasped my wrists, prying my hands away from each other. I struggled against his iron grip, Penn and Gerans blood still soaking my skin.

"I have to get it off! I have to get it off!" I yelled at him, water splashing around us. His grip held firmly and tight, his grey eyes catching mine. His face was wet and drops of water ran down his cheeks and danced over his scars. His handsome face was twisted in fear, sadness filling his eyes and colors.

"There isn't anything on you, Lorn." He said quietly, gently. He gently raised my hand to his face and kissed my palm, then kissed the tips of each of my newly freed fingers. When he finished with the one he moved to the other. His gentle touch and kisses wiped the blood from my hands. My body sagged, exhaustion melting deep into my bones. Cals touch calmed my raging mind and shattered heart. I realized now what the water around us was red with. I had cut open my wrists from scrubbing. They were red and raw, blood oozing from my wounds. My body sagged with exhaustion as Caligan pulled my naked body into his arms and held me.

I had never let anyone see me cry. Not even Penn. But there, in the safety of Cals arms, I sobbed heavily, crazily and frantically. My pain too much to bear, too much to control. My burned soul within was too heavy to hold anymore. I let my tears fall, without embarrassment or shame. Cal had said so himself, sometimes things are too much for one person to feel on their own. I had felt enough in my lifetime for dozens. And I let it all out, my heart too tired to contain it any longer.

Chapter 24

Caligan continued to hold me as I cried, gently stroking my back as I curled into his chest. When my eyes finally dried and my mind cleared, I lay still, relishing the feel of his warm skin. I became very aware of every stroke of his fingers. The contact sent shivers down my spine and heated low in my stomach. He wasn't touching me out of desire, but out of worry. His colors were somber as he did his best to comfort me. It was strange having someone care for me, but also not being able to convince myself otherwise. I could see how he felt around me, see how my emotions effected him.

"Are you ready to get out?" He asked softly long after I had stopped crying. I nodded, knowing I would need to explain to the group why I had freaked out and lost control. He lifted me gently from his lap and climbed out from the water, his clothes clung to the grooves of his body. My cheeks heated seeing the muscles in his back flex as he left the cave. He returned shortly in dry clothes and a set of my clothes in his hands. He set them on the floor and waited outside for me to change. When I emerged he guided me to his workshop and wrapped the cuts and scratches I had dug into my skin.

"Thank you." I said softly as he fastened the cloth around my wrists. He gave me a small shrug.

"No need to thank me." He sat down on the floor in front of me. With him being so tall we were almost at eye level, even with me sitting on the edge of the small bed. I came to the conclusion that it was in here for when others were hurt and needed his attention, much like I did right now. "We always take care of each other. You're apart of our family whether you want to accept it or not." He said, nudging my foot with his. My heart warmed at his words. I was still annoyed with him for his recent behavior, but not as much as I was this morning. "You should go talk to the others. They're all worried about you."

My heart sunk. I didn't want to face them. I didn't want to explain that those deaths were on my hands. But Caligan was right. I owed them all an explanation. He wrapped my hand gently in his and guided me from the building. He led the way across the soft grass and into the barn, Cals hand still wrapped firmly and warmly around mine. When we reached the door, he dropped it, holding it open for me. Grey whirled around me at the lost contact.

Grady was in the kitchen preparing dinner. The delicious aroma of spiced meat and vegetables filled the air making my stomach growl. The others sat by the fire, cloaks and leathers gone as they all lounged silently together. Their heads snapped to me as I entered, Caligan trailing behind me. Ziggy zoomed eagerly to my side, his furry wings brushing my skin as he landed on my shoulder. He rubbed my cheek affectionately in welcome.

"I missed you too buddy." I whispered to the dragon. He responded with a low purr. I stood silently, watching the worried faces and colors of the men around the room. Silas patted the cushion on the floor next to him, inviting me to sit. I joined them and tucked my feet under myself. It took several moments before I found my voice.

"The human woman hanging was Mrs. Pennly. The woman who took me in when I was a child." A lump formed in my throat. "The man next to her was Geran. We grew up together. Penn would buy his wool and goods for the inn." I took a calming breath. The clan sat quietly and patiently as I collected myself. Cal's grey eyes watched me from across the room, his arms crossed and shoulders tense. Grady had stopped cooking and joined us by the fire. "The witch with the purple skin, tried to get me to kneel on Prospers Day in the square. She was afraid for me. And the guard next to her, I stole his horse to escape to the edge of the territory." The room remained silent.

"Mortala killed them because of me." I looked between them, my strength replenishing as I spoke. "She killed them just for knowing me. They were innocent." The guard not so much, but I continued. "She's evil and for some reason she wants me dead. She hung them as a message to me and I'm done letting her control my life. I'm done running." Anger built within me. "I want to make her hurt. I want to make her burn." My voice was strong with fury and determination. "I will not allow her to continue hurting innocents. Human, sorcerer, or anyone else." The room fell silent as they took in my words. "I know I can't do it alone. But I can't expect you to help me. I don't want any of you to get hurt."

Caligan was right. They had all become my family. I don't know what I would do if any of them were to end up hurt or killed because of me. She had already taken away my people, the people who shared my blood and magic. I couldn't let her take my new family. But with them by my side, we might be able to destroy that evil being called queen. The men in front of me all exchanged looks. Asher turned his eyes to me.

"All in favor?" Every hand in the room rose into the air. Except Caligans. His arms remained across his chest, his gaze hard as he watched me. My heart sunk. He had the power to overrule, and he seemed to be using it now.

"One condition." He said, his voice even and steady. My spirits rose once more as hope blossomed in my chest. "You officially become one of us." My eyes widened. The group shared agreeing smiles, their colors a hopeful blue. Caligan leaned against the back of the chair Ciprian had occupied. "You are apart of this clan, Lorn. With the brand, we will take an oath to protect you." His eyes were pleading as he spoke. "And we will follow you to hell and back." He promised. The way his eyes gleamed, made me feel his words deep within my heart and soul. The room fell silent once more as they all awaited my answer.

Could I accept the brand? Could I accept my place within the group? I knew in my heart that I could.

That I already had. This place was my home. These men were my home. The only family I had ever truly had. I realized now that I had been hoping all this time that I would be able to stay. They had given me a new chance to start a life. Not one I was forced into or had to fight to get from day to day. But one where I was safe. One where I could find peace and joy. The cracks in my broken heart glowed with warmth as I smiled softly.

"Okay." The room erupted into bright golden light.

Chapter 25

The next morning Silas and Lagan shoved me into my cottage and instructed me to stay there until they came and got me. The day passed by painfully slow and I ran out of things to pass the time quickly. Ziggy kept me company and relentlessly pressured me to play with him. I dragged my fingers through the blankets on my bed, his big green eyes intrigued by the fast movements. But even he grew tired and bored. He curled up on one of the pillows and drifted off into a deep sleep.

I sharpened my weapons blades and buffed my boots. I tried to read but my mind was too excited and curious to focus on the words. I had gotten through all the books Caligan and Cip had gifted me, each one describing beautiful lands and adventures documented throughout the lands history. But even they couldn't hold my attention. As it got later and later, I became nervous. I changed my shirt twice, worried that the first one was too old and worn for such an occasion. They all seemed to take this branding very seriously. Which I understood, they were adding a new member to their clan. My palms started to sweat as I checked myself over in the mirror. My hair was still too long for my liking but I didn't have enough time to shave it. I had no idea when they would be coming to get me. My weapons belt lay beside my bed and my chest plate was hung on the wall. I wouldn't be needing my weapons tonight.

Finally, closer to dinner time, a blue bird produced by Cals magic floated into my room. My presence was now needed and welcomed down below. Wiping my hands on my pants, I made my descent, a happy Ziggy flying by my side. Within the barn, the dinning table overflowed with roasted meats, toasted bread and boiled potatoes. Pastries and cakes covered in sugar were piled into a tower at the end. Candles lay on almost every available surface, casting the room in a warm glow. Fresh flowers lay in large bouquets around the room, their sweet fragrance enthralling to my senses. Ciprian stood by the fire, clothed in bright yellow robes, a warm smile on his face. The others stood in a half circle behind him, all dressed in clean and nice clothes. Obviously only worn for special occasions.

They all greeted me with grinning faces. Ciprian took my hand and guided me to stand in the center of the group. Ziggy flew, sitting softly on Silas's shoulder. Taking my left hand in his, the warlock cleared his throat.

"With this brand Lorn, you will be bound to those who stand around you. You will be responsible for helping and protecting them as they will you." I glanced to the men around me. Their eyes light with encouragement. Their colors happy and bright with excitement. "Their pain will be yours. Your heart will echo the beating of theirs. Their prosperity, will be yours to share. By accepting this brand, you accept a life full of peace, protection and family. You will not lift a hand to harm another, nor will they you. For if you shall, the bond between you will cease to connect you." He paused, a warm smile wrinkled the skin around his eyes. "Do you choose to accept?" I squared my shoulders, my heart racing. I had never been so sure about anything in my life than I was in this moment.

"I do." With a nod, he turned and retrieved a branding iron from the fire behind him, the tip glowing red. I rolled up my sleeve and held out my wrist. I prepared myself for the oncoming pain. Quickly and fiercely, Ciprian grabbed my wrist and placed the burning metal to my forearm. I hissed loudly, grinding my teeth to avoid yelling out. My skin seared and sizzled under the intense temperature. My chest suddenly felt as if it had been kicked, a great pressure weighing on my heart and ribs.

My heart felt like it was growing, getting larger with every beat. I released a sharp gasp as the pressure released suddenly, leaving me stunned. The cracks that had formed within my heart and soul from all the years of pain and fear, now felt as if they were reforming. The weight that had latched itself onto my shoulders all of these years felt lighter. It was like I wasn't the only one baring it anymore. After a second, I realized that was exactly what was happening. I was now connected to the people standing around me. Our hearts in synch, our burdens and troubles shared.

Ciprian raised the iron from my skin, the same swirling lines that I saw on the others was now traced into my own. But the lines were thick and black, not from being burned but it resembled ink instead of chard flesh. My brow furrowed as I turned to Ciprian who only smiled kindly before placing a warm hand on my shoulder.

"Magic affects everyone differently." He reassured me. "Welcome home, Lorn." He said with a small bow. The room exploded into a roar of cheers as I was swarmed by my family. I received aggressive hugs and large smiles. Silas gave me a long hug and a firm kiss on the cheek, his face turning bright crimson. I was handed a large glass of rum as everyone toasted to the newest member of the clan and drank deeply. Asher surprised me by pulling out a beautiful violin and filled the air with sweet music. Grady took my hand and set my glass to the side. He pulled me to the center of the room and began spinning and twirling me around in a sloppy dance. I didn't know how to dance and obviously neither did he but neither of us cared. I laughed and spun anyway, happiness glowing brightly all around me.

Soon we all danced together in careless joy. Ciprian it seemed, was the only one who knew how to properly dance but enjoyed the sloppiness of our dances just as much a the rest of us. The air was warm and bright. We passed around spiced rum and drank deeply from the bottles. My body soon felt warm and fuzzy, adding to the bliss of the evening. Ciprian sat, soon too tired from the dancing. The rest of us continued to dance, eat and drink. Cal stood by Asher, his eyes on me. I was glad he had the power to hold wards up around our home. For if he wasn't here now, I don't think I would be as happy as I was.

Grady had outdone himself with tonight's meal. The meat fell apart tenderly with every bite and his pastries dissolved on my tongue in a puddle of sugary sweetness. I had released a small moan after biting into my fourth one when Caligan slid to my side.

"Careful." He said, his voice low in my ear over the loud music and laughter. "Don't let Silas hear you make noises like that or he'll try to kiss you for real." I rolled my eyes, but giggled anyway.

"If he weren't so young I would think you're jealous based on how often you bring up his advances." I said, the rum making me smile wildly as I teased him.

"Why would I be jealous? And he's over a hundred years older than you." His grey eyes gleamed, his colors swirling into night. I refilled my glass and tried to ignore the fire within me.

"Oh please, you forget I can see what you are feeling." I eyed him over the rim of my glass. His eyes darkened. "And I've seen these colors before." The memory of his hands on my body flashed through my mind. Based on the violent movement of the night around him, I knew he was thinking about it too. Before he could speak I twirled past him and let Grady spin me around the floor once again. We danced for several songs, Elias cut in surprising everyone in the room with his lightness of foot. Ziggy had claimed a pile of food for himself and ate happily. I caught glimpses of Caligan every now and then. He sat next to Asher while the blacksmith fingered the instrument on his shoulder. Caligan drank from his glass. His eyes never leaving me.

Lagan and Silas, both with way too much alcohol in their systems, stumbled across the floor together in their best waltz and failing miserably at it. The room laughed all the same. The room burst with laughter as Silas dipped Lagan dramatically and spun him back into his chest. As he swung back to his partner, Lagan's shoulder bumped mine and sent me toppling back into Caligans lap. The contents of my glass spilling down my shirt, I giggled.

Hoping to tease him, I trailed my hand dangerously high across Caligans thigh and stood. Stumbling slightly, I made my way out into the night. I clumsily climbed the winding staircase, pausing a few time when the twisting became too much. I smiled to myself, hoping my touch had the same effect on Caligan as it did on me. I floundered into my room and took a fresh shirt off the shelf and pulled it over my head. The door banged open and Cal stumbled through the threshold. I giggled as he straightened and shut the door behind him.

"Tell me Cal, how did you learn to be so smooth on your feet?" I teased.

I walked to his side and stumbled. He caught me before I could fall, his hands stayed on my waist as he waited for me to steady myself. My heart raced and my skin tingled where his hands lay. His gaze was hard, his colors black as night. My own colors turned to match his, swallowing us in our hunger. My body ached, needing more of his touch. I needed him to need me just as much. His eyes darted to my lips then back to my eyes, his own darkening.

"You think you can touch me like that without me doing something about it?" His voice was low and rumbled through his chest. Excitement and desire flared through me. My body sang with relief as he crushed his lips to mine fiercely. I pulled his body flush to mine, desperate to feel more of him.

He placed a hand on the base of my neck and picked me up with the other. I gasped and wrapped my legs around his waist as he carried me backwards. His lips and tongue tasted like rum and sugar and they fought with mine for control. Sharp pain shot down my spine as he slammed my body into my door. The pain added to my burning desire. His hand moved, wrapping around to grasp my throat as he slowly set me on my feet. My body sliding down his sent jolts of pleasure through me as my breasts moved against him.

I ran my hands down his chest, relishing in the feel of his muscles under his shirt. I didn't realize how badly I craved his touch, his kiss, until now. How had I gone so long without feeling him, without tasting him? His hand left my throat and grabbed my wrists quickly before pinning them to the door above me. The heat between my legs intensified. He pulled away from me, his lips swollen and eyes greedy with desire. He held my wrists with one hand and pulled a knife from his belt with the other. His eyes never left mine as he stabbed the blade into the door below my joined wrists.

I flinched, a small pang of fear mixing in with my hunger for him and spreading through my colors. I looked up and found the blade wedged under my hands, slicing through the sleeves of my shirt; holding me in place. I couldn't move unless I wanted to cut open my wrists on the sharp blade. I looked back to Caligan, shock on my face. He looked like an animal ready to pounce. And I was his prey. My excitement flooded back with a vengeance.

"I may not be able to see your emotions," He bent his head low and dragged his tongue down my neck. Sparks of pleasure shot through me as I squirmed against him. "But I can feel everything going through that dreadful head of yours." He pulled back and gave me a wolffish grin before kneeling before me. He held my gaze as he undid my pants and pulled them down, exposing me to him. I was suddenly completely sober and aching for him intensely.

With the first drag of his tongue, I was nearly undone. I moaned loudly, my back bowed off the door. He pressed his hand to my stomach and pushed me back flat sharply before hooking my leg over his shoulder, granting him better access. He flicked his tongue and drove it into my center. I moaned loudly with pleasure as he drove deeper and more quickly. Climax neared, pleasure building as I climbed higher and higher. His fingers replaced where his tongue had been and began working me as he stood back to face me. He licked his lips and leaned close to me, his lips brushing mine.

"I want to see you cum." He snarled, his fingers moving faster. His words sent me over the edge. His lips crashed to mine, swallowing my scream of ecstasy as release found me. Pleasure rolled through me as his fingers drove me through my release. My body sagged against the door. He bent and pulled my pants back up around my waist and pressed his forehead to mine and clasped my face in his hands. "Ive never wanted to protect, fuck and kill something at the same time." His words and touch followed me well into the night, distracting me from the laughter that filled the air of the barn when we returned. I don't think I'll ever be able to forget the way he had touched me, the things he had said to me. I definitely made the right choice by staying.

Chapter 26

The next morning, the small village was silent. Everyone dragged their feet, squinting at the harsh light of the morning sun. No one dared speak or make any noise for fear of upsetting our bodies further. The affects of the alcohol from last night ran painfully through our heads and twisted our stomachs. I walked carefully into the kitchen, carrying my boots to avoid any unnecessary sounds to contribute to the violent aching in my temples. Grady, Lagan and Elias sat at the table with their heads on its surface. None of them ate. I plopped Ziggy onto the table next to a plate of bacon and let the dragon eat. Asher and Silas lay on the floor, grimaces on both their faces. Caligan lay sprawled on the couch, his arm thrown over his eyes. My cheeks flushed at the memory of his mouth on me and his touch.

I joined the two on the floor with a small groan. I closed my eyes, hoping the room would stop spinning. Ciprian sat in his usual chair, reading and drinking coffee. He seemed to be the only one free from sickness as he chuckled at the group of us.

"You all need to learn how to hold your liquor." He teased with a smile. Grady hissed at the sound of his voice, Silas clamped his hands over his ears. Elias slid from his chair and slumped to the ground beside me.

"You are hundreds of years old, you've had plenty of time to build a tolerance. Don't make us feel bad for being young." Lagan groaned at the old warlock. I smiled, despite the banging in my head at the sound of their voices. Ciprian may be older than all of us, but the others weren't young by any means. At least not by mortal standards. Ciprian laughed heartily. Caligan launched a pillow at him which only made him laugh harder. Once he stopped laughing he clapped his hands together loudly, making all of us flinch.

"All of you get up, we have a lot to get done today." He walked to the dinning table and took a seat while the rest of us slowly and painfully followed. My brain felt like it was being squeezed and my stomach turned dangerously as I rose. Grady passed around a pot of coffee and we waited silently for our turn to fill our cups. Ciprian waited to begin speaking until we all had a mug full. "We need to discuss plans on our rebellion against Mortala." He turned his attention to me. "What are your thoughts, Lorn?" I took a large gulp and set my cup on the table in front of me.

"First, I want my intentions to be made very clear." I looked at each of the faces around me. "This isn't about justice or saving the kingdom of Willowmore. I have no desire for any of that. My only intention is to hurt Mortala. To burn her kingdom around her and then destroy her for good." My anger hardened within me. But nobody objected. I turned back to Ciprian. "We want to attack her throne first. Her power, her hold over the people. She uses fear to control her subjects. No amount of magic could compel and entire kingdom to cower before her every word. They fear her, so they obey her." I took another drink of my coffee, the bitter liquid clearing my mind. "Killing her won't be enough, we have to take away the only thing she loves and cares about. Her position of power."

"So how do we do that?" Asher asked dryly.

"We make the people of Willowmore fear something greater than her. Something far more terrifying. We take their fear, so *we* hold the power. Not her." I said simply. Ciprian leaned forward in his chair, his eyes wild and his smile wide and crazy.

"What do you have in mind?" I gave him my own wild grin in return.

The next several days were spent discussing plans of possible attacks to ambush the queen and her kingdom. Once we had decided what our first assault would be, Silas, Lagan and Ciprian spent the days in the destruction twins workshop on something Ciprian thought could help. The rest of us stayed in the barn most of the time to work on strategy and prepare fully for the planned attack. We ate around maps and plans, not taking breaks unless to sleep. Caligan and I started patrolling at night, only staying out for half the time we usually would so we could continue working on preparations still needing done.

We split up, each taking a side of the pasture, never going more than half a mile deep into the forest. I had the south perimeter tonight, while he had the north. Neither of us had spoken of the night of my branding and what had occurred between us in my cottage. But I couldn't help the fire that sparked to life within me every time I caught his grey eyes watching me. He trailed light touches over my skin while we sat around maps or passed each other on the stairs. I ached and hoped for time alone with him again, but I hadn't found the opportunity yet.

Patrolling had been enjoyable so far, never meeting more than two Damned at a time. I handled myself well, but hated the sticky black blood that coated my skin every night when I returned back home. I checked my watch in the moonlight. Almost two in the morning, it was time for me to head back. I marched through the forest, keeping my footsteps silent and listening for any movement.

At the edge of the perimeter, just a few feet from the lush pasture, I heard moment. Quick and heavy footsteps barreled around the side of a tree. I unhooked my axe and brought the heavy blade up to defend, but a warm, calloused hand wrapped around my wrist, stopping my attack. A large hand gripped my waist and pressed my body firmly to the trunk of a tree. My heart raced and jumped at the sight of Cals wicked grin flashing in the moonlight.

"Don't go killing me yet sweetheart, we have a queen to destroy." His voice was rich and low, my body shivered.

"Don't call me sweetheart." I crushed my lips to his, sighing with the satisfaction that flooded through me. I had craved him, ached for him. His hands held me firmly, almost painfully as he claimed my mouth with his. My hands dragged over the exposed skin of his neck, traced over his muscles bulging under his shirt. He pressed his body flush to mine. I moaned as I felt his hard length press to my belly, straining under his clothes. His mouth tasted of sugar, his scent of lavender put me into a hungry trance. The kiss was fierce, wild and frantic. Both of us not knowing when the next would come.

I almost whined, begging for more when he pulled away, both of us breathless.

"I will never be able to get enough of that dreadful mouth of yours." His words sent a black and gold glow shifting through the air around me.

After days of barely any sleep and working day and night, it was time for us to make our move. It was well into the night when I strapped my blades to my hips and chest. With my cloak around my shoulders, I met the others by the fire pit. Caligan, Elias, and Asher wore dark colors like me and had their weapons sharp and ready to go. The four of us would be entering the kingdom of Willowmore while Grady, Silas, Lagan and Ciprian stayed at home. I gave Ziggy to Lagan, his green eyes sad with my soon departure. I kissed his fuzzy head.

"I'll be back soon." I promised the tiny dragon.

I joined my three companions, the four of us stood before the others. Silas handed us each a small silver orb about the size of a pearl.

"When you are ready to return home, bite onto this and you'll be transported back here." Cip said, his voice serious and steady. We all nodded our understanding and tucked the small orbs away safely. He spread his hands wide and took a step back. "Are you ready?" He asked quietly. I exchanged looks with the small group, their faces stoney and ready for battle. With a small nod, green fog drifted from Ciprian's hands. The fog swirled around us, enclosing us from the others. The fog grew thick, blocking us completely from view from each other. A slight breeze blew in, clearing the fog and revealing the gates of the city before us. Ciprian had transported us directly into Willowmore.

The four of us exchanged silent nods and split into different directions. Melting into the shadows, we spread out and took separate alleys that would eventually lead us to the square in the center of the city. We will meet up where all of this began. Where the residents of this kingdom demanded my blood while the queen ordered my execution. I slid through the alleys easily and quietly. My surroundings familiar from my years of being a resident. I came across few people, ducking behind bins and walls to avoid being seen. My heart raced as I walked, listening and watching for any sign of the royal guards on patrol. The feeling of fear and hiding within the city walls was all too familiar.

I reached the center square just before midnight, the moon high and bright above me. I took my position at the east entrance, hidden behind a large topiary. Just as I expected, five royal guards sat on the stairs of the queens dais playing cards by an oil lamp. The same five guards playing the same game in the same spot as they have every night for the last several years. I had run into them several times since becoming a messenger. They were cruel and hated humans almost as much as the queen did. I had watched them whip and beat countless over the years, for simply being human. I had been their target on more than one occasion. They deserved every second of what was coming for them tonight.

The clock tower chimed loudly, signifying midnight. That was our cue. I said a silent prayer that my friends had made their way to their positions and stepped out into the moonlight. Three figures appeared with me, one at each of the entrances to the square. Their faces hidden in darkness, their silhouettes haunting to look at. We waited for the guards to notice us, and when they did, we pounced.

Taking off at a dead sprint, we all rushed the officers, weapons drawn. Their shouts rang through the air only briefly before we were upon them. Caligan tackled one to the ground, his scythe glinting in the moonlight. Elias kicked one in the chest, sending him backwards to the ground in front of me. I leapt onto him, knife in hand and slammed it into his chest, tearing through skin and muscle. Grabbing another from my chest plate, I slid it across his throat, blood squirting onto my face and neck. The guard stilled underneath me.

I turned to find two officers dead at Caligans feet. He was bent low, wiping the blood from the blade of his scythe onto the pant leg of the guards. Asher landed a killing blow to the head of another officer with his flail and Elias silenced the last with a knife to the jugular. Pride flowed through me at the sight of my family victorious and covered in the blood of the royal guards. We all stood breathing heavy as we checked each other for wounds. None of us had even a scratch. The bastards didn't even land a punch. Quick and easy. We quickly dragged the lifeless bodies onto the steps of the dais, blood pooling around our feet. Our mission complete, we all took out the small pearl like orb Silas had given us.

Elias and Asher popped theirs into their mouths and vanished from sight. Caligan gave me a small nod before popping his own into his mouth and disappeared with them. I palmed mine and turned back to the dead warlock guards at my feet. An idea popped into my head as I stared at the pool of blood flowing down the steps. I dipped my hand into their blood and hastily began writing on the wall behind the platform, using the thick red liquid as ink. Footsteps came from around the corner just as I finished. I wiped the blood off my hand and onto my pants before pulling the orb from my pocket. A strange taste filled my mouth as I bit into it and the air around me became cloudy. The world seemed to tilt and shift underneath me and then the fog began to dissipate. When it finally cleared, I found myself back in the small barn.

Sighs of relief filled the room, Caligan, Elias and Asher each had a glass in hand with curious expressions on their faces.

"What took you so long?" Elias asked. He took a large drink from his cup.

"Yeah, you had the orb in your hand when I bit mine. You should have been right behind me." Caligan added.

"I left the queen a little love note." I said, wiggling my blood stained fingers in the air.

"Do tell. What did this note say?" Grady asked with a small smile. A slow wicked grin spread across my face.

"Traitors to the Damned." Their wide smiles were the only approval I needed.

Chapter 27

We began venturing to the city every night, hitting different places at different times, always under the cover of the night sky. Our attacks on the kingdom had produced the outcome we had been hoping for. The amount of guards on duty had been tripled throughout the city since our first attack. Homes and businesses were boarded up, their owners afraid their property would be the next target. A curfew was set within the cities walls, no one was allowed out past dark and if they were, they were killed on sight; warlock or human. A little harsh in my opinion, but I expect nothing less from Mortala.

We started with just taking out guards, but now we began destroying buildings owned by cruel sorcerers or those favored by the queen. We had become notorious, haunting the dreams of Willowmore's residents and leaving them in constant terror. Signs were posted around the city offering rewards for any knowledge on the radical group we had created. Through our raids we had discovered that we were believed to be the creatures of the Damned, thanks to my little note our first night in the city. The residents of the kingdom believed we, the creatures, were enraged and taking it out on the queen and her people for the injustice done to us. Which wasn't exactly false. The queen had obviously tried to squash these rumors, but it only increased the growing theory of her inability to stop us. The people believed her to be weak compared to the creatures wrecking her city and filling her people with fear.

In the span of a few weeks, we became the most feared thing in the land, holding more power over the kingdoms residents than the queen herself. We were able to keep up the facade of being the Damned creatures with the help of Caligan and his talents with leather. He had crafted each of us masks that covered the bottom half of our faces that perfectly resembled the jaws of the Damned. Using paint and real teeth from the bodies we had killed in the woods, they were perfect replicas. The fear on the guards faces whenever they saw us were priceless. We had shared stories of the different reactions we had all received, laughing so hard tears fell from our eyes and stitches had formed in our sides.

Grady and Lagan joined the group of us to go to the city while Cip and Silas stayed home. The two continued to make the transport orbs and create new bombs and weapons for us to use on our raids. Our days were filled with preparations, training and resting. Caligan and I had yet to find time to truly be alone longer than a few moments. Stolen glances and slight touches was the extent of our personal interactions. Throughout our days, his gaze igniting the fire that always sparked to life when I was around him. Every time we returned home, I hoped we would find a free minute so I could be alone with him, but there was never a moment to spare. When we returned we were all always too tired to do anything but sleep for several hours.

Silas had started becoming restless, relentlessly asking if he could go on the next mission. He was always told no, just because he was needed to make weapons. But I knew the real reason nobody said yes was because we were all secretly too afraid to let him go. We worried about everyone that went, fear filling us at the thought of being caught, hurt or killed. But it was different when it came to Silas. He was so innocent and kind, I don't think any of us could bare the thought of losing him.

Every time we left it seemed more and more nerve racking and stressful. Not knowing how many guards we would be facing throughout the night. When we departed earlier tonight, tears lined Ciprian's eyes as he hugged each of us before sending us away with a wave of his hand and a cloud of green fog. The fear of being caught or harmed had to be pushed aside when we entered the city gates, our minds remaining clear and on track with the task ahead of us.

Tonight we not only will be taking out whatever guards we come across, but we will also be demolishing the statue of the queen just outside the castle grounds. The six of us split up when we came into the kingdom. Weaving though streets, I made my way to the castle, killing several guards as I went. Their blood coated my hands and flecked across my mask and around my eyes. I left all of their lifeless bodies in the center of the road, out in the open for all to see when the sun rose.

I kneeled in the shadows, the gates to the castle ahead of me. The castle looming in the distance, stark and grey. Like the rest of the city, it was cold and dull. I counted twelve officers, six on either side of the gateway. I waited patiently, my palms sweaty with anticipation. I didn't know if my companions were in position, waiting like I was. I hadn't felt anything down the brand connecting us to signify anything had gone wrong. We had done this so many times over the past few weeks, the trust we laid within each other to be where we were needed, was instinctual.

The clock struck one and rang loudly throughout the quiet streets. I rolled my shoulders, loosening the tightness winding through them. Fear begged to take control, but I pushed it down, holding it back. My fear would not control me but it could help drive me to get back home safely. Instead, I gave into the frenzy of the fight that waited fo me. Gave into the part of me hoping for blood, the part of me that was eager to repay those for the cruelty they have put into the world. With a deep breath, I burst from the darkness of the alley, my actions copied by five shadows each storming from their own places. The guards were ready for the ambush, and they drew their weapons as we approached. The torches hanging overhead illuminated our faces as we rushed them. Terror flashed across their faces as our masks confirmed their worst fears; the Damned have returned.

Chapter 28

I threw my shoulder into the first guard, our bodies fell to the ground in a painful heap. I threw a jab at his jaw which he blocked and delivered one of his own that sent stars dancing across my vision. I snarled, the noise muffled behind my mask. I pressed my knee to his chest and send a left hook to his cheek. Bone cracked under the brass knuckles encasing my fingers. While he lay stunned and bleeding, I drew my hatchet from my hip and slid the sharp blade across his throat swiftly, releasing a river of dark blood. Sounds of steal and punches filled the air around me.

The rest of the officers were occupied fighting my family. My clan seemed capable of handling the rest. Seeing my window of opportunity, I sprinted to the towering statue to my left. It glistened like polished silver in the moonlight, the smooth stone replicated the queens beauty flawlessly. I glowered at it, my hatred for Mortala bubbling up within me. I pulled the small box that Silas had given me out from under my cloak. A small fuse stuck out from the side. I threw a look over my shoulder. Four more guys lay dead on the ground, their bodies stiff and wet with their own blood.

I waited, breathless and frantic for the others to finish with the last few. Soon, Caligan was the only one still in combat. Shouts and footsteps started coming down the surrounding streets, more guards coming our way. Deciding that I couldn't wait any longer, I turned back to the bomb in my hand. I let my anger blaze to life and dance across my finger tips, my power now unrestricted. I placed the deadly box at the base of the statue and watched as my magic licked its way up the fuse. I turned seeing Cal still dealing with the last guard. I only had seconds to get away before the small box went off and he and I both stood too close to the soon to be destroyed statue. I threw myself into Cals side and took him to the ground with me.

A sharp pain tore through my side, but before I could see what it was, the air exploded into light as the bomb burst to life. I grasped Caligan to my chest, shielding him from flying pieces of stone and burning fire. His arms circled me, turning me so his back was to the crumbling statue. The noise was deafening, a high pitched ringing noise filled my ears. I coughed as smoke swirled around us, my head spun as Caligan's soot covered face popped in front of mine. His mouth was moving but I didn't hear what he was saying over the ringing. He shook me, his eyes wide. My lungs ached as I tried to breath, my ribs cried in protest.

I watched as he shoved something past his lips and then moved my mask to slip something into my mouth. A small ball slid along my tongue. It was a transportation orb I realized, my mind clearing. I gave him a nod and bit down and the familiar strange taste filled my mouth as smoke surrounded us. The world tilted and we were back home away from the smoke and fire. I gasped, pain flared through me. I fell to the floor within our dining barn, the pain in my chest intensifying excruciatingly.

Cal ripped the mask from my face and knelt beside me and looked at my side. I looked down. My ribs were bleeding, a knife stuck out of my body like a broken tree branch. The last standing guard must have stabbed me before the blast. Cal got to his feet quickly and sprinted from the room. I looked at Cip, panic filling my mind. Asher and Elias crouched beside the warlock, relief filled my heart as two of my friends had returned safely. Ciprian began shouting at the others while I frantically looked for Caligan. Where was he? Why had he left?

Ciprian pressed on my shoulders and pushed me to my back. He unstrapped my chest plate and threw it to the side. He then began cutting away my shirt, slicing it around the knife patruding from my chest.

"Where's-" I choked. "Caligan?" I struggle to ask, my voice hollow and breathless. Lagan appeared at Ciprian's side with a pile of clean towels. Ciprian took them from him and began placing them on the floor around me, soaking up my spilled blood.

"He will be right back, he is getting some things to help heal you." I stared at the ceiling, gasping and clawing for air, my lungs no longer wanted to fill. Caligan returned, blood smeared and flecked his handsome face and arms. Grady came sprinting into the room with a small jar filled with a fine orange powder. Ciprian took the jar and leaned over me, his snowy eyes full of worry.

"We can heal your wound quickly with magic but we have to remove the blade first." He gave Caligan a quick look who nodded in return.

"Its going to hurt, Lorn." Cals voice was steady and calm, despite the panic flashing around him. "You need to try and remain calm and in control." He sat back on his heels. "Or we will all be dead."

His words were blunt, but true. If I didn't remain in control of my power, I could fill the entire building with flames. I gave him a weak nod. Caligan placed his hand gently on the knife and froze, his grey eyes overflowing with panic and worry, his colors swirled violently, horridly around him.

"It's going to be okay, Lorn." The room was filled with red panic, it flowed from everyone as they watched my slowly suffocating form. I ground my teeth together, trying to breathe and keep control over the panic and pain swirling within me.

"Take the fucking thing out!" I spat through clenched teeth, frustration rolling through me. Caligan's jaw flexed and with a quick tug, he ripped the knife from my side. I felt the blade scrape against bone and tear my flesh. My body bowed off the floor as I screamed. The pain was excruciating. My lungs burned and seared sharply. I could feel my palms burning, my magic fighting to break free. I curled them into fists, holding onto my flames with all my remaining strength. My skin and flesh stung and burned as Caligan cleaned the wound.

Ciprian's voice was soothing in my ear as I struggled to breathe and keep my power at bay.

"Almost done, you're almost done." He said softly. "The pain will be gone soon." I slammed by hands to the hard floor beside me. Black spots formed in my vision, my lungs heaved with effort. Darkness swirled around me, clouding my vision. It was welcoming, beckoning to me to give into it. It would be so easy to fall into it, let it swallow my completely. But I held on tightly to the pain, letting it anchor me. If I gave in, I don't think I would ever leave the darkness. If I gave in, I would be lost forever.

Suddenly and fiercely, the pain disappeared. I gasped, taking in a large lungful of air, filling me completely. The black around me began to fade. The pain that racked my body a second ago was gone as Ciprian blew the orange powder into the hole in my side. Cals eyes seemed to glow brightly as he placed his hands on the outer edges of my wound. It was like a unbearable weight being lifted from my chest. Cals hand glowed where they touched me, his magic seeping into my skin and flesh underneath. I watched as the wound slowly closed until it was nothing but a scar.

I closed my eyes, relishing in the delicious air that came to me easily now. I vowed to never take breathing for granted again. Sighs of relief filled the room around me. Silas crouched beside me, taking my hand in his. Ziggy perched on his shoulder. I could have sworn I saw tears brimming within the dragons large green eyes. I gave my furry friend and the red headed boy a small smile and wiped a tear from his freckled cheek. Lagan knelt by his side and clapped a hand on his brothers shoulder. They both studied me.

"We did it. You blew it up." His wide grin was infectious. The room suddenly was filled with grinning faces as we announced our triumph. I sat up slowly and grinned at all of them. Asher knelt to my side and pulled me to his chest in a hug. I gave him a small grin as he stood and accepted a glass of wine from Grady. Joy and relief flooded through the room. We had accomplished something huge tonight and it was definitely something worth celebrating. If the people of Willowmore didn't doubt their queen yet, they would after they see the destruction we had caused so close to the castle. Caligan helped me to my feet and leaned in close so only I could hear him.

"Don't ever do that to us again. To me again." His grey eyes were still flooded with worry as he studied my face. I gave him a small smile and nodded. While the rest of them began to celebrate, I scooped up my chest plate and mask, wincing at the tightness and ache still pounding dully within my chest. I left the warm glow of the barn and slowly walked down to the caverns. I was eager to rid my skin of the soot and blood coating it thickly. I grabbed a change of clothes from my room and practically ran to the warm pool of water. I moaned as I sank into it slowly, loving how it felt against my sore body.

Sounds of laughter echoed through the clearing, followed by the sweet sound of music. Asher must have brought his violin out again. Tonight was to be a night of celebration for our clan. I smiled to myself, thankful for at least one night of relaxation before we began preparing for our next offense. Tomorrow we will see exactly how our actions affected those within the city. We will get to see just how powerless Mortala has become.

I climbed from the warm, iridescent colored pool and tugged on my fresh clothes. My skin finally felt clean and fresh. I carried my boots and weapons belt back to my room, loud laughter and conversation floated through the air from the open doors of the barn. I had planned to drop off my things and head back to join the others, eager for some fun and maybe a few glasses of rum and wine. But my plans changed. When I entered my quarters, Caligan stood inside, waiting for me.

Chapter 29

Caligan stood next to the counter on the far wall. Ziggy lay curled up, asleep in the bed I had made him out of a box, torn fabric and a small pillow. Cal had changed into clean clothes. The blood and soot gone from his skin. I eyed the bulge of his muscles, visible through the tight black shirt he wore. He wasn't wearing his chest plate and his weapons belt hung low on his hips. He shifted nervously from foot to foot.

"Can we talk?" He asked, his voice unsure. I nodded silently and shut the door behind me. He shoved his hands into his pockets and focused his gaze on me. "You saved me tonight." His voice was low, his eyes on his feet. I had never seen him look so unsure, so... nervous.

"You would have done the same." I shrugged. I hung my chest plate by the door and placed my weapons on the table next to my bed. I turned to face him, my arms tightly folded across my chest. "Was that what you wanted to talk about?" He shook his head. His scarred hand ran through his black hair, messing the soft, inky locks into a wild mess. My heart flipped wildly in my chest.

"Its about that night you helped Silas with his nightmare. When you came to my room." My heart skipped again, but this time from dread. I didn't want to talk about what had happened that night. I had made a lot of progress when it comes to talking about my past, but I don't think I was ready to discuss that part yet. I closed my eyes and took a deep breath.

"Caligan I just got blown up and had a knife plunged into my chest, I'm really not in the mood to talk about this." I turned and started straightening a stack of books on the floor by the book case. They had started to fill up quickly thanks to the stacks Cip and Cal had gifted me over the last several weeks. The small cottage had finally started looking like a home. Weapons, books and clothes scattered throughout the room. Even a few pretty rocks and flowers I had found decorated the many shelves.

"Well I am."

"Why?" I whirled at him, glaring.

"Because I upset you that night. And after what happened tonight I want to make sure I don't do it again." His eyes blazed. He took a calming breath. "If you had died tonight," his jaw clenched tightly, his colors violent. "If you had died I never would have gotten the chance to apologize. " His eyes softened and his voice lowered. I wanted to argue, to refute what he said. But he was right. We had shared many stolen moments since then, but something felt... off. I missed how we were before, with no tense moment wavering over our heads. I sighed and nodded. I sat down on the edge of my bed and folded my hands in my lap.

"I'm sorry I made you uncomfortable that night." He said quietly. My head snapped up and my brow furrowed.

"You didn't."

He looked to his feet. "Then why were you so upset when I asked about the scar? You've been opening up about the stories of your past. I didn't know that one was different." I sighed and rolled my shoulders. My heart raced, my brain screamed for me to leave this conversation. I squeezed my eyes shut, fighting against the urge to run from the room as the panic starting to roll through me.

"Because that scar cuts the deepest in more ways than one." I snapped, frustration and panic surging through me. The room was silent for a long moment.

"Please talk to me, Lorn." His voice was closer than before, but I kept my eyes closed. I took a steadying breath.

"Its not a story you want to hear. Its not a story I want to tell." I paused. "At least not yet." He placed his hands on either side of my face, his eyes no longer holding anger.

"I understand and I'm sorry for pushing you. If you don't want to talk about it I wont force you." He dragged his thumb across my cheekbone. "I just want to know everything about you. Every story, every fight, every memory." I remaind silent. His colors pulsed around him, fear and hope swirled in the air. Whatever he was wanting to say was seriously worrying him. "Every instinct I have revolves around you. Where I stand in a room, so I can see you or be close to you. Where I position myself in a fight in case you need help. You're the only thing I've been able to think about since the night you came stumbling through the woods. Everyday I hope I can make you smile or laugh. It drives me crazy every time I see Silas kiss you or one of the guys flirts with you. I gawk every time you fight or practice because its the most beautiful thing to witness." My colors glowed around me. His grey eyes glowed, his shoulders tense. "I never want to hurt you, or upset you or become another story of your past too painful to tell. You are strong and bold and brutal, Lorn. And the most breathtaking creature I've ever seen."

Chapter 30

My heart hammered wildly in my chest. My body flooded with happiness, my colors bright and golden around me. No matter what, he would be my favorite story to tell. I had never had the luxury of loving someone, of giving my heart to someone to protect and care for. I knew that heartbreak can ruin even the strongest of people. But hearing his words, feeling his touch, I would give him my heart now and a million times over. I don't care if he breaks it. My heart is his, completely and thoroughly. I placed my hand gently on his cheek and brushed my lips against his. They moved softly with his, the feeling of his lips like velvet and sweet. My chest ached and my stomach dropped as he pulled away and turned to the door.

"You're leaving?" Panic filled my voice. Why would he say those sweet thing and then just leave? Is it because I hadn't said anything in return? I thought my actions were enough, but maybe I was wrong. I didn't know how to tell him how much he meant to me, how much of my heart was already truly his. When he reached he door, he turned to face me. His eyes were dark and his jaw tight.

"I'm not going anywhere." He reached behind him and locked the door. A jolt went through me as he stalked towards me. Desire bloomed within me, my colors swirling to night, his shifting to match. He reached out and grabbed my hand and pulled me gently to my feet.

My heart beat rapidly against my ribs. He lowered his head and gently brushed his lips across mine. A shiver went through my body as he placed a hand on my cheek and rested the other on my hip. What started as gentle and soft, quickly turned hungry, rushed, and fierce.

Our tongues danced together as his strong hands caressed my body. We both became frantic, eager to be closer. He dragged his hand down my neck and up my stomach and cupped my breasts. A small moan escaped my lips as he gently brushed them with his fingers and continued feeling his way back down to my hips. Very quickly, he picked me up and wrapped my legs around his waist. I gasped, pulling away from his kiss to see his face, now wicked and full of desire.

He spun and sat down on the edge of the bed with me straddling his lap. He placed his hand at the base of my neck and pulled my lips back to his. I moaned and pressed myself to him, feeling his arousal beneath me. His lips trailed down my neck, licking and biting as he went. His hands flawlessly undid the buttons of my shirt and tore it from my skin with a growl. The throbbing between my legs intensified as he brushed his thumbs over my exposed nipples.

He sucked one into his mouth and pulled on it with his teeth. Sparks of pleasure rolled through me as I arched into his touch. Only when another loud moan tore from me did he take his lips away.

"You have no idea what that moan does to me." My cheeks heated, his voice thick and husky. Breathing heavily, I began unbuttoning his shirt, slowly revealing the broad plains of his scarred chest. Tossing it to the side I traced the scars and corded muscles now on display. I don't know if I'll ever get used to feeling things on the tips of my finger but I know I'll never get enough of feeling his skin. His grip on my hips tightened as he lifted me from his lap and set me on my feet before him.

He toyed with the buttons on my pants and pulled me closer by the belt loop. He gave me a questioning look, asking for my permission to continue. I nodded lightly, desire thrumming through my veins. He gently undid the buttons and my pants slid to the floor at my ankles. He had seen me naked before, but this was different. That wasn't him trying to comfort and calm me. This was hunger, this was him aching and needing me. And me needing him. He pulled me gently by the waist back onto his lap. He lifted me effortlessly and spun so my back was now pressed to the mattress.

His mouth claimed mine once more as his hands roamed over my exposed body, leaving trails of sparks in their wake. My eyes fluttered shut, relishing in the feel of his lips as they trailed down and over my skin. His hand slid between my legs, I had to bite down on my lip to keep from screaming out.

"You're so wet for me, Lorn." His words rolled through me. He slid down lower and placed a kiss on my inner thigh before dragging his tongue across my center. He watched me from under lowered lashes as he licked and kissed, sending a flood of pleasure through me. I knotted my hands in his hair as he devoured me. Great moans and gasps escaped my lips. I squirmed under him as he pumped his fingers in and out of me. I bit my lip until I tasted blood to keep from crying out as pleasure continued to build within me.

Suddenly he was gone, his touch no longer burning my skin. I sat up, aching for him to continue. I was wiling to beg for him to continue, but I saw what he was doing and stopped myself, my voice dying in my throat. He had stood up and was unbuckling his weapons belt, his knives and scythe falling to the ground. His eyes had darkened further, the grey no longer visible as his pupils swallowed them with desire. I tore my eyes from his when his pants joined the rest of our discarded clothing. The curves of his muscles and scars on his body were mesmerizing. Seeing his hard length made my desire grow to dangerous heights.

He crawled onto the bed with me and pressed himself between my legs. I lifted my hips in anticipation and eagerness but he didn't move.

"We can stop." He said breathlessly. I shook my head. I wanted this. I wanted him. I wanted to feel him and connect with him in every way. My back arched as he slid into me. I winced at the pain but stayed still until he filled me. I let the pain fuel the pleasure slowly starting to build as he started to move slowly. The pressure intense and delicious. He loosed a moan as he sank back in, even deeper than before, filling me completely.

He kissed me intently, feverishly as he continued to move slowly. He dragged his lips down my neck as I hooked my legs around his waist, moving my hips with his. He started moving faster, pounding into me. I dug my nails into his back, urging him on as my climax neared. His eyes found mine, his hand placed firmly on my jaw, forcing me to look at him while the other gripped my hip almost painfully. A growl rumbled through his chest. His thrusts came faster and harder. Sweat covered his brow.

"Cum for me, Lorn." My name on his lips finally had me crumbling around him. Waves of pleasure rolled through me as he slammed into me once more before shuddering and growling into my neck as he found his own release. We lay breathless, our limbs entangled. I lay in his arms as my body came down from its high. He trailed his fingers lightly over my skin as we caught our breaths. Bruises from his fingers already blooming to life where his hands had gripped me, made me smile. I fell asleep in his arms, the sound of his heart beating the most beautiful lullaby.

Chapter 31

Waking up in Caligan's arms was a feeling I never wanted to forget. He held me firmly against his chest, my legs entangled with his. The hardness usually found in his face was calm and relaxed as his chest rose and fell evenly. Being next to him made me feel safe. Protected. This moment, was the only time I had ever forgotten the pain that had tainted my life. His touch, made me feel free of the life I had once lived and hated. Being with him now, made me realize just how much I loved being alive and living within the new existence I had found here in the Forest of the Damned.

This new life that held the promise of peace and happiness, things I never had the luxury of experiencing. Hope was always a word I hated. I'de never allowed myself to hope or yearn for things. But here, in Caligan's arms, I hoped. I hoped for a happy life. I hoped for this feeling, of being wrapped in his arms to never fade. I hoped that one day, I would be able to tell him about all the pain and scars I carried. I hoped that when he woke, I found the courage to tell him how much I felt for him. I hoped that he felt the same.

My throat and mouth were dry and sticky with thirst. I slowly slid from Caligan's grasp, careful not to wake him and climbed from bed. I pulled on my own pants and slipped his shirt on and buttoned it up. It was much too big for me, hanging almost to my knees but I stepped from the room with a small smile on my face anyway. The clearing was quiet. My family obviously sleeping soundly as the moon lay brightly in the sky above. The grass was cool under my feet as I padded down to the empty kitchen and poured myself a large glass of water. The cold freshness felt wonderful on my parched throat. I finished my first glass in record time and poured myself another. The sound of the crackling fire within the pit my only companion. I stood in blissful peace as memories of my evening with Caligan danced in my mind.

"Thirsty?" A voice said behind me, making me jump. I whirled, my hand going instinctively to my empty hip. Elias leaned against the dinning table, his face hard and tired. I heaved a sigh of relief, the fright he had given me at his sudden presence passing quickly. I had been so wrapped up in my own thoughts I hadn't even heard him enter the room.

"You scared me." I said with a small laugh. His expression remained hard. I gave him a quizzical look. He seemed off, something in his colors was wrong. "Is everything okay?" He straitened to his full height. Like his brothers, he was large in stature and built solidly with muscles from years of fighting. I had grown used to being around them, being the smallest of the group. But something with his colors and facial expression made me weary.

"The others may be fooled, Caligan may be delusional about your purpose, but I don't buy this whole act of yours." His eyes trailed my body as he slowly started walking around the table. An alarm went off in the back of my head as he approached, a deadly expression on his face.

"What are you talking about, Elias?" I asked, keeping my voice even, despite the alarm and surge of fear trailing down my spine. He titled his head to the side.

"You think I don't know what you are? What you're trying to do to my family?" He was on the same side of the table as me now. "Trying to get us to trust you so you can overthrow the queen and take her throne?" He snarled. "You're just as unnatural as she is, as *they* are." He practically spat the words. He was talking about sorcerers. But Ciprian is a warlock, why would he be talking like this about a man he trusted and that cared for him since he was a child? How could he be so hateful to Cal?

"I'm not trying to do anything. You forget that I'm one of you, I would never do anything to hurt any of you. I took the same oath you did." I growled, my body tense with anger at his accusatory words. "And for someone who was raised by a warlock you seem to dislike his kind much more than you should." His face twisted in fury as he lunged at me, grabbing my arms and caging me to the counter with his body. My heart hammered wildly and panic swirled in the air around me.

"He is a means to an end. Living here saved my life, doesn't mean he did." Anger twisted violently around him, coming off of him in thick, vicious clouds. His weapons belt hung at his hips, complete with his knives and daggers. I was completely defenseless.

"Let me go." I demanded. A laugh racked his chest.

"No way in hell I'm letting you continue living amongst us, like you belong here." His words hit me like a slap to the face. "No one will be sad to see you go. All you are is a distraction that will eventually get us killed. Caligan might be the only one who fights it seeing as you've opened your legs for him and that he believes you're the one who will give him back what's his." I snarled at him, my anger coursing through me, outweighing the confusion of his last words. I wanted to hit him, beat him until his blood stained my hands. But I took an oath, swearing to protect them. To protect him. Not to hurt. I grabbed hold of my anger coursing through me, pulling it back before I engulfed him in flames.

"Let me go, Elias. Final warning." I didn't know what I would do if he didn't, but I could always make him think I would fry him. But another cruel laugh came from his lips as he glared at me. His grip on my arms tightened painfully.

"Hurt me, Lorn. Do it. Prove me right." My blood turned to hot flames as I bared my teeth at him. He was trying to provoke me, trying to unleash the monster writhing within me. But I wouldn't give him the satisfaction. He was wrong about me, about the others.

This was my home, they were my family. I wouldn't allow him to take that from me. My body relaxed in his grip.

"You're wrong about me." Pure violent anger flashed across his features as I relaxed and met his glare calmly. With a roar of fury, his fist connected with my face. I slumped back, the coppery taste of blood filled my mouth. Black spots dotted my vision as I shook off the surprise attack and turned back to face him. He brought his arm back again but this time landed the punch directly into my gut. I doubled over and groaned in pain. Bile worked its way up my throat and splattered onto the floor at my feet. Panic and past memories flooded through my head as he grabbed a fist full of my short hair and yanked my head back.

"Fight me, Lorn. Fight me or I'll kill you right here and now and you'll die a coward." I wasn't going to die. I sent a pang of fear and pleading down the bond connecting me to the rest of the clan. Elias felt it go through him and roared in fury once again. Picking up my body effortlessly he launched me onto the dining table. The wood cracked and split under the impact of my body and broke easily. I landed on my back, pain shooting through my bones and muscles as my vision began darkening. Another punch hit my jaw and then another was delivered to my side. I gasped for air and choked on my blood. My mind screamed for me to fight back, to turn him to ash where he stood. But I wouldn't let him take my home, my family from me.

I looked up at him, my left eye quickly swelling shut. His towering figure stood above me, his chest heaving and his eyes wild. He pulled a knife from his hip and bent low over me. My heart raced, my body ached as I watched him bring his arm back, the blade aimed for my heart. His eyes were wild, his colors vicious and frenzied. I couldn't move, my body protested with each breath. He was right, I was going to die. As his arm came down, a wicked grin spread across his lips. A body barreled into him and threw him off of me.

I scrambled backwards, my body aching and screaming as I tried to climb from the pile of broken wood. Silas wrestled with Elias, trying to pry the knife from his hands. The young boy being much smaller than Elias, was thrown off quickly and slammed into the cabinets behind them. I felt the pain hitting Silas slide through me, the brand alerting me of the danger surrounding him. Grady and Asher came barreling into the room, both shirtless and hair messy from sleep. They charged at Elias and brought him back to the ground. Caligan, half naked, came sprinting in to join them with Lagan and Ciprian trialing close behind.

Ciprian knelt beside me and helped me stand as the others pried the weapons belt from Elias and yanked the knife free from his grip. He roared as he struggled and fought against his brothers, his deadly glare trained on me. I leaned heavily on Cip, the pain in my chest and face fierce. I knew I would heal soon my power now unrestricted, but I still ached and bled.

"Elias! Stop!" Asher yelled. Caligan's fist slammed into Elias jaw and the man soon calmed in his brothers hands. His chest still rose and fell quickly and his gaze never left mine but he stopped struggling against the others.

"What the fuck is going on?" Grady asked, confusion swirled around him.

"She attacked me." Elias said. I knew it was a lie but his colors flashed around him as he spoke. The heads in the room turned to me. I shook my head, unable to speak. Elias turned to his brothers, his expression now a mask of pleading. "You think I would hurt her without cause? You've known me for years, I would never hurt one of our own." I looked to Caligan and silently pleaded for him to see through his lies. "She's the one with a temper!"

Cal walked to my side and knelt in front of me, his hands gently held my battered face.

"He's lying." I croaked. His eyes searched mine and his colors turned from angry and confused to violent rage as he slowly turned back to Elias. But Elias stood his ground even faced with Caligan's angry form. He was truly terrifying with anger plastered across his face, his grey eyes murderous.

"Of course you would believe her, you've been keeping her bed warm." Elias snarled. Caligan's face twisted as he lunged but Ciprian's voice stopped him.

"There is a simple way to reveal the truth." All eyes tuned to the warlock. "Truth serum." Elias' eyes flashed, his colors filled with fear and panic.

"Why wont you just believe me? Why do you need to use magic?" He said quickly, desperately trying to ward against it. Ciprian's gaze was hard as he stared him down.

"If you are telling the truth, then you have nothing to worry about." Elias struggled against the others.

"But she has magic, she can charm her way out and make me lie." Ciprian's face was pure anger as he whirled to face him. I had never seen such anger from the wizard, never seen him so filled with violent emotion.

"No one, no matter your abilities can fool the serum. Don't worry Elias, the truth will come out." He snarled. Relief flooded through me. They would know the truth. There was no doubt they could see what really happened for themselves but they needed the truth to be said. I couldn't expect them to chose between me and their brother. But now with the truth about to be out in the open, they would have to.

Chapter 32

"I don't need a scrum to know you're lying."
Caligan growled, anger rolled off of him in waves. His
body shook with fury as he stared down his brother.
"Want to know how I know?" He asked, not waiting for a
response. He pointed a finger at me behind his back. "She
not only has the power to burn you to ash within seconds,
but we've also seen her in a fight. She has taken out more
Damned and royal guards than any of us." His hand
dropped as he took a step forward, now nose to nose with
the man who tried to kill me. "If she truly had attacked
you, you would be dead at our feet." His words dripped
with venom.

"I agree." Grady spoke up, anger flashing through
his eyes. "She's more than capable." His gaze turned to
me, his brow furrowed. " I believe that he attacked you. I
just don't understand why you didn't fight back." All eyes
were now trained on me. They all seemed confused by his
lack of injuries as well. I shrugged, pain lacing through
my shoulder and back.

"We don't hurt each other." I locked my gaze on
Caligan's, hoping he could see the truth in my next words.
"I didn't want to jeopardize losing the only family I've
ever had." I could feel my cheeks heating with the
admission, but I didn't care. They deserved to know I
cared for them, that I valued their friendship and loyalty.
Violent clouds of rage flowed from the bodies around the
room. Pouring from everyone as glares were traced back

to Elias figure. He began to panic, his colors bright and alert.

"You know me, I'm your family. Your brother!" Elias roared. He turned his attention to Caligan. "You're only taking her side because you need her to get your kingdom back!" That's the second time he had said that. What was he talking about? Was he talking about Willowmore? Everyone around the room tensed at his words. A deep growl ripped through Caligan, his body shook with fury. He made a move toward Elias, but he froze when I spoke.

"What is he talking about?" Caligan didn't turn to face me, but stayed rooted in place.

"Nothing." His colors flashed in warning. He was lying. He realized quickly I had known. He turned to me, his eyes wide, worry swirling around him. I pulled myself from Ciprian's arms.

"Don't lie to me. What is he talking about?" The room fell silent, a wicked grin spread across Elias's face. Caligan colors moved and mixed with fear, panic and conflict. "Answer me." I demanded. Caligan's body tensed, his hands opened wide at his sides.

"Tell her Cal, or should I say, your highness." I gaped at Elias' words. Cal tensed, his body shaking with fury and fear.

"What is he talking about Cal?"

Cals face set into a unreadable mask. "My name is Caligan Dolant. Son of the late king. I am the rightful king of Willowmore." My heart stopped, my stomach dropped painfully. Why wouldn't he tell me? Why would he keep something that big from me? My stomach twisted. Caligan took a slow step forward before continuing. "Your father was one of the guards that had helped me escape the castle as a child. Your mother, was the other. They came back to the city and I kept watch over them. Making sure they lived and were safely hidden from Mortala." My body froze, my blood running cold. He knew my parents? "The second you were born, I knew you would be powerful. That you would be like me." My blood ran cold.

"The second I was born?" He nodded, his face reddening and his fear growing.

"I found you just after your mother died, your father had been killed a few months prior to your birth." I thought that he had watched over them to make sure they were safe? What had changed? How did they both die? "You were alone, and you needed to be protected. You were the last of my people left, the last to exist besides me. I had to ensure you grew up normal, your power hidden." I shook as rage and sadness swirled within me. Cold seeped into me as a realization hit me. I silently prayed that I was wrong.

"Caligan, what did you do?" Sorrow filled his eyes.

"I put the casings on you, so you could hide in plain sight. So you would be safe until you got older. So Mortala wouldn't be able to find you. I took you to that orphanage, hoping it would be safe." My heart shattered within my chest, the healing that had taken place over the last few months, undone as I broke inside once more all at once.

"You thought I would be safe?" My voice was steady despite my body shaking. The others remained silent, sorrow filling their colors.

"I couldn't bring you back here, the forest was too dangerous for an infant."

"Anywhere would have been safer than that place!" My voice cracked with emotion. "Do you have any idea what they did to me? What you sentenced me to?" My eyes stung as I pulled up my shirt, revealing the deep, thick scar across my stomach. "You asked me where this came from. They did this to me." Caligan's face paled. The others grimaced at the horrific scar. Tears fell steadily and calmly down my cheeks. I didn't care if they all saw me cry. I was breaking and I couldn't stop it. "They cut my womb from me. They gutted me." I spat through gritted teeth. Caligan's shoulders slumped as tears welled in his eyes. Ciprian gasped behind me. "I was a child, Caligan. I remember the pain. I remember the blood." I took another step forward. "I remember that witch laughing, proud of ending at least one human bloodline." I dropped my shirt, rage building within me.

"My life has been anything but safe." I snarled. "I have been beaten, raped and starved. If I had my magic, if I had been able to use it, I could have stopped it all." The tears fell heavily now. "I wouldn't have had to go everyday, hoping that it would be my last but being to scared to stop fighting so it wouldn't be."

"Lorn, I'm sorry, I didn't-" I held up my hand, silencing whatever was going to come from his mouth. I turned to those around the room.

"Did you all know?" Their faces were somber and drawn. Tears fell from Silas's green eyes and ran down Asher's silently. They had known. "None of you told me?" My voice cracked again. Caligan stepped forward.

"They are bound to me. I forbid them from saying anything, they couldn't stop it." I returned my glare to him. "Lorn, please." I gritted my teeth, my heart and soul fracturing within.

"Was everything you told me a lie?" My chest ached with the question.

"Not everything." Cals voice was low, sorrow dripping off every word.

"You damned me Caligan. Not the king, not Mortala. You. You sentenced me to a fate worse than death." I threw his words back at him from my first night here. I turned my attention to Elias, a wide grin still plastered across his face. I walked to his side, letting my anger roll from me and swallow him. "You were wrong. I will not hurt any of you I swore to protect. But you were right about the monster within me." Fear swirled around him as he stared at the death promised in my eyes. "Hope that I'm not the one to decide your fate. Or you will see exactly what me and my power are capable of."

I stormed from the barn and ran to my cottage. I could hear the others calling my name, Caligan's voice being the loudest, but I charged up the stairs and slammed my door closed behind me. I locked it and shoved my desk and bedside tables in front of it. Caligan wasn't getting in tonight. I turned to my bed, tears still falling freely. Ziggy's sleepy head popped over the edge off his bed. My bed was unmade, the tangle of blankets a reminder of the evening I spent with Caligan. My heart broke completely then. Sobs racked my body as I curled in on myself and slid to the ground.

The one time I had let myself hope, let myself love, it broke me. Broke me worse than any other violence I had faced. It was the first time I had ever found happiness and now, I didn't know if any of it was real. Did he really need me to stay to answer questions? Or was I kept just so I could be used? Did Caligan really care for me? Did any of them care for me? Or was that all a part of his plan? Did he know that I would eventually seek revenge on Mortala?

I cried until there was nothing left to fall, until my throat was horse and dry. I ignored the knocks on my door and stayed on the floor, staring at the wall. Ziggy sat in my lap, nudging me with his fuzzy face, trying to comfort me. I fell asleep against the wall, my heart aching worse than ever before. Sometime after I had fell asleep, I woke slightly to the sounds of distant screams. I knew from the bond that they weren't from my clan. I hoped it was Elias. I hoped he was in pain. I hoped he felt what I was feeling inside. Sadness dragged me back to sleep, guilt washing over me.

Chapter 33

Tap. Tap. Tap. The soft noise pulled me from sleep. I sat up on the hard floor, my body stiff and aching from sleeping on the hard wood. I looked to the window where the noise came from. Asher and Grady's faces peered in from the glass. Their faces were pleading, their colors filled with sadness and worry. My chest ached, my stomach turned with the memory of last night. But Caligan was the one to blame, not the others. I pulled myself from the floor and made my way to the window. I pushed it open and stepped aside to allow the two inside.

Asher pulled me into a hug and held me tightly. I squeezed my eyes shut, holding my tears at bay. Lagan placed a hand on my shoulder.

"We're sorry, Lorn." His voice was heavy with remorse. I pealed myself from Asher's warm grasp. I shook my head and glanced at their faces. Their eyes were warm. I could feel their worry through the brand, see it in the air around them.

"You guys have nothing to apologize for." Lagan placed his hands on my shoulders and ducked his head down so we were at the same eye level.

"Not everything was a lie. We all love you, Lorn. You're our family. That was always real." I nodded, my eyes stinging even more.

"What happened to Elias?" I asked. The two shared an angry look.

"His brand was removed and then-" Lagan began.

"We fed him to the Damned." Asher finished. I nodded, the realization settling within me. They had chosen me. They had been telling the truth about that. Cal had been telling the truth.

"When you're ready," Asher said softly. "you should hear Caligan out." The sound of his name sent a pang through my chest. I looked at my feet, not trusting myself to reply. Lagan cleared is throat. "We know last night was rough. You're injuries seemed to have healed though." I almost forgot. Without the casings, my magic is unleashed completely. I heal faster now. I looked at my skin and felt my face. No swelling or bruises. Lagan cleared his throat.

"We brought you this." He pulled a small tin out from his pocket and handed it to me. Inside was a cream, light and fluffy and smelled of sugar. "Its shaving cream." My eyes shot to his. "We thought you maybe wanted to shave your head. Especially after last night." Tears ached, fought to break over the edges of my eyes. They knew me so well. Better than anyone ever had. I gave them a small smile and went over to the mirror sitting above my small counter. Asher gave me a canteen full of water and a small bowl and set them before me.

"Do you want help?" Panic shot through me at the thought of someone else touching my head. I shook my head quickly. The two sat on the floor and played with Ziggy while I spread the sweat smelling cream over the short outgrowth on my head. With every scrape of the small blade against my scalp, I could feel myself falling back into place. I could feel my strength replenishing, feel my armor that had been broken last night reforming around my heart. I watched myself in the mirror when I had finished. I watched as my eyes grew hard, my soul fighting back against the pain thrashing inside of me. I had escaped violence and beat death. I could survive the heartbreak Cal had caused.

I turned back to my two companions, their eyes traced my newly cut hair. I could feel their relief to see me look like myself. I watched as they noted the strength burning within me.

"Much better." Asher said, dimples appearing on either side of his lips. The two climbed to their feet, Lagan placed his hands on the weapons belt hanging loosely from his hips.

"We came to check on you, but also, we have news.." My eyes darted to his. "We need to go down."

I grabbed my weapons belt while the two cleared the way to my door. The three of us raced down to the kitchen. Ziggy zipped through the air happily beside us. The others were crowded around the dining table, now repaired probably by magic, over looking a map of the city. Conversation died as I walked into the room, all eyes turning to me. Relief flooded through the room, Silas gave me a tight hug before returning to his seat. Caligan stood by the counter, his eyes rimmed with dark circles, like he hadn't slept all night. I blocked out his emotions, not wanting to be bothered with trying to decipher what he was feeling. I swept my gaze away from him and moved to the table next to Ciprian.

"So, what's the big news?" I asked, breaking the silent tension in the room. Ciprian took a sip of his coffee and turned to me, a smile across his wrinkled face.

"There is complete unrest within the kingdom. Riots and protests have been happening all morning." I raised my brows. "I used a seeing charm to take a peek within the kingdom's walls just a little while ago. Mortala is going to publicly address the kingdom, in the square, tomorrow at mid day."

"Isn't she worried about an attack?"

Silas and Lagan grinned. Grady shrugged. "Apparently she isn't too concerned about it since they will be only gathering during the day. Curfew is still in place."

"And since we only attack at night," Asher began, but I nodded, knowing exactly where he was going with his thought.

"So she won't expect an attack during the day." The table fell silent once more. Ciprians hand fell over mine.

"This could be our best chance at finishing this." His eyes were filled with worry, but eagerness swirled around him. "But if you aren't up for it, or if you've changed your mind-" I shook my head quickly.

"No. You're right, its the perfect opportunity. She will be out of the castle and not expecting us to show up. Its perfect."

"Well, almost perfect." Caligan chimed in. I tensed at the sound of his voice, but drew my gaze to his. His grey eyes held mine as he walked to join us at the table. My heart ached at the sight of him. "We are going to have to blend in to the crowd to get into the city." I nodded, his statement rather obvious.

"And?" He crossed his arms over his chest and straitened to his full height.

"And you're the only woman in the entire kingdom with a shaved head."

I shrugged. "I'll just dress like I did when I lived there." His jaw clenched. Grady shifted beside me, ignoring his brother.

"What do you need?"

I thought for a moment, remembering what my routine of dressing was like when had been within the kingdom. "I need a long stretch of fabric, preferably nothing itchy." I tapped my thumb to my collar bone. The lack of metal felt odd. "and some drawing charcoal." I used it to sharpen the edges of my jaw and face to make it seem more masculine. Nobody had ever questioned my disguise unless I spoke. I would blend in perfectly. Asher and Lagan both nodded and left the barn to gather the supplies that I requested. My heart skipped at the thought of what we were planning to do. We were going to the city tomorrow, to kill the queen. Mortala's reign will end tomorrow. Her death will be the key to freedom that I, my clan, and others have so desperately wanted for so long. Excitement and fear mixed together inside me, swirling through my colors.

I walked to the end of the table where Ziggy sat eating a small bowl of berries Silas had brought him. I petted his fuzzy head, lost in thought while the others talked about what our plan of attack should be. I didn't even notice Cal as he stepped to my side, his presence sending a jolt of pain through my heart. I watched his grey eyes, as sadness and anger swirled in the air around him. Bright, hot fury ripped through me. How dare he be angry at me, I'm not the one who betrayed and lied to him. I turned my eyes straight ahead, watching the rest of my clan.

"How are y-" I cut him off, not allowing him to finish.

"What was his name?"

"Who?" I could see his confusion in the air around him.

"My father." There was a pause, his body tense.

"Zigmund." My heart flipped. I closed my eyes tightly, holding back the fresh tears in my eyes. *Ziggy*. He had told me it was the name of an old friend. And I had made fun of it.

"And my mother?" I asked, my voice low and shaky with emotion.

"Lacuna." Ziggy and Lacuna. It felt odd to hear their names, to learn them so late in my life. "You look like her. But you have your father's eyes." My heart squeezed. I had never missed them, for I never knew them. But hearing their names, hearing about what features I had of theirs; it made me miss them. I opened my eyes, calming my aching heart. I let my anger come back to life, let it burn away the sadness in my chest for the moment. I hated him in that moment. Hated Cal. Hated that he withheld information about my family. Hated that he had lied to me. Hated that he had tricked me. Hated that he had made me fall for him.

Cal brought his hand up as if to touch my cheek, but I didn't give him the chance. I grabbed the front of his shirt and slammed him down onto the table and pressed the blade of my axe to his throat. The room fell silent and still. I bared my teeth at him, anger and pain ramming through my chest. I resisted the urge to light him on fire.

"You're getting what you wanted today. You'll have your precious throne back. But you and I are done. Touch me again and you'll burn."

Chapter 34

The crowds were ridiculously large. Everyone was furious, angry and demanding the queen do something to stop the band of rebels from attacking and killing. I had my cloak pulled tightly closed, hiding the axes and knives at my hips. I left the hood down, which made me feel incredibly exposed, but it would look like I was hiding if it were up. Fall had finally come thankfully, or wearing the cloak would be too odd and way too hot. The cool breeze was felt but the crowded streets made it hard to appreciate it.

I walked calmly with witches and warlocks alike. Nobody sneered or spat or glared in my direction, the magic within me was different but with so many sorcerers around me, I became virtually invisible. It was weird walking through a city that once was so dangerous, but now it seemed harmless. They all feared me and what I had accomplished within these walls. Soon, they would fear me far more.

Our clan had split up, all walking to the square on separate streets. Silas had been allowed to come after much debate, but we needed our bomb maker for a day like today. He and Lagan were off together placing little surprises throughout the city. Ciprian was the only one that stayed back in the forest. Fear kept trying to creep into my heart and mind. Fear for innocent, sweet Silas. For goofy Lagan. For Asher and his kind heart. For Grady and his wide grin and light. For Caligan, and the love I still carried so deeply for him.

But fear will not control me today. Today, we succeed in ending Mortala's cruel reign of Willowmore. My family will make it out alive. They will make it back home safely. I could heal my broken heart after. But right now... now was time to control my emotions and use them to start a new life not just for me and my family, but for everyone.

I squeezed past witches and warlocks, all in deep, angry conversations about the state of the kingdom. I made my way to the back of the square and took my designated spot. I searched the crowed for the others. Grady, Asher and Caligan all stood along the same wall as I did, our spacing several yards apart. Silas and Lagan would join our line soon. My heart raced as I looked to my family. I knew that today was going to be dangerous, the likelihood of all of us returning home was very slim. But I refused to allow one of them to be hurt. If anyone was going to die, it was going to be me. I'll make sure they all remain safe. I'll make sure I don't lose the only love I've ever had.

My body jolted as trumpets began to sound, announcing the queen's arrival. A large train of royal guards came in from all entrances. Obviously, our nightly ambushes had gotten under her skin. The number of guards had been tripled since the last time I had stood in this square. Mortala finally came through the entryway, her beauty still undeniable. Her gown was deep purple, her silver hair twisted into elaborate curls and braids at the top of her head. Her wings still gleamed just as brightly and perfectly as I remember. The crowed slowly quieted and kneeled as she walked to her throne atop the dais. Her people were slower to kneel than last time, anger rumbling throughout the crowd. But they all lowered as their fear overshadowed their anger. I pulled my mask over my mouth and returned to my still position, my family mirroring my movements.

Mortala sat atop her throne and turned to her people and the sea of kneeling subjects. Her face hardened, her colors swirled with anger and fear as her attention snagged on the six standing figures in the back of the square. Asher, Grady, Caligan, Silas, Lagan and I remained on our feet, our faces the image of the Damned.

Chapter 35

The square remained silent as they waited for the command to rise. But it never came. Mortala's eyes never left mine peaking over the mask covering my mouth and jaw. Slowly, the witches and warlocks around us turned, following the queens gaze. Fear erupted through the square, filling the crisp fall air in thick red clouds. Screams rang loudly, wizards and humans pushed and shoved trying to flee. They didn't get far.

Cal snapped his fingers, magically igniting the bombs hidden throughout the city. Explosions went off, ringing throughout the twisting streets of the kingdom. Four in total. One at each end of the city. Large fires and smoke billowed largely in the air. We wanted them to see this, we wanted them to see the downfall of their queen. We wanted them to see their city crumble. We wanted their fear, because that means we have her power. The screams continued as the six of us slowly started walking forward, the crowd frantically rushing to get as far away from the square as possible. With a silent command from the queen, guards charged. I threw my cloak to the side and palmed my axes. I kept my eyes on Mortala, but I could see my family moving, revealing their own weapons.

I loosed a roar as we hit the wall of guards with a fury. Steel clashed against steel. The sound of torn flesh and dripping blood joined the screams that echoed through the air. I ripped through one guards throat and lodged my blade deep into the chest of another. My face, hands and handles of my axes quickly became slick with blood. I let the craze of the fight take over. I let my rage burn to life and dance across my palms. I ignited those who came too close and smiled as they burned before me. I loosed another roar of violent fury, eager for my next opponent. I spun, taking out two guards at once, a flaming blade in each hand. I whirled and sliced through the air, not stopping or even feeling the cuts and punches delivered to my body by others. I let the pain fuel me, I let it drive me.

Raw, dark power fell from Caligan in dark waves, suffocating and killing more guards as they came charging in from all sides of the square. My heart jumped at the sight of his power, the full vast range of it. My clan had taken down most of the guards thrown at us, the large crowd still coward together, desperately fighting to get away.. Streaks of spells flew past our heads, missing us by inches. We moved too irrationally and fast to be hit. Mortala screamed from atop her throne and stood. She threw her arms out wide, blowing the walls of the courtyard to the ground, allowing the rest of the bystanders to flee. The commotion was enough to break the concentration of me and my companions. Silas and Lagan were taken down by three guards, their weapons wrestled from their grasp. Asher and Grady followed shortly after. Caligan was hit by a spell to the chest. His body was thrown back into the wall, the stone cracking under the impact.

His body twisted at sharp angles, his body bending in ways it shouldn't be. Raw screams erupted from his throat, veins straining in his neck and the exposed skin of his hands. I felt the alert of pain down the brand connecting us, my heart constricting at the sight of him hurting.

Another spell was thrown at me. Without knowing how I did it, I threw up my hands and a wall of violet fire blocked my body, the spell deflected by my flame. When I brought my hand back down, and the flame died away, my heart plummeted. The rest of my clan were held by guards, their weapons cast aside. Their faces revealed and free of the masks. I turned my glare to Mortala who had descended the steps of the dais and slowly made her way across the square.

"Release him!" I shouted, my voice angry and rough. I pointed to Cals tortured figure.

"Lay down your weapons, or your friends will die." She said to me, her voice cold. I glared at her, my colors violent. I dropped my axes to my feet, my eyes trained on her. She waved a pale hand. "The mask." I snarled but removed the mask, my face free. Cals body stilled next to me as she released him of the painful spell. I watched recognition light in her eyes, her face twisting into cold anger as she approached.

"You."

I smiled. My knees were kicked from behind, a blade pressed to my throat as a guard forced me to the ground like the others with me. Another bound my hands behind my back. "Everyone kneels eventually." She mocked as I snarled at her. She walked closer, her gaze traveling down her nose and looked at me in disgust. "So you're the one responsible for all the trouble being caused." I smiled once again.

"Did you miss me Mortala?" Her body tensed, her white teeth flashing behind her blood red lips. The guard behind me hit me hard on the back of the head.

"She is your queen!" He snarled.

"You're not my queen!" I spat at her feet. Her face twisted with rage. A bright blue ball of magic formed in her hand and flew directly into my chest. Intense, excruciating pain shot through my chest, up my neck and down my legs. My muscles spasmed, a scream flew from my throat as sharp, torturous pain ripped through my body. My vision faltered. I writhed like a worm, trying to get away from the pain.

"Lorn!" Asher and Lagan yelled, their voices soon cut off by the guards rough hands.

"No!" Caligan's voice bellowed. Mortala raised a hand, the pain immediately gone. I gasped, my body aching, my mind numb from the agony I had just felt. Mortalas gaze fell to Caligan. Blood ran down a cut below his eye and from a gash in his arm. He would heal quickly, but my heart still ached to see him hurt. The false queens eyes widened as she stepped to him, her boney hand traced the line of his jaw. I saw the fury flow from his shoulders as he tried to pull away from her touch.

"I'd know those grey eyes anywhere." She knew him? "You look just like your father." Her head tilted to the side as she inspected him. Anger flared within me. "You have your whore mother's mouth though." Caligan snarled and spat at her. I stared at them both, infuriated by Mortalas hand still on his skin. "What's your name?" It was Silas who responded, not with his hands, but with his mouth. The voice that came from him, obviously didn't belong to him, but it belonged to someone. Someone I knew.

"His name is Caligan Dolant, son of King Dolant and rightful heir to the throne of Willowmo-." His words were cut off for a blade made from magic, sliced clean through his throat.

Our screams filled the air as Silas' head fell to the ground. We felt the line of his life sever, felt it in our bones, in our hearts. A deep, aching sadness welled within all of us. Caligan's head fell to his chest, a roar of fury echoed from his lips. Grady and Asher thrashed against the guards holding them. Lagan managed to escape the hold of his guard but only briefly. He managed to make it a few steps closer to his brother before being tackled back to the ground, a cry roaring from deep within his chest. I knew as soon as I heard that voice, that it wasn't Silas. I watched as the head fell to the ground, the transforming spell disappearing before it became still. Ciprian's wild green hair was matted with blood, his eyes dull and grey.

The others watched as the truth was revealed. Ciprian had taken Silas's place.

The sight of Cip, of his pale, dead eyes, made the flame within me erupt. I let the flame consume me, engulf me. Violet flames devoured the guard behind me and burned through the ropes binding my hands. I shot a ball of flamed at the guards holding my family, freeing them from their prisons. Grady, Asher and Lagan ran to my side, our weapons back in hand. Caligan wasn't where he was a moment ago. Instead he kneeled before Mortala, his hands still bound and a blade held to his throat. Mortala smiled viciously.

My eyes fell to Caligan's. Those grey eyes I have fallen in love with. Those eyes that held mine every time I walked into a room and that started a fire within me. His face was pale, his colors were deep with grief and pain.

"Weapons down, or I kill your precious king." Mortala sneered. I gave into the violent anger, I didn't care if it consumed me. I wouldn't let her hurt Cal. The blade against his throat slid slowly, a small trail of blood forming against the skin of his throat. "I wont repeat myself." I froze, her words an obvious promise.

"Lorn." Caligan whispered. Tears stung my eyes and panic filled my heart. "Forgive me." His eyes glowed bright and green smoke surrounded his three brothers and myself. I realized too late what he was doing. I tried to lunge from the smoke but when I emerged from the thick cloud, I didn't find Caligan before me. Instead I fell to the grassy pasture of our home. We were back in the Forest of the Damned. And Caligan wasn't here.

Chapter 36

I fell to the ground, my heart pounding and my lungs unable to take in enough breath. He wasn't here. He was still with her. I could still feel his lifeline through the brand so I knew he wasn't dead but he was gone. He had sent us back. *Forgive me.* The last words he said. My heart ached, screamed with anger and pain. Asher got to his feet and began looking around the clearing.

"What did he do?" He asked, disbelief filling his voice. Blood ran from several cuts on his face and body. Grady and Lagan were both bleeding and injured as well. Grady buried his face in his hands, sadness weeping from him in pools.

"We lost Cip and Caligan."

I crawled to his side and placed a hand on his shoulder. He brought his green eyes to mine, they were brimmed and red with tears.

"We didn't lose Caligan. He's still alive. We *will* get him back." I promised, my voice heavy with sadness and determination. Asher and Lagan agreed quietly. We sat silently for a moment, each trying to muddle through the events that just took place. Ciprian was dead. Caligan remained with Mortala. Caligan was the son of the king, held by the false queen who killed his parents and his people. *Our* people, I corrected myself. Lagan shot to his feet suddenly, breaking me from my thoughts.

Silas came sprinting to our group, a wide smile across his lips. Lagan wrapped him in a bear hug and tore him from the ground. Tears of relief and happiness flowed down his face at the sight of his best friend. Grady and Asher both gave the smiling boy hugs and I gave him a kiss on the cheek. He seemed very confused by the amount of affection, but then we told him what happened. His colors faded from golden to grey and dull at the mention of Ciprian's death. He rubbed the brand of his wrist, as he put the pieces together. Asher placed a hand on his shoulder as a tear fell from his cheek.

"We will get Caligan back." Silas perked up at that and began walking to the barn, waving for us to follow. We all wiped our tears and trudged tiredly after the red headed boy. He ushered us into the barn, but once inside, we all became on high alert once more.

Within the building stood, and sat over two dozens elven soldiers. Their pointed ears giving them away. Their chest plates gleamed and shined. Weapons hung from their sides. They were larger than even my family, towering several feet above us. I palmed one axe and let my flame blaze to life in the other hand. Asher grasped his flail, Grady his whip and Lagan his sword. Silas stepped in front of us. His eyes wide and his hands out in front of him.

No! He signed. *Ciprian sent for them before he left.* None of us relaxed. Silas waved to one of the giant men behind him. He had black hair that hung to his waist in a long braid. His eyes were a dark brown, almost black and his skin seemed to have been kissed by the sun itself. His face had deep scars across the one eye and down his jaw, disappearing behind a thick beard. His hands were weathered, scared and calloused. He was obviously a seasoned warrior even thought his armor was like polished silver, not a scratch to be seen. He gave me a warm smile, his eyes crinkling at the edges. Ziggy sat happily on his shoulder, a wide toothy grin across his fuzzy face at the sight of me. As the elf approached, the tiny dragon zoomed through the air to my chest, his green eyes happy.

"My name is Feareth, general for the southern kingdom of Norkin." His voice reminded me of gentle waves, smooth and crisp. His warm eyes took me in, he stared down his crooked nose at me but not a hint of smugness could be found in his features or his colors. "You must be the empath I've heard so much about." His colors were pure, no hint of deception hidden within him. I doused the flame in my hand and held it out to him. He grasped it firmly.

"Lorn." I lowered my axe and pointed to the men behind me. "This is Lagan, Asher, and Grady. I can see you've already met Silas." The freckled face boy smiled wildly, my heart warming at the sight.

"Where is Ciprian and the young king?" Feareth's brow furrowed as he found our group short. My heart constricted.

"Ciprian was killed. Cal was taken by Mortala." My voice was rough with emotion. The elf frowned.

"Ciprian was a wonderful person, and a great friend." A lump formed in my throat. "He and the king told me a lot about you, all of you." When had they talked? "My kingdom was an ally to the late king Dolant." He gestured to the men crowded within our small barn. "We have come to help you achieve your goal of overthrowing that dreadful woman who calls herself queen." His voice was strong, his jaw set with determination.

I eyed the elf. If we planned on succeeding in freeing Caligan from her grasp we were going to need help. We also need help when it comes to killing her, based on how badly we failed today. But I didn't know how well he and his men would work with our small clan. I replaced my axed at my hip and crossed my arms.

"I'm not good at following orders. Neither are the rest of my clan." The elf shook his head quickly.

"You misunderstand me, we are here under your command." My brows rose. "You and the king are the only ones left of our old friends, our allies. You are the answer we've been waiting for." My stomach flipped. The elf then did something I would never have expected. He knelt in front of me. His entire small army followed suit. I stared, not knowing what to do or say. His brown eyes were now eye level with mine and held them steadily. "You will lead us, and we will follow." My face heated, embarrassment flushing my skin.

"Okay, deal, just please don't kneel like that." Several of the soldiers laughed, as did Feareth. They rose.

"So, are we planning on saving the king, or is he not our priority?" I flinched at his words. My anger spiked within me.

"We are going to get him back." Asher said his voice low.

"Soon." Lagan added.

"First." Grady growled.

"If anyone gets to kill him, its me." I mumbled, gaining me laughs from my clan but granting me strange looks from the elven warriors.

"Well then Lorn, what do you need from us?" I considered his question and thought about what it would take to achieve our goals. First, freeing Caligan and second, destroying Mortalas throne. I was getting Caligan back. Despite his lies and the pain he caused me, I couldn't let him stay within her grasp. He belonged with us. With me. I met the elves eyes.

"I need your anger."

Acknowledgments

Holy shit. I wrote a book. Holy shit. There are so many amazing people that I need to thank because without the love and support of my friends and family, this dream of mine never would have come true.

First and most importantly, thank you God for answering my numerous prayers. This is a something I've talked to you and asked you for since I was thirteen. Thank you for pushing me, guiding me, and giving me the tools I needed to accomplish this.

To my loving husband, Drake. Thank you for encouraging me to "Just write it!" Thank you for listening to my long rants, ideas and character descriptions. Thank you for correcting my hundreds of grammatical errors and for supporting the craziness that is me. Without your support and encouragement, I never would have started writing. I love you and appreciate you.

Thank you Natalie, my best friend, my little bird. Thank you for your excitement and enthusiasm, it was much needed for me to have the confidence to write this book. I'm sorry for all of the shitty drafts you had to read until the finished product. Thank you for being the confidence boost, helpful suggestion, and late night excited phone call that helped me get this finished.

To my dog, Jack, who inspired Ziggy and gave me supporting cuddles during late night writing sessions.

To my bookworm mother who introduced me to books as a child and grew a love within me that led me to this goal and dream. Thank you also for your green eyes for they played a big role in my characters descriptions.

To my loving dad, who isn't a big reader but is supportive of all my crazy ideas. Even if you never understood my desire to do the things I do, you have always been my number one fan. Thank you for being the inspiration for all the goofy and funny pranks pulled within the small group of people I created.

Thank you Hunter and Doak. The very real destruction twins.

Bell, thank you for being a role model and the inspiration behind Lorns confidence and sassy attitude. I know this book will take you forever to read, but I appreciate that you did it for me.

To the rest of my family, thank you for not laughing when I said I was writing a book. Thank you for your supportive questions and enthusiasm.

Finally, thank you to everyone who has hurt me in the past. Without the pain you caused, I never would have created a world where I was able to find peace and healing. Fuck you, but thank you.

Thank you Lorn, for to me you are real. Through healing you, I healed myself and was able to find peace with the ghosts of my past.

ABOUT THE AUTHOR

A.R. Stirn does not like her picture being taken, but believes that you can't write a book without an "About the author" section. So enjoy this awkward picture of her while she does one of her favorite things, reading. She also does not like talking about herself, so here are some random facts about her.

She enjoys reading, sleeping and watching movies. She hates being in public and being the center of attention. This probably wont end up being in the book, because she is writing this section, and like I said, doesn't like talking about herself.

Printed in Great Britain
by Amazon

67811969R00173